The LAST COON HUNTER

Book I of the Ryland Creek Saga

JOSEPH GARY CRANCE

ISBN: 978-1-4834-6983-6 (sc)
ISBN: 978-1-4834-6985-0 (hc)
ISBN: 978-1-4834-6984-3 (e)

Library of Congress Control Number: 2017908042

Lulu Publishing Services rev. date: 09/12/2019

Praise For
The Last Coon Hunter

"It was Painted Post, after all," is a joke, turned into a signal, turned into a clue, turned into legend. Crance layers in hints of a deeper mythology—the inextricably woven bond between the local folklore and the tragedies and triumphs of the Ernst family.

— Mattea Orr, Writer

Joseph Gary Crance is a masterful storyteller. He weaves together history and legends with present day life to create a saga not soon to be forgotten. You'll become friends with his characters. I have found a story that produces tears stays with you for a long time after. Thankfully, the saga continues in his upcoming books. Write on, Joseph Gary Crance!

–Judy Janowski, author,
Life is A Garden Party

"What a great book! There are a lot of unexpected twists and turns that keep the reader riveted and makes it hard to put down. I can't wait for the sequel! I highly recommend this book."

- Lisa S. Arnold, Author, *From Chaos to Calm*

Such a great book and a great writer!

-Ernest Stephens, Vice President, Orleans County (NY)
Houndsmen and Conservation Club

Dedication

This book is dedicated to my father,
Gary Clayton Crance,
New York State Forest Ranger, Retired,
the greatest coon hunter and dog man I have ever known.
And I've known quite a few.

Acknowledgments

There are so many . . .

Special thanks to author Judy Janowski {*Life is a Garden Party*}, Gloria Upchurch Williams, Carey May Stephens, Shari Lynn Heffner, Ann-Marie Feedham-Morgan, Flora Hensman, David Moorhouse, Cheryl Ward, Tracey Yorio, Tara Schulze, and Chanon Landenberg—all of whom provided constant encouragement to continue writing after I shared some stories of the outdoors.

To my daughter, Samantha, for always being my personal cheerleading squad.

A heartfelt shout out to Mrs. Michelle Pointis Burns and her family for their support of the entire Ryland Creek series of novels.

A very special thanks to Dr. Cherri Randall for her constant and patient tutelage during this novel's editorial review.

A call out to my copy editor and proofreader, Ms. Joyce Mochrie (http://www.one-last-look.com), for her superb professional review of this manuscript.

Grateful thanks to my wife, Brendalyn, who knowingly dared to love a man drawn to chasing a pair of hounds in the darkened forests.

Finally, I would be remiss not to mention the mystical woodland hollows of Upstate New York.

There is a magic in these places—if you know where to look.

Contents

Chapter 1

A Good Hunt

1976

"Treed," Jacob Ernst pronounced in his usual quiet but steady manner for his sons to hear. The thin, tall man with short-cropped, black hair listened intently as he stood motionless in the dark forest. He leaned on an oak walking stick and carried a .22 caliber rifle, secured by an old leather sling that hung diagonally across his back.

The nearly thirteen-year-old boy could not see his father on this pitch-black fall night for he kept his small, two-cell flashlight off. He knew, even at his young age, to save his light source's meager battery power. The mighty spreading red oaks in this forest still held most of their leaves, creating a canopy that made the moonless night seem even darker.

But Nathan Ernst did not need his father's deep voice confirming what the boy had clearly heard. Their black and tan hounds, Luke and Moses, had been trailing their prey, a raccoon, for the better part of ten minutes with a long-bawled "trail" bark. The coonhounds had finally settled down to their "treed" bark, a rapid, short bark, indicating they had located the coon; the critter had likely climbed one of these majestic oaks to make its escape.

Next to Nathan, his younger-by-two-years brother, Mead, rustled his feet nervously. The siblings were wiry thin, and the cooling night air of a typical late October in Upstate New York was soaking through their worn coats and boots. Both boys sported long hair that helped keep them warm. Nathan had his father's dark hair, while Mead's light brown hair came from their maternal side. Walking to the hounds now meant warmth from the physical exertion, but they waited patiently to follow their father's direction. Both boys knew never to complain about the cold, or any physical discomfort, as they were mindful of their father's intolerance for such petty whining.

Jacob Ernst was a hard but fair man.

"That's a tall hill," Jacob spoke again. It was a matter-of-fact statement—a simple acknowledgment of the terrain which was akin to the many hills in their hometown of Painted Post. He scanned the darkness in the general direction where he knew his sons to be. A widower since his wife, Rose, had died during Mead's birth, Jacob recalled when he, too, had stood in the darkness as a child, awaiting his father's final decision to move on to their treeing hounds. Jacob knew that chasing ringtails through these hills would form much of his sons' characters, and patience was chief among the virtues instilled.

Jacob reached down to his headlamp's battery on his hip and switched it on. A bright beam of white light from his hard-plastic helmet atop his head pierced the night. "Are you boys ready?"

"Yes, Pa!" they both exclaimed in unison.

"Come along then," Jacob said as he turned in the direction of the hounds.

As excited as they were, both boys knew to stay at least six feet apart to avoid having any low-lying tree or brush branch snap back in the dark to slap them painfully in the face.

"Go ahead, Mead," Nathan instructed, ever protective of his younger brother. Nathan took the last position in line as the men moved quickly in the night. Judging by the volume of the dogs' barking, the hunters were within three hundred yards of their final destination.

It was the year of the United States of America's much-celebrated bicentennial. Many of the tall oak trees, whose thick branches the trio passed beneath, were undoubtedly young saplings when Native Americans of the Iroquois Nation, likely Seneca, traveled through these same woods centuries ago. At forty years old, Jacob had climbed this hill for more than three decades, and he was confident that this mountain had not lost a single inch in altitude since the signing of the Declaration of Independence.

As the hill's grade steepened, the boys would often grab a tree to assist their ascent as they struggled to keep up with their long-legged father. Nathan and Mead knew, however, if Jacob did outdistance them, they would be guided by the continuous barking melody from Luke and Moses.

Mead then tripped on a branch and went down hard to the forest floor. He let out a small yelp, and while his eyes watered, the boy stoically held back any tears.

Even over the hounds' singing, Jacob heard the stumble of his youngest son into the dirt, and he looked back to see the small boy bravely lifting himself up with Nathan's help.

"It's okay, Pa," Mead said quickly to reassure Jacob. "I just bruised my knee a bit."

"Good boy, Mead, you're a tough one," Jacob said. While neither boy could make out their father's face beneath the glaring white light now trained on them, they could detect an unmistakable pride in Jacob's voice—a father's tacit approval at both Mead's grit as well as Nathan's quick response to assist his younger brother.

Each one knew the other two men were all he had in this world.

Jacob turned back and resumed walking to the beckoning hounds, but he offered one last observation. "Besides, boy," Jacob said over his shoulder, "that bruise is a long way from your heart."

In another five minutes, they crested the steep hill and traveled the last few yards to the two sleek-coated hounds. Climbing the grade had warmed them considerably, and the boys were no longer mindful of the cooling air but thought only of the drama ahead.

There was little doubt which tree the hounds believed the raccoon had climbed. Luke and Moses ran around a monstrous oak's base and periodically jumped up to place their front paws on its ancient trunk, barking all the while. Moses was the oldest and dominant of all the hounds in Jacob's kennel. Before this hunting season would end in late winter, the nearly ninety-pound Moses would be eight years old. The younger dog, Luke, had been "broke in" by Moses, the experienced hound showing the neophyte how to hone his natural talent to track the wily ring-tailed creatures. Luke would turn four years old next summer, entering his prime.

As hard as the dogs were barking up the tree, Moses suddenly stopped, ran to Mead, placed his huge paws on the boy's chest, and licked the youngster's face. Mead patted Moses on his broad head, comforting the hound that the young boy had safely made the climb, and all was well. The hound looked the child over for one last check and, once satisfied everything was okay, ran back to the tree to resume his steady treeing alongside Luke.

Jacob silently watched Moses's display of affection as he had often witnessed the unbreakable bond between boy and dog. The seasoned coon hunter knew well that Moses would teach Mead many things about life.

Yes, many things, Jacob thought.

Knowing the routine well, Jacob, Nathan, and Mead spread out and began shining their lights up the tree. With most of its fall foliage still clinging to this ancient oak's branches, the hunters knew that they likely would only catch the telltale reflection of the raccoon's eyes shining back in their lights as two small amber orbs. The men never doubted their hounds, confident there was a raccoon there. Now it became just a matter of finding where it hid amongst the tree branches.

In less than a minute, Nathan shouted excitedly, "Got him, Pa! Right here he is!"

Jacob and Mead converged on Nathan's location and looked to where the eldest son held his light, and they too espied the raccoon's eye shining back through the leafy maze. Jacob patted Nathan on the back without saying anything, but the father did not have to offer overt praise; Nathan understood Jacob's way of showing approval.

"Can I shoot, Pa?" Mead asked, surprising both Jacob and his older brother. Mead had diligently honed his marksmanship for the past several months, but he had never asked to shoot the game.

"Nathan?" Jacob asked. By rights, Nathan had located the coon and would normally be afforded the shot.

"Sure, Pa, let Mead shoot," Nathan said magnanimously. With

both their lights trained on Mead, they could see the excitement in the youngest boy's countenance.

"All right then," Jacob said as he unslung the rifle from his back, loaded the magazine into the bottom of the gun, and ensured that the weapon's safety was on.

"Mead," Jacob instructed, "once you shoot, if the raccoon comes out of the tree alive, you keep this gun's barrel pointed straight up in the air. Moses and Luke will do the rest. Understood?"

"Sure thing, Pa!" Mead shouted, unable to curb his enthusiasm any longer.

The rifle was outfitted with a scope, and while the device did not magnify the target's image, it did show a single, bright-reddish dot to guide the hunter's aim. The gun was relatively light, and Mead was strong for his age, precluding the need for any assistance when Jacob handed the weapon to the young boy. Mead held the barrel aloft and waited patiently until his dad and brother stepped behind him.

Jacob knelt close to Mead while Nathan dutifully held his light on the raccoon, with the furbearer continuing to stare into the lights, unknowingly giving away its position.

"Okay boy," Jacob spoke slowly, "put the red dot on the coon's eye. Remember what I told you—control your breathing and squeeze the trigger. The raccoon isn't going anywhere, so just take your time."

Mead raised the barrel of the gun, peering through the scope. His aim was steady—the firearm felt natural in the crook of his shoulder. Following his father's guidance, Mead exhaled slowly, aimed precisely, held his breath, and gently depressed the trigger.

The semiautomatic rifle cracked sharply, and the audible report of impact told Jacob that the bullet had found its mark.

Both coonhounds stopped barking while still looking up the tree. The raccoon, dead instantaneously from the well-placed shot, crashed through the oak's branches. With a final thud as the furbearer's body hit the forest floor, both hounds pitched into unmoving form but instinctively knowing there was no life left in this ringtail.

"Good shot!" Jacob exclaimed.

"Way to go, Mead!" Nathan applauded.

Mead dutifully handed the weapon back to his father, and Jacob quickly removed the magazine and emptied the remaining bullet that had been automatically loaded into the rifle's chamber.

Nathan walked over to Moses and Luke, who still had their jaws latched onto the raccoon, and shouted, "Dead coon!"

The well-trained black and tans knew this command, and they subsequently released their grips, stepping away from the motionless raccoon.

Nathan let his flashlight's beam play over the critter a moment to ensure it was dead, but like Jacob, Nathan had known Mead's aim was true. This creature had felt no pain—its race in this life was over. He hoisted the ringtail by its hind leg from the leaves littering the forest floor. "It's a big coon, Pa!"

Moses began treeing again with his front paws on the old oak tree.

Luke turned his human masters, and back to his canine mentor, the younger hound looking somewhat befuddled.

"Moses!" Jacob said in a loud voice. "Come off that tree now!"

With his feet still on the tree, Moses looked Jacob directly in the eyes and knew to obey. With a snorting, frustrated half bark that sounded like "harrumph," Moses dropped his paws to the ground, seeming somewhat dejected, and walked slowly around the other side of the tree out of sight.

Jacob Ernst, not being a wealthy man, turned back to the dead raccoon, and smiled at the night's take. He would use the money from this season's fur sale to buy his sons new coats and boots.

Jacob removed a small silver chain and his razor-sharp knife from his hunting jacket. Threading part of the links through its small ring to make a loop, he pulled it taut to hold the coon's hind foot. Securing the chain's other end around a nearby sapling to suspend the carcass chest high, Jacob began skinning the animal. Luke stood patiently next to Nathan, while Moses guarded Mead as all watched the skilled hunter expertly remove the ringtail's hide—tail and all—in less than two minutes.

Handing the prime pelt to Mead, Jacob pocketed his chain and knife.

Mead dutifully stuffed the large, primed fur into the game bag attached to the back of his father's jacket.

Jacob then looked to Nathan. "Which way is it to the truck, son?"

"We went in east, Pa—so we need to go back west." Nathan quickly responded.

"Yep, but which way is west?" Jacob persisted.

Nathan stabbed his finger pointing back to the way that he thought they had just arrived.

"Might wanna take a look at your compass," Jacob chided.

Nathan dutifully took out his compass from his coat's front pocket and carefully oriented its needle to magnetic north, only to find that west was in the exact opposite direction than he had just indicated! Without looking at his compass, Nathan would have suggested going away from their truck.

"It's all right, boy," Jacob said in a comforting tone. "We all get turned around out here in the dark."

"But you weren't lost, were you, Pa?" Mead's question stung Nathan's ego a bit.

"Not tonight, Mead, but on any other night, without looking at my compass, I might just have easily pointed in the wrong direction. It's not hard to lose your way in these hollows, boys—always rely on your compass.

"It's getting late. Nathan, hook Luke on your leash and lead him out," Jacob directed. "Moses will follow us."

Using the leather strap that he had been carrying over his shoulder, Nathan put the snap onto the metal ring on Luke's collar, and the hunting party headed back down the hill.

When they arrived at their vehicle twenty minutes later, Jacob dropped the old truck's tailgate, and both hounds jumped up into the well-constructed dog box perfectly fitted to the truck's bed.

Nathan then turned and asked, "Pa, why did Moses go to treeing again once the coon was dead on the ground? I don't recall him ever doing that before."

Jacob smiled at his son's keen observation. "He was telling us there was at least one more raccoon sitting up in that tree."

"Really, Pa?" Mead asked.

"Yep," Jacob confirmed.

"Well, why didn't we take the other raccoon then?" Nathan asked with a hint of being upset.

"You gotta leave some coon for seed, son, so there's some to hunt next season," Jacob replied.

Nathan gave a begrudged nod.

Moses, from his cage, as if he understood the conversation, gave another loud, audible "harrumph," indicating that the old hound shared the boy's frustration.

Still, Nathan had to admit, with one big hide taken, it had been a good hunt.

Chapter 2

A Sight to Behold

Nearly seventeen years hence . . .

It heard them, and the rage that came so naturally to it now unleashed. The hounds were easy to locate as their trail barks filled the night air. While it had been in this part of the forest for only a few weeks, it already had full knowledge of the lay of the land.

In its primitive mind, it knew that the Enemy would not be far behind the hounds. With its sheer power now, there was nothing it feared in these woods—nothing it could not rend with its tusks. Its massive, five-hundred-pound frame moved effortlessly through the snow, which masked the sound of its movement.

This night there would be a reckoning.

———◆———

The present . . .

Nathan's eyes popped open. The hunt the night before was still fresh in his mind as he lie in his warm bed beneath a handmade quilt his late mother had made a long time ago. He could imagine Luke and Moses treeing the raccoon—the sounds and excitement of the chase. The thoughts of the hounds brought to mind his daily chores. He turned his head slowly to see Mead still sound asleep in the bed directly across the small bedroom.

Nathan slipped silently out of bed and quickly donned socks, flannel shirt, and blue jeans with a matching denim jacket. The young boy finally threaded a brown leather belt through his pants' loops and slipped his feet into his boots—still moving quietly to be sure not to wake Mead.

Nathan reached for the door knob and turned it slowly.

"Tell Moses I'll be there in a bit," Mead said as the younger sibling spun quickly in his bed, already smirking.

Nathan rolled his eyes and shook his head, realizing that Mead had been awake the entire time as he had painstakingly tried to dress silently. "Will do," he said, returning the grin. He exited the bedroom to look down the hall. Jacob's bedroom was dark. It was the weekend, so his father did not have to get up early to work at the local feed mill. Nathan slipped past Jacob's room to the stairs leading down to the first floor of the small farmhouse.

At the base of the stairs, Nathan looked up to see the picture of his mother, Rose, hanging on the wall. It was a small, simple frame "like she would have wanted," he recalled Jacob saying once, situated in front of a large window facing the rolling hills that ringed their small farm.

Rose had been a stunning beauty, and Jacob had never sought the company of another woman since her death. At times, Nathan would find his father staring and smiling silently at Rose's picture. Nathan believed a conversation was being had, or at least remembered, in Jacob's mind. He could not specifically recall his mother's company, for he had been too young when she died, but the boy innately felt a great emptiness at her loss.

Nathan paused to reflect, but the thought of his chores came rushing back to the forefront of his mind, and he opened the door to the beautiful world outside.

Their little "gentleman's farm" was still a working farm and constituted almost two hundred acres—nearly half of the acreage a field, with the other half, oak woods. Next to the house was the garden whose vegetables, except for some large, bright orange pumpkins, had been harvested the month before and canned for the upcoming winter. Jacob may not have made a lot of money, but he wasted nothing, and the boys always had a good meal on the table.

A small barn not far from the house sheltered an old mule named "Butch." In his younger days, Butch had carried Jacob's father through the woods many a night chasing raccoon. As the mule had grown older, the animal had become quite cantankerous.

Dozens of chickens roamed loose across the yard. Jacob would allow the birds to run free for a few more weeks and then confine them to the coop for their protection. As Painted Post's winter set in, wild predators would begin looking for easier meals. More than one pile of feathers of a former prized hen or rooster had served as a grim reminder to the Ernst family to be wary of hungry raccoons, foxes, weasels, and an occasional coyote.

Just to the side of the barn were the coonhounds' kennels. The wire pens were well constructed and the wooden coops sturdy. "Airtight," Jacob had always insisted as he inspected the dog coops before each winter for any signs of wear requiring repair. Jacob was a true "dog man," and while he had lost hounds to old age or even a vehicle accident, on rare occasion, he ensured his dogs were always cared for and well fed.

Nathan entered the barn, filled a bucket of dog food from the feed hopper, and turned on a spigot to a hose that he used to fill each dog's pan with fresh water. He took a moment to look at the walls of their barn to see many implements hanging there—old farm tools, large, two-man, wooden-handled logging saws, and even dozens of leg grip traps that had been just recently "boiled and waxed" for the upcoming trapping season.

"You're up earlier than I expected." Jacob's voice startled Nathan's reverie. His father's tall frame filled a doorway of a small side room in the barn.

"Morning, Pa," Nathan said, happy to see Jacob and suspecting that his father had been watching him since he exited the house.

Jacob had risen early to prepare the coonhide taken the night before and now wore a brown canvas apron and a pair of long, green rubber gauntlets that covered his hands and reached to his elbows. The tall man held a long, two-handled, curved fleshing knife down at his side. Using that special blade, he could easily remove the considerably excess white fat that the raccoon had gained to get through the cold winter. Jacob would next comb the fur and place the hide on a wooden stretcher.

After allowing the hide to dry for a few days, the coon hunter would roll the fur from nose to tail, place it in a plastic bag, and put it in an old chest freezer in the back of the barn. There the entire season's take of hides would remain until sold to the local fur buyer.

"After morning chores, we'll go to town to get a part for the tractor at the hardware store. Play your cards right, and we might even stop and get some ice cream." Jacob winked at Nathan. A smile grew on the boy's face at the thought of the sweet reward.

Then Butch snorted at Jacob from his stall.

"What do you want?" Jacob asked in an annoyed tone while looking at the old brown mule. Butch responded with another snort and turned in his stall to walk away.

"Damn mule," Jacob muttered.

While Nathan did not understand the complete history between his father and the ornery animal, Butch was one of the few things that could consistently make Jacob curse aloud.

Without further words, each turned back to continue the tasks at hand—Nathan to the dogs with Jacob putting the finishing touches on the coon hide.

The hounds heard Nathan coming. Luke and Moses, tails wagging, barked the loudest at seeing their young master with the food. Two more hounds also came out of their coops: Katy and Maud. These female hounds were also black and tan like Luke and Moses. Katy was the youngest and the liveliest—jumping in her kennel with seemingly endless energy.

Maud, however, moved slower than the other dogs in greeting Nathan as she carried pups sired by Moses. Jacob estimated the litter was due in nearly two weeks. Nathan and Mead were excited at the thought of puppies soon to be on the ground again—another generation of hounds to play with and eventually train.

As Nathan opened the latched kennel doors, he patted each dog on the head gently, saying his or her name, while providing fresh water from the hose and a scoop of feed. Maud wagged her tail reservedly, while Luke eagerly awaited his feed and immediately drove his muzzle into the food pan once filled.

Moses waited last in line, displaying an uncommon amount of

patience, allowing his young master to finish the routine. The hound nuzzled the boy's leg, and boy and dog stared into the other's eyes.

Nathan knew that Moses was thanking him for the previous night's hunt—each having performed their roles superbly. He smiled back at Moses, patted the hound's head again, and began the last task of cleaning the kennels.

This last chore was something that Jacob insisted on, often saying, "You can tell how good a dog man is by how clean his kennels are." Nathan often found Jacob, true to his word, cleaning the kennels several times a day. Nathan reckoned his father must be the best dog man in the world!

Dutifully, Nathan took an old square-nosed shovel with its solid ash handle and cleaned the kennels. The young boy inspected the kennels once more, ensuring nothing was missed.

Satisfied that he had accomplished the job well, Nathan began to close the last kennel door and accidentally pinched his hand in the metal catch. Reflexively, he threw the shovel to the ground and kicked the door. He looked up surprised to see Jacob, without the fleshing apron, staring at him from several feet away.

"I'm sorry, Pa. I didn't mean to get so mad," Nathan said, embarrassed at his sudden outburst.

"It's all right, son. You come by it naturally—you just need to learn to control your temper," Jacob said solemnly. "Finish up now. Mead will have breakfast ready soon," he added on a lighter note.

"Will do, Pa," Nathan said. The boy watched Jacob walk to the house and enter. Nathan picked up the shovel and returned it to the exact place where he had found it. He then ran to the front porch, his empty stomach reminding him that breakfast would be a welcome meal.

Upon entering the doorway, the smell of frying bacon greeted Nathan, putting a smile on his face. Nathan walked into the kitchen to find Jacob already sitting at the table. With the morning paper spread before him, he could only make out his father's eyes, with Jacob now sporting a dirty, brown, fedora-styled hat atop his head.

Nathan turned to see Mead at their old gas stove, standing on a small step stool to compensate for his height and a wooden spatula in hand as he concentrated on a cast-iron pan with frying bacon. Mead turned to Nathan, seeming to expect him to arrive precisely at that moment.

"Nate, do you mind making the toast?" Mead asked politely.

"Sure," Nathan replied, and he immediately proceeded to the far side of the kitchen and placed several pieces of white bread into an old silver toaster.

"Scrambled eggs okay, Pa?" Mead asked.

"Yep," Jacob replied without so much as moving the paper an inch. Mead looked at Nathan, and his older brother nodded. Taking six large brown eggs from a basket that Jacob had filled this morning courtesy of their chickens, Mead cracked the eggs into a large bowl, added a little milk, and scrambled them with a fork. He poured the mixture into the same frying pan that he had cooked the bacon. Within minutes, the youngest boy placed a platter full of bacon and another one of eggs on the table.

Jacob folded his paper and set it aside as he watched his two boys sit down on the opposite side of the table facing him.

"Say grace, Mead," Jacob instructed quietly.

Both boys folded their hands, closed their eyes, and bowed their heads.

"Dear God," Mead began, "thank you for this food and this family and your bountiful blessings." He paused for a second and then continued. "And thank you for the good hunt last night, too."

Nathan opened one eye to first look at his brother and then to his father, who was also peeking at Mead. They shared a grin at the ad-lib prayer supplement while Mead remained solemn with his eyes closed.

"That's a good thing to be thankful for, Mead," Jacob finally said.

"Thanks, Pa," Mead said as he opened his eyes and simultaneously reached for the bacon. Each man filled his plate quickly and began polishing off the tasty victuals.

"Pa?" Mead asked at one point.

"Yes, Mead?"

"Do you reckon Ma is in heaven looking down at us right now?"

The question caught Jacob a bit by surprise, but after a short pause he said, "Yes, I reckon she does every meal."

Mead smiled but continued, "Do you suppose you'll see her again in heaven someday?"

"Yes, someday—assumin' that I make it to heaven of course," Jacob said with a grin.

"Yep—assumin' you make it," Mead responded now satisfied as he resumed eating.

Both Jacob and Nathan looked at each other and laughed softly.

With the breakfast dishes cleaned, the men loaded into their truck and headed to town. The fall leaves were spectacularly colorful—golds, oranges, reds, even purples—and both boys stared at the high hills surrounding Painted Post and could not help but wonder how many raccoons the forest held.

The ride to town was less than fifteen minutes as they pulled up to the large, old building with a sign that proudly displayed in bold black letters the words "J.P. Smith's General Merchandise & Hardware Store." Even though it was still before nine o'clock in the morning, there were already several vehicles parked outside, attesting to the store's popularity with the local community.

Jacob and his sons walked up three wooden steps, and Jacob swung the store's front door open as bells clanged noisily announcing their arrival.

The store was relatively large, with one section catering to the tool and implement needs of the rural community. Another part of the store sold clothing that ranged from durable denim clothing for hard farm work to the finest suits and dresses for the most well-to-do families in Painted Post.

Sitting behind a large brass cash register, wearing a blue jean apron over a white, short-sleeved shirt, was the current and somewhat corpulent proprietor, J.P. Smith, Jr.

Jacob noted that J.P. did not immediately proffer the friendly greeting that he usually provided to all his customers. Instead, J.P. had his eyes fixed toward the back of the store where a man and a boy stood in front of an elderly woman, evidently blocking her way in the narrow aisle.

Jacob immediately recognized everyone. The woman was Miss Penelope Wainwright; she had been an elementary school teacher some years back. All in Painted Post knew her to be a mild-mannered school marm who would go out of her way to be kind and never cause problems for anyone.

Unfortunately, the man in front of her was known to be a problem to everyone.

Well, every town has one.

"You know where I like to park!" John Allen all but screamed in Wainwright's face.

John was an alcoholic and a bully. He had two of his former wives leave him, and it was anyone's guess, and many a private bet, when the current live-in woman would come to her senses and follow her predecessors out Allen's front door.

A small boy, Larry, a son from Allen's first marriage, stood nearby, enjoying the spectacle as he watched his father berate the timid teacher.

Like father, like son.

"J-J-John," Penelope stuttered, terrified at Allen's belligerence, "I didn't know anyone had their personal parking spot at this store!"

"Oh, you knew all right! I park there every Saturday morning," Allen continued.

By this time, Jacob had walked to the counter beside J.P., who then noticed Jacob's tall figure. Nathan and Mead followed closely behind. "Boys," he instructed without taking his eyes off the growing-ever-louder ranting of John Allen, "stay here with J.P. for a moment."

"Yes, Pa," they both answered, but each boy looked bewildered at their father's bidding.

"Morning, Jacob. Sorry, I didn't see you come in," J.P. began. "I was watchin'. . . ."

"I got it," Jacob interrupted, nodding knowingly at the store's owner as he began to walk toward the irate Allen.

"Now if you ever . . .," John commenced in a scolding tone, wagging his finger at Miss Wainwright. Then he heard a steady, low voice behind him.

"If she ever does what?"

John turned quickly to see the lean figure of Jacob Ernst looking down at him. Recognition, and then fear, registered in Allen's eyes.

"J-Jacob," John stammered nervously, "I was just. . ."

"You were just leaving." Jacob finished the sentence for Allen in a not-too-subtle tone. "Sorry, ma'am," his voice quickly warmed as he looked beyond Allen at a relieved Ms. Wainwright. "Apparently, there was some misunderstanding," Jacob said with an unmistakable venom in his voice as his steely gaze returned to Allen.

"Yes, there was!" the bully, revealed as a coward, readily agreed and tried to work his way around Jacob. In an exaggerated effort to not touch Jacob, Allen knocked over some dog food cans on display, which clattered noisily onto the floor.

"Pa!" Larry Allen protested, trying to get his father to come back to save some scrap of dignity. Larry's eyes rested on his school classmates, Nathan and Mead, who were witnessing the entire scene. He knew that his father could not leave like this—running scared—in front of his peers!

"C'mon boy before I whip your hind end!" Allen screamed, trying to find some sense of his manliness as he turned his vitriol on the only person within earshot that he safely could.

"Leaving so soon?" J.P. asked sarcastically as Allen hastily went out the door saying nothing, offering only a glowering look at the storeowner.

The shamed man and boy jumped into their run-down vehicle and quickly sped out of the parking lot and out of sight.

Jacob bent down to pick up the dog food cans spilled across the floor as he engaged Miss Wainwright in friendly banter.

While Jacob was still in the back of the store conversing with the retired teacher, J.P. leaned over the store counter and half-whispered, in a confiding tone, asking Nathan and Mead, "You ever see your pa in a fight, boys?"

Mead spoke up immediately. "Pa says we should only fight if we have to, sir. 'Turn the other cheek,' he says."

"Well," J.P. said with an approving nod, "your pa is right about that, of course." Smith was quick to add reverently, "But when it does happen, when Jacob Ernst finally does decide to fight, let me tell you, it's a sight to behold." He grinned and winked at the boys.

"A sight to behold indeed," J.P. repeated, keeping an awed tone.

The boys waited proudly and patiently, watching as their father went about the store getting certain items like nothing unusual had transpired.

Ms. Wainwright stepped up to the counter and unloaded her small basket of items. She gave Nathan and Mead an appreciative smile, but they knew the gesture was not so much for them as it was for their father's chivalry. After she had finished purchasing the goods, she turned to look at both boys and mouthed a silent, "Thank you." Both boys nodded politely, and Ms. Wainwright stepped out of the store.

Jacob finally returned to place some assorted pieces of hardware on the front counter. J.P. merely smiled as he rang up the purchase.

"Has J.P. been telling you ghost stories?" Jacob asked as he looked at his two sons.

"Ghost stories!" Mead exclaimed, more excited than terrified if there was still but a hint of the latter in his voice.

On cue, J.P., living up to his widely known reputation for improvisation, placed both of his large hands on the counter and smiled. "Why, did you boys ever hear the legend of the Hell Hound of Painted Post?"

"No, sir!" Mead quickly spoke up.

"Well, well, well. . . ." J.P.'s tone sounded almost disappointed as he shook his head, if perhaps a tad overexaggerated. "I'm somewhat surprised, with as much time as you spend in the forest around here, that you haven't heard of this terrible creature!"

J.P. then handed Jacob the total for the merchandise, and Jacob reciprocated by giving the store owner a twenty-dollar bill.

"Well, what is this thing, J.P.?" Mead asked, completely enticed, while Nathan looked on somewhat skeptically.

"Allow me to explain," J.P. began, sounding like a scholarly lecturer preparing to expound on a complex subject. "Back in the early 1800s, before there were many settlers in this region, there was a man, a great bear hunter, by the name of Jedidiah Smith—"

"Was he any relation to you, J.P.?" Mead interrupted.

"Well, there's rumor to that effect, Mead," J.P. grinned, "but I can't say for certain one way or the other. Now, where was I?"

"You were saying he was a great bear hunter, this Jedidiah Smith, sir," Mead replied politely.

"Oh—yes, yes, yes!" J.P. reaffirmed. "Jed, that's short for Jedidiah, tracked and killed many a troublesome bear through these hills in Painted Post once upon a time. However, there was one bear, a huge bruin topping eight hundred pounds, that had become a man-eater! They called him 'Old Three Paws' because this particular critter had lost one of his feet when he was a young cub to a trapper. Legend has it that Three Paws had killed and eaten more than ten people, and that he might have been a grizzly bear that came from out west!"

"No!" Mead all but shouted with Jacob grinning at J.P.'s legendary tall tale telling ability.

"Oh—yes, yes, yes! So, the few people around here back then asked Jed to see if he could track this monster down and kill it. Jed agreed, for a handsome price, of course."

"Hmmm. I'm beginning to think more and more you may have been related to Jedidiah," Jacob quipped, looking down again at the store receipt with a smirk crossing his face.

"Tsk, tsk!" J.P. snorted at Jacob and then turned his attention back to the young child. "Now where was I, Mead?"

"Jed had just agreed to hunt down Old Three Paws." Mead quickly responded. "Did Jed have any hounds, J.P.?"

"Well, I'm just getting to the best part, young man! He had one faithful hound by the name of Samuel. Now, Sam—that's short for Samuel—was a great big dog. Some say he topped the scales at nigh over a hundred pounds, which is quite believable considering the occupation of hunting bear and all."

Mead let out a low whistle, imagining the dog's size.

"So," J.P. continued, "one night, after one of the settler's cows had been killed, Jed found Three Paws' tracks, and put Sam on that stupendous creature's trail.

"It became quite the chase! The old timers say Jed and Sam chased Ol' Three Paws over all the hills within sight of Painted Post and finally caught him on what we now call Denmark Hill, near the top.

"As Jed walked with his old flintlock musket, following the sound of the baying Sam, he knew that Three Paws must have finally turned and decided to fight. However, Jed noticed something else—they were on a Native American holy site. Jed didn't want to trespass here, as he had the highest respect for many of his Indian friends, but he realized that he had little choice in the matter.

"Then he came upon Three Paws, and that old bear and Samuel were fighting viciously, but Sam was too fast for the big old bruin to sink his teeth into him. Jed took careful aim and fired his musket. And he hit that bear right square with his musket ball, but did you think that Three Paws died right then and there? No, sir!"

"That's one tough bear!" Mead squealed with glee.

"Some say uncannily so!" J.P. paused to wink at Jacob and Nathan. "In fact, Three Paws then charged Jed, who was in the process of reloading that old muzzle-loading gun of his. But the distance was too short to reload in time, and Jed watched helplessly as the big bear bore down on him.

"But when Ol' Three Paws' jaws were but inches from Jed's throat, Samuel jumped into the fray, knowing that he had to get between Jed and the bear if'n there was any chance to save his master.

"And that was Samuel's final mistake because he could no longer maneuver in the short span, and with a mighty swing of his paw, the bear threw the hound into a large oak tree and killing Samuel instantly."

J.P. paused and looked down for a protracted moment out of respect for the loss of the loyal hound.

"So, did Jed shoot and kill Ol' Three Paws, then J.P.?" Mead begged the storeowner to continue.

"No, sir! Jed never managed to load his gun in time," J.P. informed the young boy.

"So how did he kill that ol' bear?" Mead asked, clearly exasperated.

"Oh, Three Paws died that day for sure, but it wasn't Jed what killed him." again J.P. paused, drawing out the drama.

"Well, then who did?" Mead begged.

"Well, Samuel might have made a mistake, but it seems that Three Paws made a greater one that day! For that old bear had, knowingly or unknowingly, killed Samuel on that holy Native American ground.

"And suddenly, Samuel stood up, seemin' to come alive again, but ol' Jed could see something immensely different in this creature from what had been but moments before his beloved hound!"

"What did he see?" Nathan even surprised himself as he asked the question eagerly.

"Samuel's eyes had turned pitch black, and it looked like his muscles grew five times of what they should have been! Then Samuel let out a terrible howl, and years later Jed swore it sounded like it came directly from the fires of Hell itself!

"Of course, Three Paws turned away from Jed at hearing that dreadful sound! But before that bear could turn to run, Samuel—or leastways what had been Samuel—grabbed the bruin by the throat, and in one mighty bite, tore out the bear's throat ending the menace that was Old Three Paws.

"Jed wanted to call Sam to him, but then thought better of it, since he knew that whatever this fearsome creature was, it was no longer his dog. Thus, as this vengeful hell hound rendered Three Paws into small pieces, Jed quietly left the scene.

"Of course, with nothing to show for his ordeal, he couldn't get paid," J.P. added as a matter of practicality. "But the old ones around these parts say whenever evil enters the forests of Painted Post, you can hear Samuel howl, warning the evil to stay away from this land."

Jacob turned to J.P. and smiled with an approving nod. His old friend had come through and delivered yet another superb ghost story.

"Pa, did you know about this? Did you ever hear Samuel howl when you were coon hunting?" Mead asked, still caught up in the tale.

"Oh, I do believe so," Jacob said, quickly manifesting a serious look as Mead turned to him. "From a distance, I do believe so.

"But know this, son," Jacob added with an enigmatic gleam in his eye as he looked out the store's front window at the seasonal opalescence of the forest's maples and hickories, "evil does not fare well in the hills of Painted Post."

"Well, what if you are a bad person and enter these woods? What happens then?" Mead asked, turning to J.P.

The large man who was J.P. leaned over the counter and gave Mead a long wink. "That would be a story for another time."

Mead looked slightly disappointed, but he knew that coming to J.P.'s General Merchandise & Hardware Store was a regular occurrence. He would be sure and ask J.P. when they made their next trip to town.

"C'mon, boys. We'll leave J.P. to run his business." As the older man held the door open and his two young sons went beneath his arm, Jacob smiled and said, "Thanks for everything, J.P."

"A pleasure as always, Jacob, and thank you for taking out the trash this morning, if you know what I mean," J.P. said, grinning at Jacob and then quickly turning to another customer who had arrived at the front counter.

As Jacob and his boys exited the store, they found a tall, handsome black man in an immaculate beige uniform, a .357-caliber revolver strapped to his side, leaning against the Ernsts' truck. The police officer watched the trio as they came up to their vehicle.

"Anything wrong, Sheriff?" Jacob asked.

"Now you tell me, Jacob," responded Sheriff Sean Covington, widely known as the "toughest man in Steuben County." When Sean stood to his full height, if a few pounds heavier and all muscle, he could look Jacob square in the eye.

"Why is it that trouble just seems to dissipate when you're around?" the sheriff continued as a broad, approving smile crossed the police officer's countenance.

"Just lucky, I guess," Jacob said as he smiled back at his lifelong best friend.

"I think Ms. Wainwright was the lucky one today. She told me what happened with John Allen in the store. He's been a bully as long as either of us can remember. Doubt there's much that can be done to change that." Sean shook his head.

"Reckon not," Jacob agreed.

"Thanks just the same for making my job a little easier," Sean said, putting his hand on Jacob's shoulder. Then he turned to the two boys. "Did you boys go coon hunting last night? Seemed like a perfect night for it."

"Yes, sir!" Mead spoke up. "We got us a big 'un, and we're headed out again tonight!"

The sheriff could not help but grin at the young boy's enthusiasm.

"Well, you listen to your pa. There's not a better coon hunter in these parts." Sean's voice indicated that he sincerely meant what he said.

"Yes, sir!" came the response from both boys this time.

"We'll see you in church tomorrow then. And I expect to hear all about the hunt after Mass."

"That's a promise, Sheriff," Nathan spoke up this time.

"I believe that I owe you boys some ice cream," Jacob said.

"Yes, sir!" Both boys were ecstatic at the thought of their favorite treat. With that, the family jumped in their truck and headed to a nearby ice cream stand.

While life was not always easy, the boys could only count themselves as lucky to be the sons of Jacob Ernst.

———— ◆ ————

The flashlight beam shining on Ronnie revealed the blood splattered on his cheeks. The gunshot had been at point blank range, and while the silencer on the pistol had muffled its sound, the impact from the high-caliber weapon was still just as deadly.

"Do you mind getting that light out of my eyes?" Ronnie asked as he viciously grabbed the small flashlight from the young man, not much more than a boy, who held it.

The cooling corpse of a minor local drug dealer, who had wanted too much, lay at their feet.

"Sorry, sir," the young man quickly apologized. Ronnie was the upstart within the drug cartel based in Chicago, and it was understood not to upset him.

"You okay?" Ronnie inquired, his violent temper seeming to dissipate instantly. This foray was the young man's first time witnessing an "enforcement action."

"Yeah. Yes, sir. I'm okay," the youth replied.

Ronnie reached into his coat pocket and pulled out a handkerchief to wipe the dead man's blood from his face. Stuffing the soiled cloth back into his clothing, the hit man then trained the flashlight on his apprentice. Instead of finding a look of horror, Ronnie discovered his partner was smiling.

Good, Ronnie thought, *this kid will be very useful to me in the years to come.*

"What do we do with the body?" the amateur asked, still elated at the misdeed that they had perpetrated.

Ronnie looked about in the night's darkness. They were on a rural, dirt back road with not an artificial light in sight. Even if his weapon had not been outfitted with the silencing device, no one would have heard it.

"Leave him," Ronnie said.

"Leave him?" the young man asked incredulously.

"Right where he lies—right where he can be found." Ronnie's voice had a slight uptick, signaling his growing impatience. He reminded himself that this young man was still quite naïve. "We want to send a message, my friend," he explained.

"Do you think these country hicks in a town named Painted Rock will get the message?" the rookie asked.

"This place is called 'Painted Post.' And yeah," Ronnie said confidently, looking at the grizzly scene, "I'm bettin' they get it."

Chapter 3

The Black Oaks of Ryland Creek

J acob looked up at the darkening sky. This night somehow felt ominous, and not a star poked through the thickening clouds, which could mean only one thing.

"Suspect we may get a little wet tonight, boys," Jacob said, looking at his sons, who, even after that pronouncement, simply smiled back, indicating their enthusiasm remained regarding this night's possibilities.

They were coon hunting once again, parking their truck near the small bridge on Ryland Creek Road, and had subsequently released both Moses and Luke to find a raccoon. The creek that flowed beneath the small bridge gurgled and sputtered as the water washed over the many jutting, grayish rocks. Jacob chose this spot because he knew that the raccoon found hunting for the small creek's frogs and crayfish as irresistible draws to the ever-hungry omnivores.

Jacob's thorough understanding of ringtail habits was rewarded when Moses's bawl soon filled the night air.

"Give Moses first strike, Pa!" Mead shouted, prancing about joyfully.

Luke's voice soon followed behind Moses, and the chase was on.

"Bet you a quarter Moses will tree first, Nate!" Mead challenged his older brother.

Nathan had to think about that offer for a moment as a quarter was a hefty percentage of his dollar-per-week allowance, but with his father quietly grinning beneath the headlamp, he felt obliged.

"You're on!" Nathan replied, matching Mead's zeal, and each boy spat in his palm and grabbed the other's hand, sealing the deal.

Onward the two hounds went, chasing the ringtail through the hills, loudly singing the story of the hunt. Further, this chase was long—unusually long.

"This coon has been dogged before," Jacob informed his sons while they listened as the hounds' voices became distant. "He doesn't want to go up just any tree. He's likely headed for a safe haven if he can get there ahead of the hounds."

"Do you think he'll make it, Pa?" Mead asked, sincerely concerned that their prey might win the night.

"We won't know till we get there, son," Jacob said as his eyes fixed on the small, craggy hill where the hounds seemed to be heading.

However, Nathan sensed something else in his father's voice that his younger sibling did not. "What's the matter, Pa?"

Jacob startled a bit and shook his head, reminded that Nathan had inherited his mother's keen intuition.

"Well boys, those hounds are headed for the Black Oaks," Jacob explained. The seasoned coon hunter then pointed in the general direction of the hounds and a small but distinctively separate knoll that stood out from the surrounding hillside.

"What?" came the simultaneous chorus from both boys who were perplexed at their father's reference.

"Well, black oak is a species of tree—just like a sugar maple or even a red oak. But the Black Oaks of Ryland Creek tell of a legend that has nothing to do with the kind of tree they are."

At this point, both boys knew their father's "storytelling voice," and they were immediately intrigued as they had not heard this yarn before.

"What legend, Pa?" Mead asked after Jacob's intentional pregnant pause. Before Jacob could speak, Moses's loud bark once again filled the air, closing on the very location Jacob had indicated moments before.

"The story goes," Jacob began, "that there once was an Indian chieftain, whose name has been lost all those many years ago, who camped beneath those oaks. He was a good chief, a great warrior, hunter, as well as a fair and honest man. Furthermore, he treated all in the tribe with respect and dignity, and he possessed great wisdom.

"But as with any people, the chief had made some jealous rivals who wanted to become the chieftain themselves. These wicked men knew they could not openly challenge the chief for the tribe's leadership, as the older man would beat them in any honest debate due to his great wisdom. Other members of the tribe would see them as young fools and reject any claims that they might make on becoming their new leader. Therefore, they plotted to kill him somewhere away from the prying eyes of their fellow tribesmen.

"So, he came, all alone, up what we now know to be Ryland Creek to hunt deer."

"It's still good deer hunting here, huh, Pa?" Mead, while absorbed with the tale, could not help but interject.

"Why yes—yes, it is," Jacob readily agreed as their coonhounds continued to trail the stubborn raccoon. "So, after a long day of hunting, he took a nice buck, skinned it, and prepared the meat. By the time the chief had finished all that work, it was getting dark, so he decided to make a small camp for the night before returning to his people.

"When the old chief did not return that evening, five, some say as many as six, of his rivals figured this was their chance to kill the old chief where no one but them would know."

"But Pa," this time it was Nathan who interrupted, "which of the five, maybe six, would be the new chief?"

"That's a fair question," Jacob conceded. "I suspect, just like many who intend ill will, they got caught up so much in their schemes that they didn't think to look very far down the trail of their own making!" Jacob paused to allow the ad hoc lesson to sink in and then continued in a grave tone.

"When they came upon the chief beneath the Black Oaks, his enemies thought he was asleep. However, the chief was still the keen warrior, and he had heard them approaching. When they came into the firelight, the chief rose up from his blanket and said, 'Why are you here? What evil purpose has led you through the dark of night to my campfire?'

"At this point, the other braves didn't know what to do, but they knew they had to act quickly. So, one of them pulled out a tomahawk and threw it at the chief. The weapon caught the old chief right in the head and killed him instantly.

"But now they realized that they had not thought out their plan very well. Anyone else from the tribe could easily track all five, maybe six, of them to the very place of the murder and find the chief's corpse. To hide their evil deed, they chopped up the chief's body into small pieces, which is a desecration."

"What does 'desecration' mean, Pa?" Mead interrupted innocently.

"It means 'an unholy act,' son," Jacob explained in his ever-patient manner but then continued. "And they buried the pieces of the chief's body beneath those black oaks."

"Did anyone ever catch them and punish them?" Nathan asked, now as wholly absorbed by the tale as his younger sibling.

"Well, it's said that no *living* person caught them," Jacob teased and then continued. "Just as the bad braves expected, other members of the tribe did find the chief's camp the very next day. While there was much blood, many of these good tribe members thought that the blood they found had come from the deer that the chief had taken. With no body, they concluded that he had disappeared into thin air. 'Taken away by the Great Spirit,' said the evil brave who had thrown the tomahawk and killed the chief. And all those who did not know the truth believed this bad man's story."

Jacob paused a moment to listen to Luke's bawl. He could tell that the hounds were getting closer to the raccoon by the excitement in the dogs' voices.

"So, they got away with it," Mead said dejectedly, thinking that Jacob had ended his tale.

"Not at all!" Jacob said in mock chastisement. "For that night, as the bad men sat around the council fire debating who should be the next chief, the spirit of the chief rose from the ground. One by one, his spirit grabbed those evil men. The other tribe members were horrified, since they could not see the chief's spirit, as they watched these men, one by one, get dragged off into the night, kickin' and screaming, until there was only silence.

"Well, that's all they could see, except when it came time for the man who had committed the crime of murder."

"You mean to say, Pa, that the one who killed the chief was left to live?" Nathan asked, incredulous.

"Oh—no, no, no!" Jacob quickly corrected. "You see, up to this point, the tribe still didn't understand what was going on. Now, when he was the last, the wicked man who wanted to be the new chieftain confessed to all who could hear that they had murdered the old chief. So, this man challenged the chief's spirit to open combat as he figured that way he would be seen as the legitimate leader.

"In response, the chief's spirit rose out of the tribe's council fire, and now all could see the old chief's body as a walking flame. As they fought, the evil brave's tomahawk passed harmlessly through the chief's spirit. But when the chief struck with his fiery weapon, he drew the evil man's blood! One particularly vicious cut left an ugly scar down the center of the last bad man's face!

"Slowly, the man became so weak from the many cuts that he could no longer raise his arms. It was then that the old chief's spirit swung his tomahawk and in one fell swoop cut off the murderer's head!

"But it wasn't over.

"The tribe watched as the chief's fiery hand reached into the dead man's body and pulled out the man's spirit. The man's ghost screamed as the old chief returned to the place where they had murdered him. The chief took the evil one and forced him into the twisted black oak beside the other wicked ghosts."

"Wow!" the boys said in hushed awe.

"To this day, they say when the winds blow, it's the black oaks that seem to creak louder than any other tree in the forest." Jacob pointed to what was assuredly going to be their destination. "Some say that noise is those evil men's spirits crying out from the torture of being trapped within the Black Oaks of Ryland Creek."

Just then, Moses's tree bark sounded loudly in the night air.

"Treed," Jacob announced. "And Nathan, I do believe you owe your brother a quarter." With nothing more to add, Jacob turned and began walking toward both hounds sounding their find.

With the story of the old chief and the ghosts of those evil men still trapped on the very hill where they were headed fresh in their minds, quarter or no quarter, Mead looked at Nathan and said, "You first!"

In about fifteen minutes, the brothers had joined their father and the two baying hounds beneath an ancient oak. Its gnarled branches looked unusually contorted—clearly seen even in the night's darkness. When they gave a quick look at their father, with something of a gleam in his eye, he confirmed their fears.

"Yep, that's a black oak," Jacob noted.

With their breath now stolen away, Nathan and Mead began playing their lights on the large oak, looking for the telltale reflection of the raccoon's eye.

"I got 'im." Jacob finally declared after but a few minutes.

"Can I shoot, Pa?" Nathan asked.

"Sure. C'mon over," Jacob said, using his light to show Nathan where the raccoon was in the tree. He then handed Nathan the firearm.

The gun was familiar in Nathan's grip as he had been taught long ago how to safely use the weapon and to respect its lethalness.

"Remember, when that coon comes out of the tree, dead or alive, you're out of the hunt," Jacob said.

Nathan nodded his understanding, raised the .22 rifle, took careful aim, and squeezed the trigger. The impact of the bullet sounded with a solid "thud," and the raccoon came crashing down through the black oak's branches to land at the base of the tree.

However, Nathan's shot had not been exact—and this raccoon still had plenty of fight in him. Further, this coon was somehow different, for down its face ran a jagged scar, even evident in the hunters' artificial light, from some unknown battle long ago. The wounded animal positioned itself with its back against the base of the tree, standing on its two hind legs and snarling viciously at the two hounds attempting to flank it.

This raccoon was certainly somehow—different.

"Let's get him!" Mead charged into the standoff. In his abandon, the young boy could not see a large, partially hidden branch in the dark, and he tripped and went headlong into the small expanse between the strange raccoon and the dogs.

"Mead!" Jacob yelled as he moved toward his fallen son.

Mead was now on his back, within two feet of the oddly marred ringtail. A raccoon usually would want nothing to do with a human, and a normal wild creature would have instead focused on the two hounds.

Yet this particular raccoon was somehow—different.

The coon growled at the prone young boy, and then it leaped at the helpless human child. Time seemed to slow for Mead, watching with his eyes wide and mouth agape as the raccoon's body, and more importantly, its gleaming white fangs, began to arc downward.

In a blur, the large hound Moses also jumped and caught the raccoon in midair perfectly in his strong jaws but inches from Mead's face.

The raccoon snarled, not out of fear, but in utter rage.

Moses landed on his feet with the raccoon's throat clamped tightly, and with a vicious shake of the mighty hound's head, the raccoon's neck broke, and its body went limp.

It was over.

"Are you all right, boy?" Jacob reached down to pull Mead up by one arm.

"I'm okay, Pa," Mead said, although the ordeal had clearly shaken his resolve. The young boy then turned and ran to Moses, who had released the raccoon and now stood guard, daring it to come back to life. Mead grabbed the large hound around his neck, hugging and praising him.

Moses stood stoically through the boy's display of affection and eventually gave his typical, "Hurrumph!"

Nathan joined them and looked down at the dead raccoon and the unusual disfigurement that ran across its head.

"What do you think made that scar, Pa?" Nathan asked.

Before Jacob could offer an explanation, Mead interjected. "Do you think maybe this was one of those evil braves come back as a coon, Pa?"

Jacob's eyebrows rose slightly indicating that he too was puzzled by this strange phenomenon. "Hard sayin'," was the best explanation that Jacob could offer that night.

As Jacob had predicted, it began to rain hard, and the deluge thoroughly soaked the hunters and hounds on their return trip to their truck.

As if Painted Post was trying to cleanse itself of an evil thing.

The next morning was Sunday. The boys diligently completed their morning chores and then slipped into their "go-to-church best," which consisted of some newer jeans with no holes.

When Nathan came downstairs, the young boy found his father at the kitchen table, staring intently at the morning newspaper's front page.

"Is everything okay, Pa?" Nathan asked, quite aware that something Jacob was reading had disturbed him.

"I'm fine, son," Jacob said as he surreptitiously folded up the newspaper so Nathan could not see the front page.

"Run along and make sure Mead is getting dressed properly for church."

"Sure thing, Pa," Nathan responded, a bit confused by his father's request. Mead was more than able to get himself ready for church, but he went upstairs as asked to check on his younger brother.

When Nathan left, Jacob opened the newspaper and re-read the short article again. He knew that his boys would hear about this terrible news soon enough, but it could wait for later.

Soon afterward, all three men piled into their pickup truck and headed to church. Jacob traded in his brown fedora for a cleaner, gray version of the same hat. Mead wore an old baseball cap, while Nathan went without any hat whatsoever.

The Ernst family arrived on time for Mass at the quaint Roman Catholic Church named for Saint Catherine of Sienna. The small stone building was built in the late 1800s and located not far from the Canisteo River in Addison, New York. The large maple trees nearby were showing off their bright red foliage, accentuating the beautiful fall morning.

The boys quickly ran ahead of Jacob from the small parking lot to enter the church and select the pew in which they would sit.

Once through two large, wooden doors at the back, the boys saw the oaken pews, evenly divided by the green-carpeted center aisle. The pastel colors of yellow and blue inside gave a sense of intimacy with the stained-glass windows reflecting a rainbow spectrum. The boys dipped their hands in a small vessel of the holy water, with Mead making a sincere, if somewhat overly dramatized, genuflection.

While Nathan knew the importance of the Mass, the youngster also hoped to catch a glimpse of someone. Knowing to look at a habitual spot toward one side of the church, he found whom he sought.

Kneeling next to her mother, Miriam, Sharon Ann Helm, a school classmate, had her head bowed and her hands folded in front of her. The pretty little brunette with the shoulder-length hair, dressed in a modest blue dress, seemed angelic to Nathan. While he knew that she made him feel good inside, he could not begin to pretend to understand his emotions.

Nathan and Sharon had grown up together. The Helms were the Ernsts' closest neighbors, the very next farmhouse on Ryland Creek, about a mile apart.

Then, Sharon had been a tough tomboy—and she could whip all the boys her age in a wrestling match—except Nathan. Time after time, she would challenge Nathan to a grappling contest when they were children. Always did Nathan win those matches and would likewise ensure to never hurt her, unlike the other boys who would take a cheap shot at Sharon versus the humiliation of losing to a girl.

However, Sharon had changed. She was becoming a woman now, more mature than the boys around her age. She quickly lost interest in those other immature children and their silly antics. None of them caught her fancy except for Nathan Ernst.

Besides being rough-and-tumble mates once, these young people shared a similar sad story. Sharon had lost her father, Kenneth Helm, a teamster, in a truck accident just a few years earlier. Nathan had attended her father's wake; the first funeral that he could recall.

Miriam, only slightly taller than Sharon and wearing a yellow dress, was an undeniably comely woman. Like Jacob, Miriam had not remarried. She worked as an accountant for a small company in town, earning a livable wage for herself and her only child Sharon. While the small village of Painted Post was awash with rumors of Jacob and Miriam possibly marrying one day, these innuendos were mostly just the hopes of well-meaning people.

Sharon opened her large, brown eyes and turned her head to look in his direction, somehow sensing Nathan's gaze. Before the pre-teen realized that he was staring, Sharon smiled prettily and waved at him. Feeling his cheeks flush, Nathan managed to return a shy smile and attempted a quick, covert wave back.

Mead punched his older brother in the arm. The younger boy had witnessed the short exchange between the two friends and was letting his older brother know there was going to be some merciless ribbing on the way home after the sermon today.

Nathan could only sigh, roll his eyes, and mentally chastise himself for not being a tad more secretive about his glances toward the girl. He also caught another sight in the pew immediately behind the Helms. Sitting there alone in an expensive, red dress and black high heels was Stella Wharton.

Stella was close to both Miriam and Jacob in age, and she, too, was a widow, going on two years now, but most of the similarities ended there. In her youth, Stella had married a man of substantial wealth who was also considerably more advanced in years. There was little doubt amongst the jealous local gossipers that the highly voluptuous blonde had married for the love of money and not for the affections of the old tycoon.

As Nathan looked at the wealthy widow, he recalled something his father had once said: if you marry someone for money, you'll earn every penny of it.

Now financially well off for the rest of her life, Stella made it clear that her sights were set on none other than Jacob Ernst. She would often flaunt her wealth in front of this simple man who struggled to raise two boys and make ends meet.

Father Simmons, the tall parish priest, dressed in green vestments, finally entered from the rear of the church and proceeded to the apse to begin the ceremony. As the Mass went on, both boys caught themselves daydreaming several times. This Sunday, Father Simmons spoke about the Ten Commandments in his sermon, explaining how God had delivered these laws to humanity, and how, when obeyed, real happiness could be achieved in everyday life.

When the Mass ended, the congregation emptied the church with plain talk of the weather and the upcoming deer season. As Nathan and Mead walked out, they found Father Simmons shaking everyone's hand. Knowing Jacob's challenge of raising two young boys without their mother, the good priest took a pastoral interest in the Ernst family.

"Good morning, Father," Nathan greeted.

"Good morning, Nathan. And how are you this fine morning?" the jovial Simmons asked as he shook the young man's hand.

"I am well, thank you." With that perfunctory politeness met, Nathan walked outside of the church, hoping to catch a glimpse of Sharon as she exited.

Now it was Mead's turn to shake the good priest's hand. "Mornin', Father Simmons," he said as he firmly gripped the tall man's hand.

"And how are you doing this day, Mead?" asked the priest, mildly surprised at the strength in Mead's grip.

"I'm well, Father. And I need to tell you, Moses saved me last night!"

The priest cast a puzzled look at Jacob, who was right behind Mead, but then returned a kindly gaze at the young boy. "You mean, Jesus saved you last night, right my son?" Father Simmons prompted, thinking that perhaps the young boy had confused part of the sermon that the priest had just given on the Ten Commandments.

"Well, Father," now a very ancient ten-year-old stared directly back and used his free hand to reassuringly pat the priest's hand that still gripped his in a handshake, "I'm fairly certain that Jesus was right there whispering in his ear telling him what to do, but Moses was the one the Lord did it through last night!"

Mead then released the priest's hands, slapped his baseball cap on his head, and pranced quickly out of the church, leaving a baffled priest standing with mouth agape. Father Simmons turned back to Jacob for an explanation.

"I can explain, Father," Jacob quickly stammered, looking a bit flustered. "Last night—"

"Well hello, Jacob!" Stella Wharton broke in, and it may have been one of the few times in Jacob's life that he was genuinely relieved to see her.

Stella hooked Jacob's arm, pulling the tall man out of the church while passing by the priest with a wicked smile. Father Simmons turned his attention to saying goodbye to his other parishioners as they exited the church.

"You owe me, Jacob," Stella confided with a sly grin.

"How are you, Stella?" Jacob, always polite, asked as he donned his gray fedora.

"Lonely," Stella admitted. She was nothing if not frank.

Jacob nodded silently.

Stella may have married once for financial security, but she was not a shallow or necessarily an unkind person. In her heart, the rich widow knew that she was competing with the memory of Jacob's wife, Rose, even with her passing over a decade ago. Stella found his steadfast loyalty even more attractive. Enjoying a challenge, unaccustomed to being denied anything, Stella became more determined to win over this particular man.

"Aren't you lonely, too?" Stella pressed harder for a response as they walked into the church's parking lot where she felt confident that they were away from any eavesdroppers.

"I've got my boys." Jacob's answer did not necessarily surprise Stella, but it did sting her on another level, as she was childless and therein had another sense of fulfillment unmet. She did not blame anyone for her situation; Stella owned the choices that she had made in her life. Still, she hoped that future children of her own were not out of the question.

"Jacob, you are entitled to so much more in this life," Stella said as she stepped in front of him to look up into the tall man's eyes. Her perfectly manicured hands reached to touch his callused fingers.

"I'm entitled to nothing," Jacob said politely. "I do the best I can by my sons. Some days that effort is good enough. Other days, I have to work even harder."

Stella knew that, like her, Jacob blamed no one for his situation, and in that brief exchange, she felt a kindred spirit.

"I understand," Stella said and truly meant it. The lovely blonde had plenty of would-be suitors, but their motives were highly suspect and likely linked to the hopes of an affair and perhaps even access to her wealth. Stella believed that if Jacob ever did find an interest in another woman again, he would pursue the value of the woman herself and not a bank account.

"Well, you have a great week, Jacob. Please tell your two handsome boys I said hello." Stella ended the conversation with a sincere sentiment as she slowly walked alone to her shiny black sedan.

Jacob briefly watched her depart before he started to look for his boys in the parking lot now filled with parishioners. At last, he caught sight of Mead surrounded by several kids his age. Jacob smiled as he could tell by Mead's animated gestures and his crowd's wide-eyed gawking as they listened, that his son was retelling the previous night's hunt and how his hound Moses had saved him from "near certain death."

True to his word, Sheriff Sean Covington was amongst Mead's audience, caught up in the excitement of the coon hunting story. Now dressed immaculately in civilian attire, the police officer reacted with the same enthusiasm as the children around Mead.

"Such a big kid," Jacob muttered to himself and chuckled at the thought of his best friend Sean, the toughest man in Steuben County.

Jacob recalled the front page of the morning paper, the brutal murder reported, and suspected that Sean and his deputies were already working to solve the crime. He thought better of asking any details of Sean, particularly after just leaving the Sunday service. With some effort, he pushed the horrific event from his mind.

It took Jacob a while longer to espy his older son, but he found Nathan at the other end of the asphalt parking lot talking with Sharon Helm. The children were not far from Miriam, who was tugging on her old truck 's door, attempting to open it. Jacob walked over to her. "Need a hand?"

Miriam recognized her good neighbor immediately. "Yes, Jacob! This old truck is starting to wear out."

"Aren't we all?" Jacob joked. He reached for the handle and almost effortlessly opened the door, much to Miriam's surprise. "You have to pull more straight out. You're kinda," Jacob hesitated, not sure how to phrase his words due to Miriam's height, "sort of pulling more . . . down."

She laughed at his awkwardness. "It comes with the territory of being short, I suppose."

"Yes, ma'am," Jacob agreed.

Both parents caught sight of Nathan and Sharon, and while it was clear that young Sharon was carrying the conversation, it was equally obvious that Nathan was enjoying just listening.

"How are your boys doing?" Miriam asked.

"As well as can be expected." Jacob thanked her with his smile. He had been very good friends with her late husband.

"How's your farm doing?" Miriam continued.

"We're makin' that work, too—mostly chickens, the hounds, a few cows, and one stubborn old mule."

"Butch? You still have your father's mule?" Miriam asked, astounded.

"Yes. Unfortunately," Jacob said with no small amount of frustration, causing Miriam to laugh.

"We sold all our livestock when Kenny died," Miriam said. A brief flash of pain crossed her face at the memory of her spouse—a feeling to which Jacob could relate.

"Well, if'n you need anything fixed around the house, be sure to let me know," Jacob offered.

"I might just take you up on that, Jacob." Miriam smiled. She was a proud woman, but she understood everyone had limitations.

Jacob tipped his hat to her and, turning to oldest son, said, "C'mon, son, it's time to head home."

Nathan looked both a little embarrassed and reluctant to leave Sharon's side. He uttered a polite "it's been good talking to you" to the young lady, who likewise returned the farewell, and the young man moved to leave with his father.

Sharon watched Nathan walk away as she climbed into the old truck with Miriam.

Mead's crowd of boys his age, and even Sheriff Covington, were visibly upset when he too had to respond to his father's call, but Mead promised to tell them other coon hunting stories at school the next day.

As the doors to their truck closed, Mead could not resist teasing his brother. "Nate and Sharon sitting in a tree, K. I. S. S. I. . . .," he began but never finished.

"Dah!" Nathan smacked his younger brother on the back of the head, knocking his baseball cap to the floor of the truck. As he reached over to pick up his hat, Mead howled with laughter, knowing that he had successfully goaded his brother. Nathan glanced at his father, and they shared a laugh.

Then Mead took on a serious look. "Pa, can we go see them?" he pleaded.

"Yes—yes, we can," Jacob responded, knowing what his young son was asking of him.

Shifting the truck into gear, Jacob pulled into a cemetery less than half a mile from the church. He drove slowly, respectfully, passing many headstones till they reached a far corner of the graveyard that was graced by a large sugar maple tree. Jacob pulled the vehicle to a stop, and all three men exited the pickup.

Mead ran ahead of his father and brother to stop and stare at three particular headstones.

Beneath that maple tree, the graves were partially covered with some of the bright yellow leaves that had already fallen. The names on the tombstones read:

Paul Ernst
Mary Ernst
Rose Ernst

Even a casual observer would notice that both Paul and Mary Ernst peculiarly shared the same beginning and ending dates on their grave markers. Jacob focused on the end date, recalling the day that his parents had died in a car crash one winter night.

The family said nothing for a while in this solemn place until Mead finally broke the silence. "Grandpa Ernst was a great coon hunter, huh, Pa?"

"I never knew a better dog man in my life, son," Jacob confirmed. "He taught me a great many things about chasing raccoon and the woods in these parts." Jacob then hastened to add, with a gleam in his eye and a knowing smile of remembrance. "Of course, he did leave a thing or two for me to learn on my own."

"And Grandma Ernst was a great cook, right, Pa?" Nathan now spoke.

"The best!" Jacob readily confirmed.

"Kinda wish she'd taught you a bit more about cookin', Pa," Mead said so earnestly but innocently that both Nathan and Jacob could only chuckle at the well-meaning, if unintended slight, to Jacob's culinary prowess.

Mead then looked at his brother and father, and with no need for words, they slowly turned and headed back to the truck. The young boy then quickly knelt in front of the headstone that read "Rose Ernst," and like his father, he stared hard at the last carved date that he knew so well.

"I'm sorry, Mama." Mead spoke in a tone just barely above a whisper. *We are never truly alone in this world, my little boy.*

The voice in Mead's head was not his own, and although he could never truly aver that his ears had heard that voice before, he knew in his heart exactly who spoke to him.

"Thank you, Ma," Mead said. When he turned, the young boy realized that he must have spoken loud enough for Jacob and Nathan to hear him, as they had both stopped to look at him curiously.

Mead offered no explanation but instead stood up and walked by his father and brother. Nathan and Jacob looked at each other and shrugged.

They climbed back into their truck and began their banter about the continued prospects of the coon season as they headed home down the back roads of Painted Post.

Chapter 4

Rewards

J acob watched the moisture from his breath rising in his headlight's white beam. The inch-deep December snow crunched noisily as he shifted his weight while leaning on his trusted walking stick.

The clear sound of Luke and Moses treeing this night should have brought a smile to his face, but both Mead and Nathan could easily read their father's concern.

"What's the matter, Pa?" Mead broke the silence between the men with the hounds' constant ringing tree barks coming from the side of the darkened hill.

"I know that mountain," Jacob explained as he had coursed the dogs' location correctly, "and those hounds are very near a cliff. With the snow and ice, that is going to be one tricky climb. Be careful, boys! It's very easy to go over a cliff at night if you're not paying close attention."

"Well, those hounds aren't getting any closer, Pa. Let's go!" Mead exclaimed.

Nathan and Jacob grinned at Mead's enthusiasm and simple wisdom.

Jacob was grateful as this hunting season had so far been very successful. The next day, the fur buyer would visit their farm to purchase their coonhides, and with Christmas just a week away, that money would go to buy his sons new, warm winter clothing.

Jacob led the way as usual, with his sons evenly spaced a dozen feet behind each other. He located an old game trail that he knew well, and while the hill's grade did increase sharply, they easily traversed the trek to the hill's top.

The men found their hounds treed on an immense eastern hemlock. Its many boughs with their flat pine needles prevented the men from any hope of seeing the raccoon's body. They slowly began to spread out around the tree with the familiar hope of catching the amber reflection of the coon's eye in their lights.

Jacob fished deep into one of the front pockets of his canvas hunting coat. He pulled out a small device, a coon squaller, to produce a loud, reedy-pitched noise to hopefully cause the curious ringtail to look down at the ruckus. As he looked up, Jacob quickly noted the direction Nathan and Mead were taking to get around to the other side of the tree.

"Boys!" Jacob said sternly, and both of his sons immediately stopped in their tracks to look at him. "Remember what I said about the cliffs? Look carefully right in front of you."

Both boys shone their flashlights in front of them to reveal that their hounds had indeed treed near the edge of a steep decline. Nathan estimated the near-vertical drop at thirty feet. With the lesson learned, the boys nodded a silent "thank you" to their father, and they gingerly changed direction to shine their lights up the tree in a safer location.

Jacob blew into the call, making a chilling sound, and less than a minute later, the coon hunter caught sight of his prey. "I've got him!" he exclaimed, unslung the old rifle from his back, and loaded the weapon. "Boys,' Jacob said, 'I'll take this one. Nathan, hold Luke. Mead, keep Moses back. If this coon comes out alive, I don't want the dogs chasing it over that cliff."

"Got it, Pa," Nathan responded, and both he and Mead grabbed their hounds and pulled them back a safe distance from the tree.

The gun's sharp report once again heralded Jacob's outstanding marksmanship as the lifeless raccoon crashed through the limbs to land on the far side of the tree. Jacob immediately began unloading and focused on making safe his rifle.

"Nice shot, Pa!" Mead said, as he released Moses and moved to pick up the dead ringtail.

When he looked up from finally slinging the unloaded weapon on his back again, Jacob shouted with alarm, "Mead, back away from that raccoon—now!"

Confused, Mead stopped to look at his father as he was nearly at their prize. But then he realized that his forward momentum had not ceased, and in fact, the boy was slowly slipping toward the edge of the cliff. Mead began windmilling his arms in the air in a desperate attempt to maintain his balance. But the lack of any traction was too much for his worn boots, and he fell to the hard, icy ground.

"Pa!" Mead called out in terror, clawing at the ground.

"Mead!" Nathan shouted as his sibling slipped over the edge of the cliff and out of sight.

"Nathan!" Jacob commanded. "Use your leash and tie Luke to a tree." Jacob then looked around for Moses, only to see the old hound rush with abandon and slip over the cliff's edge where Mead had just disappeared.

"Pa! Nate!" Mead's terrified voice shouted in the night.

While hearing Mead's voice brought temporary relief, Jacob did not know if his son was hurt, and he knew getting the boy off the cliff would be no easy chore.

"Nathan," Jacob explained as his eldest son ran up to him after having secured Luke to a small sapling with his leash. "I'm going to lie on my stomach and inch over the edge and see where Mead is. I want you to keep a hold of my boots as I could slip over that edge just as easily."

"Will do, Pa," Nathan said.

Jacob removed the rifle from his back and re-grasped his oak walking stick leaning against a nearby tree. Then Jacob walked as far as he could before he started slipping on the steep grade. With Nathan beside him, and giving a quick nod to proceed, Jacob dropped to his stomach and finally inched to the edge to look over.

As planned, Nathan anchored himself with his boot heels digging into the snow, grabbing his father's ankles tightly.

There, perhaps only five feet below the edge, Mead stood, holding on to an oak sapling. Luckily, while the cliff here was very steep, it was not completely vertical. Jacob's light revealed that had Mead slipped just another five feet, he would have gone over the truly sharp edge to a twenty-foot drop onto a cold, frozen creek's bed with certain fatal results.

Next to Mead, but able to secure his claws into the icy cover for a firm hold, was the ever-faithful Moses.

"Are you okay, boy?" Jacob asked.

"I'm okay, Pa, just a little scared." Mead's voice cracked somewhat. "I lost my flashlight."

Jacob breathed a second sigh of relief. "Good and don't worry about the light," he said. "Now listen to me. I'm going to hand you one end of my walking stick. I want you to grasp it and pull yourself up, hand over hand. Don't worry—I'll have the other end, and I won't let go. Can you do that, son?"

"Yes, Pa!" Mead shouted.

"Good boy, now here we go." As planned, Jacob held out the walking stick to Mead with his arm fully extended.

"Pa, what about Moses?" Mead asked.

"Son, don't worry about that hound—he'll be okay. Now, grab the stick!" Jacob said louder.

Mead took one more look at Moses standing nearby and then reached for the stick. But to the dismay of both Mead and Jacob, the walking stick was about a foot too short for Mead to grasp.

"I can't reach it, Pa! Not without letting go of this sapling. And if I let go, I'll slip over the cliff for sure!" Mead sounded on the verge of tears.

"Listen to me, boy," Jacob said calmly. "I want you to get down on your stomach and use your feet to push against that sapling. That should close the distance by just enough for you to get hold of the stick."

"All right, Pa, I'll try!" Mead said, although his voice remained laced with uncertainty.

Nathan's boots slipped just a bit in the snow, and both Jacob and his eldest son slid another inch down the hill.

"Hold tight, Nathan!" Jacob shouted over his shoulder.

"I will, Pa," Nathan reassured.

Gingerly, Mead lie down on the ground, securing his feet on the base of the sapling, and then pushed himself slowly up the grade toward his father. While he could just touch the end of the walking stick with his fingers, Mead could not get a hold on the staff. "I'm still too short!"

Mead then felt something grasp the back of his clothing. Moses had clamped his powerful jaws onto Mead's coat collar and, with a powerful jerk, lifted the boy the precious last few inches, allowing Mead to get a solid grasp on the stick.

"I got it, Pa!" Mead shouted for joy.

"Thank God," Jacob called out. "Now, pull yourself up, and then climb up my body to your brother."

"Will do, Pa!" Mead responded. As instructed, he pulled himself up quickly on the walking stick, breathing heavily from the exertion. When their faces were close together, with Mead now grasping Jacob's strong arm, he looked his father in the eye with the boy's tears beginning to flow. "I'm sorry, Pa."

"It's all right, boy. Just keep climbing, please," Jacob said.

Mead smiled at his father's encouragement and began to reach higher. Climbing up a little more on Jacob's back, the boy placed his knee over the cliff's edge to safety.

Then Mead heard Moses next to him, and the frantic sound of the hound's claws trying to find purchase on the icy slope. The hound had his front two feet over the cliff's edge, but with the lack of traction, Moses started to slip helplessly over the steep overhang once more.

"No!" Mead shouted as he watched his beloved hound slide backward. With his free hand, the boy thrust his arm out and firmly grasped the dog's collar.

Years later, many of Painted Post residents would point to this adventure as the first evidence of Mead Ernst's incredible strength.

The young boy suddenly heaved the large hound over the cliff's ledge to safety. Completely over the glazed brim now, Moses quickly dug his nails into the side of the hill and successfully made the climb to join Nathan, who was still holding Jacob's boots.

The whole scene had happened so quickly that Jacob had no time to react, as he would have told Mead to save himself. Moses was a good hound but not worth his son's life!

Mead quickly scrambled up the hill.

With Nathan's help, the brothers extricated Jacob from the awkward position. All three men then sat beneath the large hemlock, with Moses near Mead and Luke looking on, still tethered to the sapling.

Finally catching his breath, with Jacob and Nathan holding their lights on the youngest boy's visage, Mead exclaimed, "Father Simmons and the kids at school are never going to believe this story!"

The next day was a flurry of activity as the Ernsts continued their preparation for the sale of their coon hides. Pulled from the chest freezer in the barn, and then carefully thawed over the past few days in their cellar, Jacob expertly combed the pelts with a small wire brush. He instructed the boys to place the bevy of fur in neat piles by size, grouped from "small" to "extra-large."

The men had just finished their work when they heard a loud knock on their front door. Jacob went upstairs while the boys waited patiently.

"Good morning, Jacob!" the fur buyer greeted his old friend.

"Good morning, Rich. It's good to see you again."

"How have you and your boys been? How many coons you take so far this season?" Rich asked.

"We're fine, thank you. And we've taken ninety-eight, including the one we worked for last night," Jacob replied, pausing unintentionally for a moment as he relived the cliff saga with Mead. "I think you'll like the quality of these hides."

"Whoa—that sure is a lot of ringtails! You must have some impressive hounds. And I sure hope the fur is good, Jacob. I've not been impressed with the quality from my last few stops. Shoot! The market is hungry for good fur, and I can't locate enough."

"Well, I hope we can serve your needs. Follow me."

Jacob led Rich down into the cellar, and the expert furrier produced a small pad of paper with a pencil and immediately knelt before the various piles, sorting each hide while scribbling notes on the writing pad the entire time. Jacob and Rich would occasionally haggle over the size of one or another, but each knew the other to be an expert judge of fur, so the banter remained friendly and businesslike.

Rich continued to make computations furiously on the paper for nearly a minute after he had graded the last hide.

The boys watched, each holding his breath, knowing that their Christmas gifts were predicated on this sale.

"These are the best hides I've seen so far this season!" Rich exclaimed happily. "And Jacob, I'll give you a twenty-dollar average for them. Do we have a deal?" Rich offered Jacob his hand.

"We have a deal," Jacob said, pleased with the price proffered. Both Mead and Nathan whooped at the thought of presents under the Christmas tree this year.

"Can I get your boys to give me a hand taking these furs to my truck?" Rich asked, producing a thick wallet to pay Jacob the cash owed.

"Boys, please give Rich a hand," Jacob said.

"Sure thing, Pa!" Nathan spoke first.

Placing the hides in large burlap sacks, the boys made several trips, taking the load to the furrier's truck. With the last of the furs placed in the back of Rich's old pickup, and the December air quite frigid this late morning, Nathan and Mead turned to go back into their warm house.

"Boys!" Rich called them back. He handed each a crisp, ten-dollar bill. "Thanks for helping me get these hides in my truck. This payment is for your service, and you both have a Merry Christmas!"

"Thanks, sir!" Mead shouted as he stared happily at the folding money.

"Merry Christmas," Nathan said in return.

That afternoon, Jacob took his sons down to J.P. Smith's General Merchandise and Hardware Store. He wanted to get Nathan and Mead coats and boots that fit well, and that meant them trying on the apparel first.

The store's doorbells rang loudly as the Ernst family entered the festively decorated store, which held a plethora of shoppers.

J.P. Smith walked up to greet them. "Well, well, well!" J.P. exclaimed as his beefy jowls quivered in delight. "Seeing you here now with these boys tells me that you must have sold your coon hides."

"Yes, sir!" Mead exclaimed. "Pa said we could get some new boots and a coat today!"

"Rightfully earned, I should say." J.P. returned. "And at the rate that you're growing, Mead, I should say you may need new boots and coat again come this spring!"

The boys laughed and ran off to choose their new apparel with Jacob following close behind. After several attempts to determine the right sizes for both boys, they were eventually able to find perfect fits.

The line was long at the checkout stand, but J.P. was not working the cash register. The holiday season meant he had to hire extra help, which also allowed him to mingle with his customers. When he saw the Ernst boys loaded down with the new boots and coats, J.P. once again approached them.

"Those are some mighty fine hunting duds you have there, men."

Both Nathan and Mead smiled at being called 'men.'

"You got another ghost story to tell, J.P.?" Mead asked.

"Well, well," J.P. said, quickly transitioning into his storytelling voice. "The only ghost I should be talking about this time of year should be the Holy Ghost." J.P. shot a quick glance at Jacob, who nodded his tacit agreement. "But do you know how Painted Post got its name?"

"No, Mr. Smith," Mead said rather formally after a moment. "I guess I never did hear about that."

"Well," J.P. began, "the painted post was, in fact, a wooden post. But it wasn't just any wooden post. No, sir! For what were likely centuries, the Iroquois, their allies, and sometimes their enemies, floated down these rivers. The land here was a natural place to meet because it's the confluence of the Tioga and Conhocton rivers."

"What does 'confluence' mean, Mr. Smith?" Mead asked.

"It means a place where rivers join. And in this case, the Tioga and Conhocton join to form the Chemung River. That's why they also call Painted Post, 'the land of the three rivers.' Thus, this land was a place of peace, trade, and also war!"

"You're keepin' the commerce piece alive," Jacob noted somewhat sardonically, eyeing the long line of shoppers in front of them waiting to make their purchases.

"Yes, indeed!" J.P. beamed at the many holiday customers in his store. "Anyway, the story goes that the original 'painted post,' for which our town is named, is steeped in mystery! Some believe it was merely a carved wooden post placed to mark the location where these Native American tribes would greet one another—sort of like an exit sign you see on the highways nowadays.

"Others believed our town's namesake to be a bragging post erected by a chieftain who recorded his deeds of martial conflict and revenge by carving human figures into its wood. Legend further has it the 'paint' was actually the blood of his defeated enemies."

"Well, how tall was this post, J.P.?" Mead asked.

"Some say as high as twenty feet!" J.P. exclaimed, relishing his exaggeration as he realized several other shoppers had stopped to listen to his story.

"That post sure could hold a whole lot of blood!" Mead reckoned.

J.P. could not help but laugh at Mead's reasoning. "I doubt that rendition, though," he mused. "The folks around these parts aren't particularly known for using euphemisms, and the town likely would have been called 'Bloody Post' if'n that accounting held more sway."

"What does 'euphemism' mean?" Nathan asked the question this time.

"Well, it's finding a way to describe something nice for something that truly ain't so nice!" J.P. explained. Nathan nodded as the erudite storeowner and storyteller continued.

"Perhaps more credible historical accounts have the post being a grave marker of a Seneca chieftain who fought alongside the British against our emerging American nation in the Revolutionary War. Later, the first settlers would find the post around the late 1700s.

"While replicas of the post were made, legend has it that the original post's last purveyor—that means 'owner'—became so utterly frustrated with the keepsake that he just threw it into the Chemung River to have it float away!"

"And what was the supposed name of this purveyor?" Jacob pressed J.P. with a knowing grin.

"Well, ahem," J.P. paused and cleared his throat as his large mug turned quickly red, apparently a bit flummoxed by Jacob's query.

"Rumor has it that his name was Smith."

Chapter 5

All Things End

Spring 1977

It was a warm, sunny day in early April. Spring had finally arrived in Painted Post, although in some dark, hilly recesses, snow could be found, stubbornly refusing to yield to the new season. While the oaks stayed in their winter slumber, the maples, as usual, had a head start in populating their limbs with fresh leaf buds.

Nathan and Mead were up early and dutifully finished their respective chores, for today they had a mission. They had heard frogs peeping for the last three nights now. The boys knew, or at least as folklore would have it, there would be plenty of fresh frog eggs in their farm's pond this morning. After breakfast, the boys began to get ready.

"Pa, can I take the .22 with us?" Nathan asked.

Jacob, his head hidden behind the morning news, folded the paper down to reveal a somewhat skeptical look. "Why do you need a rifle to collect frog eggs?"

"Just target practice, Pa," Nathan responded and quickly added, "We won't shoot at the water, and we'll be sure to know what's beyond our target to be safe."

Jacob said nothing but nodded approvingly and folded the newspaper back, hiding his face once again. The brothers looked excitedly at one another and began to collect their glass jars.

"Why don't you take those pups with you, too?" Jacob called from behind the newspaper. "And be certain you know where they are before you do any target shooting!"

"Sure, Pa!" Mead exclaimed and all but danced. "I'll get the pups, Nate!" Out the door Mead sprang, jars in hand, and the hounds barked excitedly as he ran to the kennels.

Nathan went to the gun cabinet, removed the .22 caliber rifle, and threaded his arm through the old leather sling to rest the strap on his shoulder. He also grabbed the gun's already-loaded magazine and a handful of shells, about fifty he estimated, which would allow for plenty of practice for the brothers and stuffed them into his pants pocket. He joined Mead, who was petting the four pups, which were now close to six months old.

Maud looked on from her kennel. Although the pups had been weaned for months now, she still had the motherly instinct and whined anxiously, seeing her litter milling about without her protection.

Ignoring their mother's concerns, the pups jumped excitedly, vying for the young boys' attention.

Well, every dog needs a boy.

"They'll be all right." Nathan moved close to Maud, reassuring her. His soothing voice seemed to do the trick, as Maud wagged her tail and quit the soft whining.

"Justice! Duke! Sam! Storm!" Mead called each of the pups by name. He went over to Moses's pen and unlatched the gate. The puppies poured into the enclosure, bouncing around the older hound, innately knowing this dog was their sire.

The habitually grumpy dog stood stoically as the pups jumped on the old hound, licking his face.

"That's okay, Moses," Mead said, gently patting the old dog's head to reward the hound's forbearance. "They don't mean anything by it."

"Hurrumph!" Moses snorted although it was evident that the older hound did not mind the extra attention.

Mead, with Nathan's help to prevent them from reentering the pen, carried each puppy out of Moses's kennel. Keeping an eye on the pups, Mead absentmindedly closed the kennel door to lock it. "Let's go!" he shouted as he picked up the glass jars, resting on the ground.

The pups, happy to run free, barked back at the youngster.

"Let's go," Nathan concurred with a smile.

The pond was only a couple of hundred yards from the house and nestled against the edge of the forest surrounding the Ernst farm. The little female pup Storm was the most energetic of the litter and independent. She sensed the general direction of the group and sprung forward, if somewhat clumsily due to her youth, into the freshly plowed cornfield.

The field was a little wet, and the mud clung to the boys' boots. They pointed to one another the different spoor left on the ground by many different denizens of the surrounding forest.

"Look, Nathan, a deer!" Mead pointed out the tracks in the soft earth. "Here's a fox!" he called out, and then spying another set, "and a coon!"

"Guess we didn't get them all, huh?" Nathan chided and knocked the small jean cap off his younger brother's head.

Mead laughed good-naturedly, bent down to pick up his cap, and then caught sight of another set of tracks as he stood.

"Nate, did we have any dogs running loose after Pa plowed the field a couple of days ago?"

"Nope. Why do you ask?"

"Well, aren't these dog tracks?" Mead pointed to the ground but also looked beyond his brother to the pups that were playing more than fifty yards away. The young boy was certain these canine tracks, quite large, had not just been made by the coonhound pups.

Nathan examined the tracks in question. "No," he said as he knelt and touched the soft mud. "A coyote made these tracks. See how the two front toes align with the back toes?" Mead nodded as Nathan continued, "That's how you know it's a coyote and not a dog. A dog's toes go all evenly around its pad."

As Nathan rose, Mead realized his older sibling was searching for something else.

Then Nathan found it. "Yep," he said, pointing a spot about ten yards away. "Here's another set of tracks—probably made by a mated male and female coyote staking out this field as part of their territory."

"Whoa!" Mead said in an awed tone.

"It's best that we keep an eye on the pups," Nathan said, sounding so much older to Mead. "You can't be sure, but those coyotes might be watching us right now with an eye toward eating our pups." Nathan, with the rifle still slung over his back, let his right hand grasp the gun's barrel, studying the woods, as though expecting to see the coyotes.

While perhaps overdramatizing his actions and showing off to his little brother, Nathan could not know at that moment how right he truly was.

The pair of coyotes had heard the commotion down by the farmhouse long before the boys had discovered their tracks and had secreted their naturally camouflaged bodies inside the edge of the forest. While instinctively fearing man, the wild canines also knew that sustenance often came easily around farms. The just-ended winter had left them lean and hungry. Using their natural cunning, strength, and speed, these "brush wolves" knew that they might easily take a stray chicken, cat, or even a small dog with little fear of discovery.

They watched as the young boys and the hound pups traipsed into the field. The dogs were too close to the humans for an opportunity to attack now, but the puppies, particularly the young female, were drifting farther and farther away from the boys, and the chance of a quick meal might offer itself at any moment. The apex predators crouched undetected in the nascent springtime verdure.

And they waited.

When the boys reached the pond, they quickly began searching for their prize. While the water covered less than half an acre and not more than ten feet at its deepest, the pond supported enormous, tasty bullheads. However, the whiskered, spiny-finned fishes were not the boys' focus today. This morning, they looked for the gelatinous masses of eggs that would eventually turn into tadpoles and then finally into beneficial, insect-eating frogs.

It did not take long for Mead to yell to Nathan and point excitedly at several masses of frog eggs floating on the pond's surface next to a small stand of cattails.

The boys moved to the edge of the pond closest to the eggs.

Mead carefully set the jars on the ground, while Nathan pulled the leather sling over his head and carefully placed the rifle on the shore to keep it from getting wet.

They quickly doffed their boots and socks and waded into the pond's murky brown water with their jars in hand. While the water was still frigid enough to make the boys' teeth chatter, they readily accepted the discomfort for the sake of their quarry.

Mead unscrewed the cap of one of the jars and handed it to Nathan, who smiled and gladly took the role of holding the lid while his brother enjoyed the hunt.

The freshly laid eggs, looking like small clouds floating in the water, were firm and contained perfectly round, little black dots, which were the developing tadpoles. Mead cooed at the sensation as he gently coaxed the mass of the eggs into the large-mouth jar. The pond water flooded into the container, supporting the buoyant ova. When he had filled the jar to capacity, Mead held it up against the sun to get a better look at his catch with considerable pride. Nathan handed Mead the container's lid, and the younger boy quickly screwed the top in place to safely transport their prize home.

They relished the idea of capturing more eggs, and both boys repeated their roles, scooping up the floating masses in another container. Soon, with their mission accomplished, and a second jar full, they slowly moved toward dry land.

While the boys had been gathering the frog eggs, the young pups had frolicked around the pond, joyously barking at the kids and each other. Storm had even attempted to join the brothers at one point, but the cold water discouraged her efforts. She quickly returned to her littermates as they chased one another.

Out of the water, the boys donned their socks and boots, the jars of eggs between them, and they sat soaking up the warm sun on the pond's bank.

"Nate, do you miss Ma?" Mead blurted out.

"Yeah, I miss her," Nathan managed to say after a long pause.

"It's my fault she's gone," Mead said looking down, his expression suddenly as cloudy as the pond.

"No, Mead—that isn't so," Nathan responded faster this time, sensing his brother's self-pity. "Those things happen in life. Pa says we can't know why they are such—we just have to bear what life throws at us. *It wasn't your fault.*"

Mead nodded, recalling those very words from Jacob on several occasions. Hearing Nathan repeat them seemed to have an added comfort—words Mead had needed to hear.

"Pa still misses her though, huh?" Mead said. Nathan hid his amazement at the younger boy's insight.

Nathan knew the accuracy of Mead's observation and acknowledged, "Yeah, he does. But they'll be together in heaven someday."

The boys sat for a long time, silently watching the water and occasionally looking down with pride at the captured eggs. They also kept an eye on the pups, now playing in the plowed field, barking loudly while taking turns piling onto one another.

Down the hilly field to their home, Moses began to howl loud enough that both boys could easily hear the faithful hound. At first, it was just a couple of barks, but then the old dog's voice became louder and his barking more frequent. Soon the other dogs began to chime in too. While not unusual for the dogs to sound off when they smelled something near the farm, there was something different in their voices this day.

The boys even saw Jacob come out of the farmhouse and scold the hounds for making such a commotion. They quieted at first, but less than a minute after Jacob had reentered the house, the coonhounds began their cacophony anew.

"What do you suppose has gotten into them?" Mead asked.

"Not sure," Nathan admitted.

But the older boy noticed something else—the pups' barking had also changed. No longer was it the carefree sound of young dogs romping about, but instead, they barked in alarm. Drawn to the new noise, Nathan caught sight of the three young males formed in a tight group. The underpinning fear in the pups' cries, and the reason Moses and the other hounds had sounded their warning, became evident as the scene unraveled.

The pups had moved to over one hundred yards from the humans. The coyotes recognized their opportunity, and leaving the cover of the forest, now tightly circled the young coonhounds. The wild canines knew that if they could separate these young innocents from their human protectors, they might take one, possibly two, of the dogs with impunity.

It would be a quick kill.

Nathan was on his feet now. He slipped the loaded magazine into the gun's bottom. Using the bolt action, he jacked a shell into the rifle's chamber and raised the weapon to aim down its iron sights.

"Shoot the coyotes, Nate!" Mead screamed, now fully aware of the danger.

But Nathan could not fire the weapon.

The coyotes were constantly moving, as were the pups, turning in tight, concentric circles, trying to maintain their protective posture. Both predator and prey knew what was at stake, and the coyotes made several fake lunges, attempting to separate one dog from the others.

While perhaps inexperienced, the young hounds were still not making it easy on the coyotes. The pups would dart a short distance back toward Nathan and Mead and then reform their defensive circle. It was not so much due to the dogs' well-thought strategy as much as fear that kept them moving closer to the safety of the humans. However, the flurry of movement continued to deny Nathan a clear shot as he tried to target a coyote and not hit the pups he was trying to defend.

All the while, Mead repeatedly screamed for his brother to take the shot.

Finally, one of the coyotes went wide in an attempt to flank Duke, who had moved away from Sam and Justice. Now Nathan had a chance. He controlled his breathing, aimed down the rifle's barrel, and began to squeeze the trigger . . .

"Don't shoot, Nate!" Mead suddenly cried.

Nathan instinctively pulled the rifle up without firing. He quickly discerned the reason behind Mead's frantic warning, for a moment later, the full-grown hound Moses plowed his considerable weight into the larger coyote that had been solely focused on taking Duke. Nathan quickly reasoned that Mead must not have completely closed Moses's kennel latch, and the old hound had forced open the pen's door and raced up the hill just in time.

The two canines, domestic and wild, tumbled under the hound's brutal impact. Moses had intercepted the larger male, but the female coyote, just as deadly if ten pounds lighter, was now fully aware of the older hound's entry into the melee. She joined her mate to face the large black and tan coonhound.

The pups meanwhile instinctively moved behind their sire as the battle unfolded.

The two coyotes charged the older hound as they knew no amount of stealth would take the experienced coonhound. Their simple strategy was to overwhelm the dog as they lunged with snapping jaws.

While Moses may have been accustomed to doing battle with smaller prey, he was still a coonhound. A deadly dance began as the powerful hound threw his weight and skill into attacking and counterattacking his opponents. Back and forth, the enemies went, lunging and biting. Both dog and coyotes inflicted significant wounds on one another, but none of the canines showed any sign of slowing.

Then the female coyote skillfully ducked below Moses's huge maw, grabbed the hound's back leg. She attempted to pull the hound off balance, allowing her mate to take the hound by the throat. Together, she and her partner would bring the old dog down and finish him.

But Moses was no ordinary hound.

While anchored by the female's efforts, his remaining legs held steady, so the hound could watch the male coyote, which had moved just out of the range of the hound's powerful jaws.

The male coyote backed off slightly, more feigning a retreat while waiting for the perfect opening in the dog's defense. That moment came as Moses, seeing the male coyote seemingly withdraw, turned to face the female still latched onto and tugging his leg. This was the moment of distraction for which the male coyote had waited. Its muscles tensed to make one last lunge that would find its jaws clamped in a death grip around the hound's throat.

A loud, sharp crack rang out, and Nathan's well-placed bullet entered the wild canine's right temple. The male coyote died instantly and slumped to the ground.

The female coyote immediately sensed what had happened: man had entered the fray. While her mind could not comprehend the concept of the firearm, she did understand that her mate was dead. Instinctively, she knew to quit this fight, for alone she was no match for the big hound. She quickly released her hold on Moses's leg and began to run.

Moses did not follow. The old hound, while not showing signs of slowing during the battle, was exhausted. Quickly, Moses's three male pups huddled closer to him as the old dog watched the remaining coyote flee the scene.

Yet Nathan knew something was not right, for the coyote should have taken a more direct path to the safety of the forest. In the periphery of the boy's vision, he quickly discerned the coyote's final strategy.

The female pup Storm had watched the struggle from a distance as she had been separate from her brothers just before the coyotes had begun their assault. While she had been lucky not to be the target of the coyotes' initial attack, simply due to the circumstance of location, she now found the remaining predator bearing down on her with frightening speed.

"Nate!" Mead all but screamed. The younger boy had also figured out the coyote's trajectory and intended target. "It's going after Storm!"

Nathan already had the rifle up and fired the weapon.

Just behind the running coyote, the gun's bullet kicked up a clod of the plowed field's dirt. Nathan quickly worked the bolt action on the rifle to chamber another shell while the distance between the young puppy and the predator shrank.

Nathan fired again but with the same effect: another plume of dirt rising just behind the accelerating coyote. He had only one opportunity left to shoot before the coyote would close the final distance. By then, there would be no way to shoot without the possibility of inadvertently hitting the young coonhound pup.

Mead was screaming, helpless to assist, and not thinking that his commotion could only distract his brother's aim.

Nathan controlled his breathing. Time seemed to slow as he focused on the rifle's front sight. The coyote started to decelerate as it prepared to pounce and kill the female pup. Remembering the lessons that Jacob had taught him, to be deliberate, Nathan slowly squeezed the trigger for what he knew would be his final chance to save Storm.

The rifle's report rang out with another sharp crack, and for the last time, the shot, although closer than the previous attempts, landed just behind the coyote.

"Nate!" Mead yelled in desperation.

The coyote, still moving at an incredible speed, opened its powerful jaws while the young black and tan pup cowered, defenseless against the wild canine's impending onslaught.

When all hope seemed lost, a thunderous explosion sounded throughout the hills of Painted Post. The noise resounded so loud that it made both Nate and Mead jump and look around to find their father, standing nearby, still aiming his open-sight lever action .30-30 rifle.

The shot was true, and due to sheer momentum of her final attack, the dead coyote's body tumbled into the dirt, finally grinding to a halt at Storm's feet.

The two boys stared in amazement at their father's marksmanship.

Jacob did not at first look to Nathan and Mead but instead kept his sight down range to ensure the last coyote was dead. He then slowly turned to his sons.

"You gotta lead 'em," Jacob said. With a smooth and practiced motion of the rifle's lever action, he then ejected the spent shell.

Little Storm approached the motionless animal, sniffing cautiously at the carcass, and then instinctively jerked back. Her male siblings joined her and were likewise skittishly exploring the dead coyote. Suddenly, Storm let out a loud and long bawl akin to her father Moses's voice. The rest of the pups also began to bay loudly at the lifeless coyote.

"All right!" Mead shouted. Like nothing unusual had just transpired, the young boy sprinted toward the pups to join in their excitement. Soon the air filled with the din of the young boy and dogs triumphantly prancing around the plowed field.

"Good shot, Pa," Nathan finally said with a slight hint of shame since he had failed to make the final killing shot.

"There's a lot of air around a coyote, son—even more around a moving one. Besides, you did get one of them," Jacob remarked smiling, lifting Nathan's spirits as he grasped his older son's shoulder.

Moses began to walk by slowly, and Nathan saw a sudden look of grave concern cross Jacob's face, as his father studied the old hound. Nathan was confused. While there might have been some blood on Moses, a moist glistening showing on the tough, old hound's leg where the female coyote had clamped her teeth, he could detect no other signs of harm.

"What's wrong, Pa?" Nathan sensed more than knew that Jacob could see something that the young boy could not.

"It's all right, son," Jacob said to Nathan while never taking his eyes off Moses. "Go and help your brother round up the pups and take them back to the house."

Nathan slung the rifle over his shoulder, gathered the jars of harvested frog eggs, and looked to where Mead and the pups were still reveling. Nathan then looked back to his father and Moses.

The hound closed the gap to within a few feet of his master, staring into the man's eyes. Jacob said nothing as he studied his worthy hound, only slowly nodding his head.

"Harrumph!" Moses let out his familiar bark and then shook his head.

The seasoned coon hunter and hound turned together to walk slowly, side by side, down the plowed field back to the house.

That night was the planting moon.

Jacob stood alone on the front porch in that full moon's bright light, smoking a pipe with his favorite black cherry tobacco. He just waited there silently, wearing his old hat, as the smoke drifted gently upward past his head.

Meanwhile, the boys were cleaning up after the dinner meal and excitedly talking about the day's events as well as their plan to monitor the frog eggs' development into tadpoles and continue the final metamorphosis into adult frogs.

However, their banter was interrupted as a loud chorus from their hounds suddenly erupted, breaking the night's tranquility. Both boys, still in the kitchen, looked at each other upon hearing the unusual sound, and ran to the porch to see what was happening.

"More coyotes, Pa?" Mead asked as the boys reached their father, who remained motionless, seemingly expecting the mournful sound.

"No boys," Jacob said, turning to give a firm but kind smile at Mead's innocent wonderment. "It's their 'last open.' It's their way of saying goodbye."

"Saying goodbye to whom, Pa?" Mead said, completely confused.

Nathan looked to the baying hounds and put the day's events together in his head.

Jacob knelt on one knee and placed his strong hands on Mead's arms, pinning them in place. He looked his youngest child directly in the eye, knowing fully how his next words would affect the boy.

"They're saying goodbye to Moses, son. Moses is dead."

"No!" the boy screamed, his tears flowing spontaneously. "That can't be, Pa! Moses can't die! Those coyotes didn't hurt him!"

The man's strong arms held Mead upright as the child's knees wanted to buckle.

"You're right," Jacob acknowledged, trying to console his son. "It wasn't anything those coyotes did to him directly. It was the effort of getting to the fight in the first place what caused it."

"I'll kill them all!" Mead shouted as the boy's tears suddenly changed from pain to rage. "I'll kill every coyote I ever see, Pa!"

"No!" Jacob's voice was stern. Mead looked up through his watering eyes in consternation to study his father's visage. "Those coyotes were simply doing what their instincts told them to do—and that wasn't evil—simply the way of things in the wild." Jacob paused, and when he spoke again, his voice softened.

"Moses went down fighting—defending his family in doing so— and you can't ask for much more than that, right?"

Mead nodded, understanding his father's words, and the boy's sobs, while uneven, were beginning to subside. For a while, the three men remained motionless on their front porch in the moon's white light, saying nothing.

Finally, Mead spoke, his voice just above a whisper, "Can I go see him, Pa? One last time?"

Jacob released his firm grip on the boy's arms and slowly nodded.

Mead sprinted into the night on the familiar path to Moses's coop and threw open the kennel door. There, lying motionless on top of his coop, appearing to be merely asleep, was the old hound's form. The boy ran to the hound, wrapping his arms around the old dog's neck, his tears wetting the hound's cold muzzle.

For nearly an hour, Mead stood motionless, holding his beloved dog with his eyes closed as the night's temperature continued to drop. When Mead finally released his grip, he rose, surprised to see both Jacob and Nathan standing there, silently watching.

Jacob's tall form leaned on an old, wooden-handled shovel.

Mead walked over to his father. To both Jacob and Nathan's surprise, Mead grasped the shovel just below his father's hands, looking long and hard at his father with a determination that defied any refusal. Jacob tacitly understood, slowly nodded, and released the shovel into the young boy's grip.

Mead turned back to Moses's body. Quickly setting the shovel aside, and in an incredible show of strength that would become legendary into Mead's adulthood, the boy lifted the dog's body off the coop and set the hound gently on his shoulders. Re-grasping the shovel, Mead walked out of the kennel and toward the field, carrying his dog.

Jacob and Nathan watched in amazement, as both knew that Moses was as heavy as Mead himself! Mead continued walking away until the boy's small form faded into the night.

After a short while, Jacob and Nathan heard the telltale sound of the shovel biting into the soil as they just stood listening.

Nearly six hours later, with the moon low in the sky, Jacob walked out into the night to find Mead asleep atop the freshly dug grave. The boy had collapsed out of sheer exhaustion of mind and spirit. He cradled Mead in his arms, lifting him up to carry him back to the house.

Jacob stopped in the fading moonlight. For a moment, the coon hunter spied in the rising mist an apparition of a large hound wagging his tail, watching the familiar man carry the sleeping child. Jacob smiled knowingly to the ethereal form as it softly dissipated into the night air.

This was not the first time that he had witnessed such a vision.

But then again, it was Painted Post.

Chapter 6

Chivalry

Nigh sixteen years hence . . .

It heard two loud cracks and felt subsequent sharp stings in its sides, and it remembered! For it had heard similar sounds before, albeit louder, the day it had come to know and hate the Enemy.

The bullets might have met their mark and drew blood, but the creature's tough hide thwarted any mortal wound coming from the small-caliber rifle. The man had brought the gun to bear when it and the dogs had separated just long enough to allow a clear shot.

The last coon hunter knew that he and his hounds were terribly undermatched against this brute. He knew unloading every round in his weapon into it would still not be enough to kill this beast immediately, if at all.

Yet, he was a coon hunter and accomplished at taking aim at small targets at night, so he leveled the semiautomatic rifle again.

———◦———

The present . . .

It was the last day of the school year in Painted Post. The warm, late June day was full of summer's promise. All the students could feel it, and Nathan and Mead were not immune to the excitement. The brothers knew the longer days meant hard work in the hayfields, but it also meant many hours of "woodsing" the pups and exploring the forest.

The bus ride home ended at the four corners of the dirt roads, and more than a dozen children piled off the bus, screaming in joy. Sharon Helm exited the bus before Nathan and Mead.

Nathan noticed Larry Allen and two other boys, whom he only vaguely knew, step off the bus. Nathan thought the strangers' presence unusual, but he figured that the two other boys were going to spend the night at the Allen household. When Nathan met all three boys' eyes, he saw a slight smirk on Larry's face, but they all looked away and headed down the road toward Larry's house. Nathan thought nothing more of it. After all, it was the beginning of summer.

The school bus drove off with the noise of its old engine fading into the distance, just as the school year moved into the children's past.

Sharon and Nathan walked side by side down the dirt road that carved its way through the forest on Ryland Creek Road with Mead following a few feet behind. Sharon was especially talkative, detailing summer plans of swimming holes and undertaking a sundry of things with her mom.

Nathan smiled coyly and nodded.

Mead occasioned to look behind them. To his surprise, he made out the forms of Larry and those other two older boys who had stepped off the bus. Mead was about to inform Nathan, but then he saw all three boys dart into the woods. Perhaps they were headed to a swimming hole or taking a backwoods path to Larry's home. No matter, Mead reasoned, they were gone now, so no need to say anything. Besides, with the boys now out of sight, Nathan and Sharon would likely chide him and say that he had imagined things.

"What will you be doing this summer, Nathan?" Sharon asked, catching Nathan off guard since he had been content to let Sharon carry the entire conversation.

"Oh, we will . . . we will . . .," Nathan stammered. Why did he always find his throat getting tight when she spoke to him? "We'll do some work on the farm and train the hounds, I suppose." Sharon stopped and moved to stand very near him, which only caused his teenage angst level to rise even more.

"Maybe we could go swimming together?" she suggested, offering a coy, almost vulnerable moment, but her beautiful brown eyes caught

Nathan's stare, and she knew the answer before he could manage to form it.

"S-S-Sure!" Nathan finally sputtered out his response.

"Mom doesn't like it when I swim alone," she explained. But the gleam in her eye belied that she would be glad just to be with Nathan, who shyly returned her smile.

Mead observed the young boy and girl with mild curiosity when he heard a loud rustling in the woods. The young boy peered in that direction, but with the bushes in full bloom, Mead could not discern the sound's source. For a moment, he thought of the coyote battle just two months ago, and a solemn thought about his hound Moses crossed his mind. Mead then realized that Nathan and Sharon had begun walking again and left him. He ran to catch up, wanting to discuss with Nathan which forest denizen might make such a noise, but he thought better of interrupting.

The conversation continued with Sharon talking and Nathan offering short, but polite, responses as they walked on the familiar dirt road. Seeming too soon, Nathan realized that the trio was at the foot of the Ernst driveway.

Mead turned toward the house and saw Jacob on the front porch, smoking his pipe.

Nathan lingered awhile longer until he was sure Mead was out of hearing. "It was nice talking to you," he finally managed to say. She turned her warm smile toward the young man, and he felt his knees go weak.

"It was nice talking with you too, Nathan." The young girl beamed. "I hope we can spend some time together this summer. We'll have so much fun!"

"That would be great," Nathan blurted out. But feeling inadequate, he hastily added, "That would be very nice."

The shy boy realized that he must look even more socially inept. However, Nathan saw in her eyes a sincere appreciation for his attempted, if awkward, civility. Before she left, Sharon reached over, grasped his hands in hers, and gave them a light squeeze.

With an impish grin, she released his hands, waved, and walked away.

Nathan just stared for a while as Sharon strolled up the road. He suspected that both his father and Mead were probably watching the whole scene play out. When he turned, as expected, they stood on the porch watching him walk up the driveway. Nathan knew by the looks on their faces that Jacob and Mead would harass him mercilessly about being "with a girl." He felt his skin flush as he moved closer.

"Pa, I was just talking to Sharon. . ." Nathan began. Before he could get any more of his explanation out, Nathan heard a loud, terrified scream. Alarm spread across his face as he looked up the road where Sharon had just walked out of sight.

"You best go see what has got Miss Sharon all upset," Jacob said.

Mead folded his arms contemptuously across his chest. "Oh, she probably just saw a snake or something."

"I'll check it out," Nathan said but stood immobile, waiting for his father's final permission.

"Well then, go, son," Jacob finally said.

Nathan wheeled and ran down the road where he had last seen the young girl. His pace grew faster when Sharon screamed again. He wondered what could continue to scare her so. Had she seen a snake as Mead had suggested? Or perhaps a bear?

The answer came soon enough when Nathan immediately rounded a turn in the road and saw Larry Allen sitting atop Sharon, now laid on her back on the dirt road with her arms pinioned to her sides. He also saw the two older boys, both clad in blue jean overalls. But instead of standing guard, they were watching the spectacle.

Larry hunched over Sharon trying to kiss her, but the spunky little brunette was having none of it and squirmed. He attempted to put his hand over Sharon's mouth to muffle any more of her screams, but he misplaced his hand, and she clamped her teeth down hard on his pinky finger.

Larry shrieked in sheer agony, convinced that Sharon would bite completely through his finger. The two older boys laughed at their partner in crime as he started hitting Sharon's arm with his free hand, trying to get her to relinquish her grip on his finger.

It was then that the closest boy heard Nathan running headlong toward the fracas. The boy's slow turn only perfectly positioned his body for Nathan to land a solid kick to the older boy's groin.

There was no warning at the onset of this fight—that simply was not the Ernst way.

Although the other boy was undoubtedly falling helplessly because of the well-placed kick, Nathan threw his fist into the kid's face, causing him to sprawl to the ground with one hand on his wounded mid-section, and the other hand covering his now-bloodied nose.

While the odds were better, Nathan had lost the element of surprise. The other boy, by far the largest, moved around the still struggling Larry Allen and Sharon so he could face Nathan and avenge his fallen comrade. This boy was fully three inches taller, but Nathan felt no fear as he tapped into his growing rage.

Nathan landed the first two punches—one to the boy's mouth and the other to his stomach. However, this boy was an experienced fighter, and he moved his body to deflect the full brunt of Nathan's attack.

Now, it was Nathan's turn to be at the receiving end of the fight as his opponent counterpunched and struck him on the cheek.

While his advantage in size made him initially confident that he would quickly overcome this little scrapper, the boy became unnerved as Nathan stepped back for a moment, absorbing the punch, and began the assault anew.

They traded blow after blow. The stamina that Nathan had gained in running the forested hills chasing raccoon worked to his benefit. Nathan landed solid hit after solid hit.

The larger boy was amazed at how powerfully this smaller kid could wallop. The elder boy's reaction time began to slow under the continuous onslaught, which allowed Nathan the opportunity to deliver even more punishing blows.

But Nathan was not unscathed. The other boy had managed to land a hard hit to his left eye, which began to swell immediately. Another well-placed punch to Nathan's mouth caused his lower lip to split and bleed profusely.

The young coon hunter continued to battle through the pain, knowing that he was defending something greater than himself.

Finally, like a logger's ax swinging for the last time to fell a mighty oak, Nathan stepped forward and drove his fist hard into the other boy's snout, resulting in a spray of blood, and his opponent stumbled backward. The first boy to fall to Nathan's attack, only now coming out of a pained haze, watched as his larger companion landed unceremoniously next to him on Ryland Creek's hard surface.

That left one more.

Nathan turned just in time to see Larry Allen, still kneeling atop the smaller Sharon, finally wrench his finger free from her mouth.

"You little wench!" Larry yelled, and he cocked his arm back to punch Sharon. Larry had been only vaguely aware of the scuffle occurring about him; nor did he care about the outcome. He wanted revenge, but the villain hesitated. For now, instead of cowering, Sharon had propped herself up on her elbows to stare at him unafraid. The girl's defiance only served to incite Larry's seething anger, and he drew his fist back even farther, brutally determined to punish her impudence.

But as Larry tried to strike, his arm was suddenly caught in a powerful grip, and he looked up to see the resolute face of Nathan Ernst.

With his free hand, Nathan struck Larry savagely in the face while using his other hand to hold Larry's arm in place to prevent any further harm to Sharon.

And the pummeling continued.

Nathan was unsure of how many times that he had hit Larry, but eventually, he realized that his foe was offering no further defense. Allen's head rolled from side to side, trying to remain conscious. When Nathan finally released the bloodied boy's arm, Larry fell to the ground in a softly moaning heap.

No longer trapped beneath Larry, Sharon quickly stood and stepped behind Nathan. Larry's partners, back on their feet again but moving very slowly, walked over to Larry. Both battered boys grabbed one of Larry's arms to pull him to a standing position. They struggled to hold their likewise beaten ringleader upright as Larry only wanted to lie back down on terra firma.

For the first time since the encounter began, more growling than speaking, Nathan said, "Get out of here, now—all of you!"

The largest boy put his free hand up, patting the empty air in acknowledgment of the command, and the bruised threesome turned to limp away.

Nathan, with Sharon at his side, watched to ensure Larry and his gang had no intent to double back.

Once the boys were out of sight, Nathan, about to turn to ensure Sharon was unhurt, saw a puff of smoke rising into the air from behind a large maple tree. On cue, Jacob stepped into full view followed by Mead at their father's side.

Jacob took his pipe from his mouth and looked into the forest as if speaking to the trees.

"You gotta punch through," Jacob said and then reinserted his pipe back in his mouth. In an instructive manner, now looking directly at Nathan, he snapped his right arm out, punching an imaginary foe, and catching his right inner elbow in the web of his left hand.

"You gotta punch through," Jacob repeated through clenched teeth with the pipe still in his mouth.

"Pa," Nathan began, "I didn't mean to start any trouble, but Larry was trying to—"

Jacob interrupted and suggested softly, "Why don't you walk Miss Helm home?" Without waiting for Nathan's response, Jacob stepped onto the road and began to walk back to their farm.

Mead, witnessing nearly the entire fight, beamed with sibling pride, and nodded, silently approving the defeat that Nathan had inflicted upon the bullies. After a short pause, Mead, eager to talk about the spectacle, turned to run and catch up with his father.

Nathan looked at the disheveled but otherwise unhurt Sharon, and the approving look she gave him scared him more than at any time during the fight. He swallowed hard.

"Do you mind if I walk you home?"

Why are my words always so lame? Nathan's thoughts wailed.

Acting like nothing unusual had happened over the past few minutes, Sharon slid her arm into his and said, "Why of course, Nathan."

The young couple walked down the road saying little as the summer sun poked its rays through the leafy canopy. Nathan's left eye was now completely swollen shut, and his split lip was following suit. In his undamaged eye, he could see Sharon assessing his wounds, and her concerned look was a warm comfort.

When they finally walked up the short drive, Miriam Helm was at the door. Her face showed immediate alarm as she saw her daughter's dirty clothes and Nathan's battered countenance and body.

"Oh, my Lord!" Miriam shouted in alarm. "Are you two okay?"

Nathan stood silently while Sharon relayed the tale of the fight to her mother, how Nathan had rescued her and beaten off her assailants.

Timid at first, Nathan eventually managed to look up to find Miriam's appreciative smile for the young man who had just saved her daughter.

"I imagine Larry Allen learned his lesson this day!" Miriam said. "Let me get you some ice for that eye . . . and that lip . . . and your hand!"

"I'll be okay, ma'am," Nathan said, declining Miriam's help.

"Are you sure? It wouldn't be any problem whatsoever," Miriam assured him.

"I'll be okay," he repeated.

"As you wish—you're certainly one tough cookie, young man!" Miriam said.

Nathan then witnessed a silent communication between mother and daughter, with Sharon punching one arm down to her side and giving her mother a look that begged the adult to go back into the house.

Miriam understood and said sincerely, "Thank you for protecting my little girl, Nathan."

Through his swollen lips, Nathan managed to say, "M-m-my pleasure, ma'am." He closed his unhurt eye, mentally kicking himself again for his seemingly endless buffoonish responses

With her mother gone, Sharon faced Nathan. Gently taking his bruised face in her small hands, she leaned over and kissed him. While the touch of her lips was light, if still painful on his swollen mouth, the entire world seemed to stop for Nathan.

Realizing his good eye was closed, Nathan finally looked up to find her smiling at him.

She leaned even closer to him. "I'm going to marry you one day, Nathan Ernst," Sharon whispered in his ear.

Before he could stumble upon another response, Sharon quickly stepped into her house and shut the door. Staring at the door for a few long moments in disbelief, Nathan turned and began the long walk to his home.

Although every step should have caused a shock of pain to course through his entire body, Nathan smiled the whole way home, never feeling a thing.

Chapter 7

The Promise

L ate June through early July typically finds farmers in Upstate New York performing the first cut of the "haying season." Jacob Ernst and his sons would harvest the nearly fifty acres of hay on their farm. Haying was arduous work beneath the hot summer skies, and the routine would continue each day for a couple of weeks, absent Sundays, and the occasional rainstorm. Nevertheless, the boys enjoyed working together and with their father. Jacob knew the hard labor would strengthen their bodies as the season progressed.

Using a small but tough tractor to haul an old mower, Nathan would first mow the hay. When the cutting was complete, Jacob used the tractor to pull a hay rake through the field to form the downed grass in fluffed, greenish-brown rows, allowing it to dry in the warm sun.

The next step was to attach the baler to the tractor to form the golden hay into sixty-pound square bundles using a strong twine. With Jacob commandeering the tractor through the field, Nathan would grab each bale and place it in a small, sideless wagon. Mead, atop that wagon, worked to neatly stack the hay. The men would return to their barn with each load, putting the bundles on an electric elevator, and would once again stack the bales in the hayloft for their livestock to feed on throughout the coming winter and sell any excess hay to other local farmers.

After a morning of haying, the boys were seated at the kitchen table relishing some cold roast beef sandwiches. Their hair was long again, with Mead's sun-drenched hair becoming slightly blond and poking out from the sides of his omnipresent baseball cap. Jacob threatened several times to take the boys to a nearby sheep farmer to be sheared, but Nathan and Mead begged off their father, who reluctantly agreed to let them "look like hippies" for the time being.

It was summer after all.

The boys talked of the young coonhounds and how quickly they were growing. Jacob, once again hidden behind the newspaper, offered an occasional acknowledgment of the boys' assessments of the growing litter.

They had barely heard it, but both boys suddenly stopped talking and looked at each other quizzically. There it was again—a light rapping on their front door!

"Well, go see who it is," Jacob instructed, still concealed behind the daily paper.

They rarely had visitors, so this was a special occasion, and Nathan and Mead nearly tripped over one another to see who had come to visit their little farm.

Upon opening the front door, they saw Sharon Helm standing there dressed in an overly large, dark T-shirt with cut off shorts. She also wore a pair of old green sneakers with dingy white laces and no socks. Wrapped around her neck was a large towel with her hands holding it in place as if fearing the towel would fly away.

"Hi Nathan," Sharon greeted shyly. "I wondered if maybe you wouldn't mind going with me to the swimming hole?"

Nathan stared for a few seconds. While his mind shouted yes, no spoken words left his mouth. Mead used his elbow to rib his brother, which jolted Nathan into realizing that he was staring and not responding.

"S-s-sure!" Nathan said. He turned around and shouted to Jacob, still in the kitchen. "Pa, it's Sharon Helm! Is it okay if I go with her to the swimming hole?"

At this news, Jacob folded down the paper. The older man's facial expression showed more curiosity than anything else, but he nodded and said, "We can hold off an afternoon of haying for a trip to the swimming hole, I suppose. Mead," Jacob addressed his youngest son, "do you want to head into town with me? I have to get some supplies."

"Yeah, Pa!" Mead shouted, knowing that the supply run would also mean a trip to their favorite ice cream stand. Then Mead turned surreptitiously to Nathan and whispered so only his brother could hear it, "No kissing!"

"Dah!" Nathan made a single swing of his hand to knock the baseball cap off Mead's head.

The younger sibling squealed with joy, scooped up his hat, and ran into the kitchen.

"Is everything alright?" Sharon asked, innocently witnessing the two brothers' interplay but completely oblivious to Mead's teasing.

"Everything is fine," Nathan said with a quick laugh, nodding his head nervously to reassure her. "Do you mind if I switch into a pair of shorts, too?" He looked down at his jeans dirtied from the haying.

"Certainly!" she said. "Can I see the pups?" Sharon had seen the young hounds playing in their pen when she walked up the driveway.

"Of course," Nathan said, smiling. "I'll meet you there shortly." He watched her turn and walk toward their kennels, and he almost fell trying to run up the stairs to get changed.

In the kitchen, hearing the frantic racket from above, both Jacob and Mead looked at each other and began laughing.

When Nathan had finally changed, he made his way to the dog pens and found Sharon kneeling by the cage with all four young pups utterly rapt with the young girl. She cooed to each, and they all poked their noses through the cage's wiring to touch and smell her hands. Nathan said nothing, merely absorbing the sight of this girl and the profound connection that she had made immediately with these young dogs.

There was something extraordinary about this girl, Nathan knew.

Breaking from her reverie, knowing he was there watching over her, Sharon turned to stare at him and smile.

"Ready to go?" she finally asked after several long moments.

"I know the way," Nathan responded, offering his hand as he helped the young girl to her feet.

The swimming hole was an oft-visited place amongst the youth of Painted Post and less than half a mile from the Ernst farm. When Nathan and Sharon reached the end of the driveway, they took a left on Ryland Creek Road.

Unbeknownst to them, another waited in the woods. When Sharon and Nathan began their walk to the swimming hole, the voyeur took a shortcut through the forest. The other would lie in wait for the right moment.

As they strolled down the hot, dusty road, Nathan was at first worried about what to say. But he soon realized that Sharon was more than happy to strike up the conversation with a plethora of topics—from the school year past, the academic year to come, and naming a few of the various trees that she recognized. Sharon would ask Nathan's help identifying the arboreal species that she did not know. Thanks to Jacob's tutelage, Nathan knew the trees of which she inquired.

"That one?" she asked, pointing to a tall tree with grayish bark.

"White ash," Nathan said and showed her the diamond pattern of the bark.

"And that one?"

"Black cherry," he replied, and so he identified nearly a dozen types of trees at her request. Sharon proved to be an excellent student as she soon was able to correctly name other examples of the trees that he had taught her.

Yes, Nathan thought, this girl is special.

It seemed like the youths had just started their walk when they came upon the worn dirt path leading to the swimming hole. The trail led away from the road into an old-growth forest with the leafy canopy of ancient oaks and maples providing some respite from the hot sun.

Nathan wondered if they would have the secluded spot to themselves. It was summer, and likely there would be other kids looking forward to cooling down in the water. After about a hundred yards, the two teenagers finally arrived at the water hole.

Their destination was just a wide part of a slow-moving creek. Large spreading red oaks ringed its sides, their limbs reaching over the water, but the sunlight still managed to warm the pooled surface. The creek's banks sloped gently to the water's edge, mostly barren of vegetation due to the many visitors beating down the path. Long ago, someone had secured an old, thick rope to a large oak whose branches hung out over the pool. With a good running start, one could swing to nearly the middle of the pool and let loose to plunge into the deep, cold water.

Nathan was relieved to see no one else, which meant they would have this secluded part of the woods all to themselves.

Sharon set her things on the ground carefully. Then, quickly kicking off her sneakers, she removed the T-shirt to reveal the upper part of a blue, one-piece bathing suit while keeping her frayed shorts on.

Nathan likewise doffed his sneakers and took off his shirt. Although Sharon did well to hide it, she nearly blushed to see Nathan's muscled upper body, toned and tanned by weeks of working in the hayfields.

"C'mon!" she said, playfully hitting his chest. "Last one in is a rotten egg!"

Seconds later, she plunged into the water laughing with Nathan chasing close behind. Nathan and Sharon were experienced swimmers, and they quickly moved into the deeper water.

"Can you touch the bottom?" Sharon asked and then quickly dove into the greenish water out of sight.

Nathan followed her, swimming into the pool's depths. While the deeper water was darker and colder, the sun's light made it clear enough for them to make out objects on the creek bottom. A broken oak branch rested on the pool's floor, and within its twiggy protection, an adult smallmouth bass watched apprehensively.

Nathan stared at Sharon, swimming effortlessly and with incredible grace, letting the water buoy her lithe body perfectly inverted. She reached down, grabbing something from the bottom of the creek, and placed it into a front pocket of her shorts.

Sharon then swam closer to Nathan till their faces were but inches apart. Her hair flowed around her like the wind had taken hold of it, and she just floated there, suspended in the water and in time, content just to be there with him. She reached out, touched him gently on the cheek, and then sprinted to the surface with Nathan again racing after her.

They burst onto the pool's surface gasping for air—neither realizing that they had spent over a minute underwater.

Sharon beamed. With a simple motion of her head, she beckoned him to follow.

When they were close to the shore in chest-deep water, she stopped. The swimming hole felt warmer here, and Sharon let the tepidness displace the chill of their dive. She said nothing. She had no need, knowing Nathan could feel her joy.

Then an impish grin came upon her face. With her palm, Sharon pushed the pool's surface to splash a surprising amount of water into Nathan's face. To make matters worse, Nathan had his jaws agape, which resulted in a mouthful of creek water!

Cocking his head up slightly, looking like a fountain statue in a public park, he spat the water out in a narrow stream. Sharon laughed long and loud while she took up splashing him more. Nathan did not respond in kind but instead slowly submerged below the surface of the water.

Sharon looked around when Nathan did not emerge for nearly thirty seconds, but then she screamed in pretend terror as Nathan now rose to the surface with her foot gently captured in his hand. He raised her leg high enough that she began to paddle slowly with her arms. Nathan looked at her with his eyes narrowed and a sly grin of his own, and Sharon craned her head forward, mimicking his look.

Nathan raised his free hand out of the water, and with his index finger, he began a corkscrew motion and making an "airplane noise" with his mouth as his hand slipped below the water.

Sharon looked at him, maintaining the same facial expression, but then her eyes revealed that she now understood his motives. Nathan's fingers found the soft bottom of her foot and caressed it gently with a few strokes. Sharon tried bravely to maintain a stoic look, but her eyes widened slightly as he continued to tickle her sole gently, and any attempt of a show of immunity quickly melted away, and the dark-haired girl completely surrendered in shrill laughter.

"You're rather ticklish," Nathan said, stating the obvious, but it was clear Sharon did not mind that he had discovered her vulnerability.

For in her weakness, she conquered.

When Nathan finally released her foot, Sharon swam immediately toward him, placed her hands on his shoulders, and lifted herself out of the water. "You brat!" she shouted.

While Nathan could easily withhold her tiny frame's weight, he understood the intent and feigned to be pushed under the water by her efforts. Again, her laughter filled the air, and the forest creatures—here a squirrel, there a deer—watched, amused at the humans' innocence playing out.

But another onlooker also took in the scene, seething with jealousy, and with the stealth of a snake, he crept closer to the couple along the shoreline, hidden by the thick brush.

Sharon let out a surprised yell as Nathan came out of the water, but this time, the usually shy boy had one arm across her back with the other arm cupped behind both of her knees as he gently held her entire frame suspended in the water. She slowly moved away his long, wet hair to study his handsome face. Sharon turned her hand and let the back of her fingers trail down his nose and then his lips, then rotated her wrist once more to rest her palm on his chest. After a few moments, she placed her head on his shoulder, knowing in her soul this boy, and someday this man, would always protect her.

Nathan paused, feeling the warmth of her body against him. Saying nothing, he carried her to the shore, gently setting her down on the bank, and sat close beside her. She leaned into him to make contact, reassured by his presence, and they sat on the creek bank, watching the sun reflect on the stillness of the water.

For a while, they said nothing to each other.

There was no need.

"What did you pick up from the bottom?" Nathan finally broke the silence after several minutes.

Sharon smiled as she reached into her pocket and pulled out a small, round stone. Nathan just looked puzzled at the seemingly unspectacular find, but he waited to say anything, and she began.

"Your mother died when you were very young?" Sharon asked.

"Yes, I was about two years old," Nathan responded to the unexpected query.

"My father died not that long ago, and I often wonder why God took him away from Mom and me. She always said I was Daddy's girl, so I don't understand why he had to leave us here alone." With that revelation, she closed her eyes and hung her head, and although her hair was still wet and dripping, Nathan knew the droplets flowing from those closed eyes were tears.

"Do you ever wonder why your mother left you and your family?" Sharon asked with her eyes remaining closed.

Nathan fell silent for several moments and then spoke. "I asked Pa that once—why did Ma have to die?" he began, stopping for a moment, recalling the conversation. But he quickly continued as he felt Sharon's intense desire to hear an answer—any answer. "Pa said there are some things in this life that we just aren't meant to know or can't even begin to understand, but everything happens for a reason. God gave us free will, to live our lives, and try to make it back home to Him. How and when we do finally go to heaven is something we can't know."

Sharon reflected on his words. "I think Daddy watches over me as best he can from heaven. Sometimes, when I get scared at night, I can hear him telling me there is no such thing as the bogeyman." She laughed, fondly reminiscing. "Do you think your mom watches over you from heaven?"

"I'm certain of it," Nathan said, staring at the water, but then he turned to her. "Do you know the legend of the Ghosts of Ryland Creek?"

"No!" Sharon said, excited and horrified.

"Oh, don't worry—they're supposed to be the good spirits," Nathan reassured her. "Pa says that during the full moon, in the woods, you can see the spirits as mist rising into the air. Sometimes, the mist will even take the form of a person, Pa says, and you can hear them talk to you in your mind." He paused, debating whether to continue, but soon resumed.

"One night, we were coon hunting on Ryland Creek beneath the brightest full moon. At the end of the hunt, Mead and I climbed into the truck while Pa loaded the dogs in the back. I thought Pa was taking too long, so I looked in the rear-view mirror.

"The moonlight came through the branches. Then I saw a mist rising near Pa, and it looked like a woman. I couldn't recall ever seeing her before, but somehow, I knew in my heart that it was Ma.

"Pa was staring at the mist, and I knew that he saw the woman too.

He nodded his head like he was talking to her. Then the fog kind of just went away, and I saw Pa raise his hand, saying goodbye, I suppose.

"When Pa got into the truck, I asked him if he was okay. I remember him looking at me with a big smile, and he said that 'everything will be okay,' like he was privy to something that Mead and I were not."

"Wow," Sharon said in a hushed awe.

"So, tell me about the stone," Nathan prodded.

Sharon smiled, looking back at the rock that she had been unconsciously rolling between her fingers. "Daddy used to say when something or someone had hurt me or made me sad, that instead of staying sad, I should just pick up a rock and throw it in the water. And when the water's ripples from the stone were gone, I should let the sad feelings go away, too."

"Does it work?" Nathan asked innocently.

"Not always," she said, looking at him. She began to giggle and broke into her full laugh with Nathan joining in. While shaking her head, the young girl repeated, softer this time, "Not always."

Sharon then stood up, and with all her might, threw the rock into the water, which landed with a solid *kerplunk!* She saw the ripples go away and watched patiently as the water's surface became placid again.

"We better start for home," Nathan said, looking at the sun's location. "Your mom is bound to be worried."

She nodded in agreement, but when they rose, Sharon had a surprise.

"Where are my sneakers?" she asked. While Nathan's pile of clothes remained exactly as he had left it, her shoes were gone. The bank was not overly steep, so they reasoned that her footwear had not slipped into the water.

"Do you think an animal took them?" she asked, continuing to search while she put her T-shirt over her bathing suit. Meanwhile, Nathan donned his boots and shirt.

"Those stinky things? I don't think so!" Nathan chided.

She playfully cuffed his head, tousled his hair, and laughed. "Well then—you'll just have to carry me piggyback!"

Sharon then quickly stepped behind him and jumped on his back. Nathan reflexively caught her legs as her small, pretty, bare feet poked out in front of him.

Although Nathan should have tired from the day's activity, he found his strength renewed as he headed back down the path.

When they broke out of the woods onto the dirt road, Nathan continued, and Sharon was more than happy to have him carry her. She did not often speak. Instead, she nestled her chin to the side of Nathan's neck, her cheek pressing against his left ear, content to be with him at that moment in time.

When they rounded a steep corner of the road, the mystery of Sharon's shoes' disappearance became apparent.

In the middle of the road, with one hand holding her green sneakers and the other hand holding a large, dead oak branch, stood Larry Allen.

"Missing something?" Larry held her shoes up higher as if Nathan or Sharon needed the elevation to see clearly.

"Those are mine!" Sharon yelled from her perch on Nathan's back.

Nathan set her down on the ground gently but held his arm out to hold the fiery brunette back. He instinctively understood Allen's kind and focused on the large stick that Larry held. Further, he was furious, realizing that Larry had spied on them while they swam in the creek.

Larry threw the sneakers underhand at Sharon in gratuitous fashion, acting like he expected thanks for returning what he had stolen. Waving the wooden stick ominously, he looked directly at Nathan.

"You won't sucker punch me like you did last time, Ernst. This time, I'm ready for you." Larry bounced the end of the makeshift club in his free hand.

"You're goin' to need that stick," Nathan said, seething as he moved toward Larry without hesitation. Sharon, still putting on her sneakers, reached out to hold Nathan back, but he was already beyond her grasp, with his eyes locked on the other boy.

When Nathan came within striking distance, Larry attacked by swinging the branch like a baseball bat.

With his forearm raised to block the oncoming blow, Nathan succeeded in stopping a direct hit to his head—Allen's intended target—but the pain caused him to wince.

Larry saw Nathan's grimace, and the sadistic bully smiled and closed in for another swing. This time, he swung the stick in an overhead fashion, again forcing Nathan to hold up his forearm.

Nathan's defense withheld, foiling the attacker's attempt to hit something vital. However, excruciating pain coursed through his entire body.

The villain swung his weapon again, but instead of blocking, Nathan punched directly at the stick. To both Larry and Sharon's utter amazement, the oak implement shattered as Nathan's fist precisely gauged the club's location, leaving Larry with less than a foot of the branch remaining.

Larry had always considered his father, John, to be shiftless and a coward. When the older man overheard his son's plan to exact revenge on Nathan, John spoke of how the Ernsts' ire was something to avoid at all costs. Now seeing the fury in Nathan's eyes, Larry began to understand that, for once, maybe his worthless father's words had been true.

And on a hot summer's day, Larry felt a chill run up his spine as Nathan moved closer. In a desperate attempt, he threw what remained of the broken oak branch.

While the stick hit Nathan in the chest, it simply bounced off and only served to stoke his growing anger. He released his rage with a series of vicious punches. The blows were hard and fast, each striking a vital area, and the now-stunned Larry Allen, only seconds before on the offense, was unable to block a single hit. With a vicious hook from Nathan connecting to the face, Larry fell on his back on the hard dirt road.

But having Larry prone was not good enough. Straddling his downed enemy, kneeling on Ryland Creek Road, Nathan curled one hand in Larry's shirt and lifted the boy's torso off the ground.

"Don't," Nathan began and punched Larry hard in the mouth.

"Ever," he said, again hitting Allen, who now had blood freely flowing from his lips.

"Touch her or her things," Nathan seethed, with his next punch to the poor boy's nose.

"Again!" As he wound up for his final strike, Nathan felt a small hand cover his balled fist, and he looked up to see Sharon. Her countenance showed alarm, not so much for the nearly senseless Larry Allen, but at his display of anger.

"I think he's had enough," Sharon said, her voice barely above a whisper.

Seeing the damage that he had inflicted, Nathan realized that she was right. The broken boy beneath him sobbed, his entire body shaking. Nathan felt pity and shame, and he stood.

Larry quickly rose and ran down the road without once looking back.

Sharon and Nathan stood watching as the would-be villain ran out of sight.

"I'm sorry. I didn't mean to. . ." Nathan began.

"I know," Sharon said as she put her hand to his lips. "It seems like you're always my protector, Nathan Ernst. But please promise me that unless you absolutely have to, you won't hit anyone again. Promise?"

Nathan looked into her eyes, comprehending the deep-seated meaning of that request. "I promise," he responded.

Sharon smiled, knowing in her heart that Nathan would keep his vow. "That's what I love about you."

Despite himself, Nathan blushed at her words.

Sharon grinned at his innocent bashfulness and then looked down to touch his swollen knuckles. She watched him flinch slightly as she applied the slightest pressure.

"You really need to toughen up," she teased as Nathan at first looked up helplessly, and they both started laughing. Sharon also examined his forearm, which had already begun to bruise from blocking Larry's makeshift bat.

With her shoes returned, she walked beside Nathan, cradling his arm. They passed the Ernst farm and continued. No words were necessary—Nathan would ensure she was safe at home before leaving her side.

Miriam Helm, clad in blue jeans and an old, tan, short-sleeved shirt, was busy putting out laundry on a clothesline as she watched the two teenagers walk up the driveway. Her motherly instincts instantly detected Nathan's wounded gait, and she quickly put down her clothes basket to intercept the young adults.

It was immediately apparent that Sharon was unharmed, for which

Miriam was grateful, but she could see that the bruised and battered warrior beside her daughter had not fared so well.

Without prompting, Sharon explained to her mother how Larry Allen had stalked them, and that Nathan had again come to her rescue.

"You're making a habit of saving my daughter, Nathan Ernst," Miriam kidded but at the same time conveyed a genuine appreciation for the young man's intervention. "Calling John Allen to tell him to take control of his son won't do any good. He's probably drunk anyway. I suspect though that the only lesson Larry will ever get through that thick skull of his is the one that you've taught him today."

"Yes, ma'am," was all the response that Nathan could manage under the circumstances.

"We better take a look at those bruises," Miriam suggested.

"I'll be okay, ma'am," Nathan said.

Miriam was impressed with his toughness, but she reminded herself that this was Jacob Ernst's son standing before her, and she should expect nothing else. "Would you like something to eat?" she offered.

"I best head home, Mrs. Helm. Pa will start to worry."

"I understand, Nathan. You are always welcome here." When she saw the young man blush, Miriam understood Sharon's deeply held attraction to this simple young man.

"Thank you, ma'am," Nathan said.

Miriam continued to stand there until Sharon gave her mother "the look," which the older woman knew all too well. "I'll be going inside then. Just right inside," she added teasingly over her shoulder as she turned to go into the house.

Sharon glowered for a moment, watching her mother disappear, and then turned to Nathan, who was confused by the exchange between mother and daughter.

When she was confident that they were alone, Sharon took his face in both hands and kissed him on the lips.

"Remember the promise," she said, so very near now.

"I will," Nathan reaffirmed.

"Do you like fireflies?" the young girl asked quixotically. Not waiting for his response, she said, "I'll see you again, soon." Sharon turned and ran into the house.

Nathan stood there in the Helms' front yard for a few moments but realized making sense of Sharon's closing words was beyond him.

Memories rushed upon him, thinking of an imitation airplane noise and her subsequent laughter.

The young man recalled how she had stared at him as he held her in the water. Then looking down at his swollen knuckles, he could hear her words again.

Promise me . . .

And as he walked home on that cooling summer day, Nathan was elated by the warm thought of Sharon Helm.

Chapter 8

The Wonder of Fireflies

F ew things require as much effort as properly raising coonhounds. And if there was one thing Jacob Ernst demanded of himself and his sons, it was a dedication to the hounds' training. The black and tan pups were growing quickly, and Jacob insisted on getting these young dogs into the forest frequently. Necessary, the seasoned hunter knew, if these hounds were ever to be successful someday.

One late July morning, the Ernst boys finished their chores early and informed their father they would take the young dogs to the woods. Jacob gave his blessing and stood on the front porch as the boys ran to the kennels to release the energetic pups.

"Want to head to the old farmhouse?" Nathan asked Mead, to which the younger boy readily agreed.

The house was the remnant of a long-abandoned farm on the far side of their property. These "hilltop farms" had been honest attempts by many farmers around the turn of the twentieth century to grow crops above the fertile river plains of the Painted Post region. Some of these farms were successful, but unfortunately, far more of these farmers found that nature had eroded the rich soil long ago, and these hills were only good for growing trees.

The boys and pups marched onto the small path that skirted the fields of now waist-high corn plants, and after several hundred yards, they entered the forest. The landscape was lush, displaying varying shades of green. Some old apple trees, part of the abandoned farm, still produced many apples each fall. As the boys passed beneath, they saw hundreds of the growing green fruit. When the time came, and the apples were ripe, they knew the raccoons would find the sweet treasures irresistible.

The young pups raced ahead and disappeared from the boys' sight. Along either side of the old path were enormous anthills—three feet high and several feet across. Mead went over to the mounds and stepped in them to watch hundreds of angry ants swarming to defend their home against the intruder disturbing their nest. He removed his foot quickly though, managing to thwart their defenses.

"You're going to regret that one day," Nathan warned his younger sibling.

"Nah!" Mead said.

"You'll be sorry," Nathan repeated.

Attempting to prove his older sibling wrong, Mead defiantly stuck his foot into another ant mound. At the exact moment that Mead stepped into the soft earth, the young pups erupted into several loud barks—impressively loud considering their age. The boys looked at each other and listened to the hounds, which would clearly tree something but then would move forward a few yards.

"They're chasing a squirrel," Nathan predicted as he listened to the hounds' cadence and movement. Many young coonhounds start their hunting prowess chasing squirrels the boys knew, so they were quite pleased.

"Forget something?" Nathan smirked.

At first, Mead did not understand what his older brother was implying, but as he followed Nathan's eyes to look down at his pants, he found his right leg up to his knee, covered with dozens of black ants. The young boy had absentmindedly left his foot remaining on the anthill as he had listened to the hound pups chase the squirrel. "Ouch! Ouch! Ouch!" Mead squawked, swatting at the biting ants, which were not only on the outside of his pants but had also gone inside his pant leg and were successfully sinking their pincers into soft flesh.

"Told you!" Nathan shouted and laughed hard as he watched his brother dance about.

At one point, Mead dropped his jeans down to his ankles to remove the relentless, stinging insects from his legs. When the boy had finally rid himself of the miniature attackers, Mead, red-faced, pulled his pants up.

"Guess we won't be kicking any more anthills, now will we, little brother?" Nathan added insult to injury.

Mead only nodded, while still scratching the tiny but painful bites.

The pups, hearing the commotion with Mead, came running back to where the boys stood. Once they saw everything was right, Nathan praised them, and the pups darted back into the forest, vanishing again. The young hounds soon resumed hunting and testing the air for new scents.

Nathan smiled, knowing the pups had passed another test. Not only were they exploring how to track game, but they were also learning to hunt with their human companions. "Checking in" to ensure each partner—dog and man—knew where the other was located.

"C'mon," Nathan said, motioning to Mead. "The old farm is only a couple of hundred yards ahead."

Both boys quickened their pace to find that the young pups had also come upon the abandoned farmstead, and with noses down, they tracked the various scents of deer, chipmunk, and the ubiquitous squirrels.

The dilapidated buildings stood solemn and gray in the forest. The two-story house had an eerie feel to it—the thing of ghost stories. The weathered but sturdy wooden frame still stood, although most of the glass windows had been broken a long time ago. The roof, at this point, had most of its shingles blown off, and the exposed, wooden rafters rotted with many holes showing. The house stood on a well-built stone foundation, which would likely remain a testament of the home's existence long after the wooden infrastructure had finally rotted away into the forest floor.

The young coonhounds once again ran as a pack and went by the boys with their noses down.

Nathan became intrigued by an old, rusting farm plow, while Mead ran over to where the pups had congregated atop a square, wooden structure. The boxed structure stood barely two feet high but completely enclosed what it sheltered. The pups' tails were wagging rapidly as their noses tried to discern the scent of some critter that had recently passed.

Mead then stood on the old, wooden structure, which groaned as he added his weight to the old planks. Time had splashed mud atop the wood, and Mead found the imprints of familiar spoor. "Nate!" he shouted, his excitement palpable, with one finger pointing down to the ground. "Coon tracks! These pups have found coon tracks!"

Nathan ended his fixation on the antique farm implement, However, assessing where his brother and the hounds stood, he shouted, "Mead! Get off that! You're standing on a . . ."

Before Nathan could complete his warning, the rotted planks made a loud, final groan and gave way to the ancient well beneath. Mead and two of the dogs, Storm and Duke, immediately vanished. Justice and Sam, looking into the now-exposed well, began barking in alarm.

Nathan ran frantically over to the well's edge to see the pups and the young boy swimming in the dark, cold water about four feet below. "You okay?"

"I'm okay!" Mead shouted, but his voice sounded more of a scream than an acknowledgment.

Nathan easily pulled the remaining planks away, which closed the gap between the two boys by a few more inches.

Green algae covered the stones that lined the well, and while Mead tried to find some purchase, his hands slipped off the slimy surface.

Meanwhile, Storm and Duke instinctively dog paddled and barked in terror, trying to stay afloat.

Mead somehow remained calm amongst the noise and splashing, but his feet were nowhere near touching the well's bottom, forcing him to tread water.

Now lying on his stomach at the edge of the well, Nathan reached down into the hole. "Give me your hand!"

"Get the pups first!" Mead insisted.

Nathan nodded, realizing his brother's request made sense from a practical standpoint.

Mead gripped the side of the stone wall, finally finding a spot that he could hold, and with the other hand, he grabbed Duke by the scruff of the neck. Again, with a strength far beyond his age, Mead lifted the puppy with one hand to where Nathan, straining, could reach his hand beneath Duke's collar.

With a loud groan, Nathan hoicked the young hound out of the well and onto dry land.

However, as the boys rescued Duke, little Storm succumbed to her lack of swimming ability, slipping below the surface of the water as Mead attempted to grab her collar. When she did not immediately re-emerge to the surface, Mead took a deep breath and disappeared below the surface of the well's water as Nathan could only look on helplessly.

The surface of the water went calm.

Dead calm.

"Mead!" Nathan shouted, his voice echoing strangely in the old cistern. Still, his brother did not emerge from the murky depths. The next thirty seconds seemed like an eon. Nathan knew if he jumped into the hole, then he too would be trapped. His little brother's well-being trumped any thoughts of common sense at this point. His mind raced as he reasoned that their father knew where they were. Although it might be awhile before Jacob arrived in search of them, the boys could remain afloat until their father came to the rescue.

Nathan prepared to jump into the well, but then the surface of the water erupted with Mead sputtering, one hand once again gripping the side of the well for support, but the other hand having a firm grip on Storm's collar. Nathan breathed a sigh of relief at seeing his brother again, and Mead's utterly soaked baseball cap amazingly remained affixed atop his head. Storm, appearing none the worse for wear, immediately resumed splashing and barking.

"Here, Nate!" Mead called out.

Once again, Mead's incredible strength prevailed as he easily lifted the runt of the litter high such that Nathan could grab her and pull her to the safety of dry land.

Nathan immediately stuck his hand back into the well, fearing that he would not see Mead, but relief flooded over him to find his younger brother reaching for his hand. Their hands gripped, and Nathan pulled until Mead was able to find solid footing on the well's sides and finally climb out of the dangerous entrapment.

Both boys, Mead panting and Nathan sighing, lie on their backs for a couple of moments.

"What is it with you, anyway?" Nathan asked. "It seems if you're not falling over a cliff, then you're falling into a well!"

"Just lucky, I guess." Mead smirked.

The puppies surrounded them, jumping excitedly and licking the brothers' faces. Storm suddenly shook the water from her coat, spraying the boys, causing them to begin laughing. Young Storm looked on, cocking her head in puppy fashion, amused at the sounds the humans were making.

Nathan, not as tired from the ordeal as Mead, stood and offered a hand to his little brother.

Mead first looked to the ground, shaking his head but also offering a silent prayer thanking God, and then looked up at Nathan. He took his brother's hand, and once standing, powerfully hugged his older sibling.

Nathan, feeling both relieved and a little embarrassed, stood back once Mead released him. "Dah!" he said, and with one hand, doing what the well had not, smacked the baseball cap off Mead's head.

Mead laughed heartedly at their brotherly routine, picked up his soaked hat, wrung it out watching the water fall to the ground, and then defiantly slapped it back in place atop his noggin.

"After wells and ants, I think we've had enough for the day," Nathan suggested.

"Agreed!" Mead said. "Let's go home."

When they arrived at their house, Mead still wet from the episode, the brothers explained their misadventure as their father listened to the boys' rendering with a concerned look.

Jacob finally smiled again, though, when Mead tried to soften the news of the potentially fatal adventure.

"But at least, Pa, they smelled a coon atop that old well!" Mead beamed.

"You never know what good there is in bad, eh?" Jacob smiled but then said seriously, "I told your grandfather years ago that we should fill in that well. I have only myself to blame for not taking care of the problem. Tomorrow morning, we'll load the old wagon with field rock and fill in that well, so nothing will ever fall into it again."

After their dinner that night, the phone rang, and Jacob answered.

"Ahem," he said. "Yes. I see." Jacob pulled the phone away from his ear, turned to Nathan and said, "This is Mrs. Helm on the phone. She's wondering if you wouldn't mind coming over to their house to help with some chores?"

"Sure, Pa!" Nathan's enthusiasm almost got the better of him.

Turning his attention back to the phone call, Jacob said, "He'll be right over, Miriam."

"You're going to see Sharon again!" Mead teased.

"Dah!" For the second time that day, Nathan cuffed his brother on the head, knocking off his brother's hat, still damp from the well episode, to have it land undignified on the floor once again. Mead howled in glee as he picked up his hat, but before he could get another barb in, Nathan was already out the door.

Although it was past eight o'clock in the evening, the sun remained, albeit quite low, in the New York summer sky. When Nathan arrived at the Helms' house, he politely knocked, and Miriam came to the door.

"Hello, Nathan! How are you this fine evening?" Miriam greeted him.

"I'm doing well, ma'am," Nathan responded.

"Always the gentleman, I see." Miriam smiled. "Sharon wants to collect fireflies tonight. I know that may not be much of a chore, but I was hoping that you would help her catch some lightning bugs. Would that be okay?"

"Why yes, ma'am. I'd like that very much," Nathan replied and silently congratulated himself for not stuttering.

"Good! It's settled then," she said. Turning to look into the house, Miriam called out, "Sharon! Nathan is here!"

Nathan could hear some commotion within the house, and Sharon soon emerged from behind her mother, wearing a short-sleeved shirt and jeans and carrying an old glass jar with some holes punched in the top of its metal lid.

"You'll help me catch some fireflies?" Sharon asked him.

"Of course I will!" Nathan responded, genuinely enthusiastic.

Sharon looked at her mother, who was still staring and smiling at the young teenagers until Sharon had to provide a subtle verbal prompt. "We'll be *fine*, Mom!"

Miriam realized that she had been doting, quickly nodded, and then closed the door, leaving the two young people staring at each other for a long moment.

"Have you ever caught fireflies before?" Sharon asked.

"Oh yes!" Nathan said. "I've even gotten pretty good at not crushing them!" he said with a laugh, which subsequently earned him a light cuff to his shoulder from the former tomboy.

"C'mon, killer," she verbally jousted. "Let's see how many you can put in this jar in one piece!"

They walked behind the Helm homestead for several hundred yards into a large, mowed hayfield. In the corner, Nathan could make out a small pond ringed with cattails. Miriam had sold their hay to another local farmer to help supplement their income, and now many square hay bales dotted the field's expanse. Dusk began to settle in. Only a few of the lightning bugs flashed here and there, but the young people knew that the real performance would start shortly.

Sharon sat on one of the bales of hay and patted the space beside her with her free hand, gesturing for him to accompany her. Nathan quickly obliged her unspoken request and sat next to her such that their shoulders touched lightly.

For several moments, neither spoke. Nathan was unsure of how he knew to remain quiet, but he sensed this foray was more than it appeared and waited patiently.

"Daddy used to take me here to catch fireflies," Sharon explained, breaking the silence, a weight seemingly lifted from her shoulders. "This is the first time I've been out here since he died." She turned her comely visage to look deep into Nathan's eyes. Sharon was grateful to find behind his boyish looks a mature understanding of what this moment meant to her.

Sharon turned and rested her head on his shoulder. Then her body shook with several sobs, and while Nathan never heard her cry aloud, he could feel the wetness on his shirt from the tears that ran down her cheek.

With wisdom far beyond his years and understanding, he sat there, hushed, knowing his presence, and not words, was all she needed from the universe at that moment.

After several minutes, Sharon looked up at the now visible stars, thankful for what the cloudless night revealed. "Remember when we talked about God and heaven at the swimming hole?" she asked, still looking into the sky. "I'll hear some kids at school sometimes say that they don't believe that God even exists." She paused and turned to look at Nathan, who was also staring up at the constellations.

"There are many nights coon hunting when the sky is just like this," Nathan began slowly, searching carefully for the right words. "When we're waiting for one of our hounds to open or tree, I often look up. When I see all those stars, or when I see the many trees and their shapes, or the animals and plants of the forest, I can only imagine there must be a God who created all this wonder. This life simply can't just be random. I reckon if everything happens for a reason, then there must be someone who put that plan in place.

"I suppose the harder question to answer becomes: how can there *not* be a God?" Nathan finished.

Then, the very quarry that the young people had hoped to capture that night alit on Sharon's shoulder. She gasped in awe as the tiny firefly crawled slowly on her shirt while emitting its pulsing light.

"I can't even understand how that bug makes a light come from its body," Nathan continued humbly. "So, I guess it follows that I can't begin to understand the God who created the universe." He then added in a more serious tone, "But as sure as I am that we're here now, I'm sure He exists."

"I'm certain that Mrs. Pleasant," Sharon said, teasingly referring to one of their high school biology teachers, "could provide a purely scientific explanation as to why these bugs glow—and nothing else."

"I hope that I never get quite that smart," Nathan said, grinning.

Sharon looked from her shoulder into his eyes, and even in the dimming light, he could see her staring back, appreciating his humor.

"This never happened before," she whispered. "I've never had a firefly land on me," Sharon said, looking back at the tiny creature.

"Maybe you smell funny," Nathan teased, and the firefly flew from her shoulder into the night, leaving a glowing trail in its wake.

"C'mon, brat!" she said, laughing. Sharon stood quickly and ran across the field while opening the jar's lid.

With no further prompting, Nathan rose from the bale to follow her.

The young couple looked all about them now. It seemed for every star in heaven, there was a firefly in the field. Together, they would excitedly point out the glowing telltale signs all about the hayfield now and hunt down the fireflies. Nathan volunteered to hold the container, fearing he would inadvertently crush the insects, and deferred to Sharon's softer touch. One by one, she would cup her hands delicately over each firefly, and then carefully deposit the flying marvels into the glass vessel.

After catching nearly two dozen of the glowing bugs, they noticed that Nathan was freeing as many insects from the container as she was capturing whenever he opened its lid.

Sharon took the jar from Nathan and gave it a gentle shake, causing the insects to fly about the confines of the glass interior. She held the jar up at eye level, and they stared at the tiny swirling light show.

The young girl then unscrewed the lid, and the fireflies continued to fly in a circular pattern until they escaped the jar's mouth. They watched as the insects flew in a myriad of different directions, vanishing into the night.

Nathan realized that they were at the edge of the small pond now as the water perfectly reflected the stars. He saw Sharon pick something up from the ground and roll it between her petite fingers. She cocked her arm back and threw the object, a small rock, into the pond.

Kerplunk!

The stone's entrance into the water caused ripples, momentarily erasing the reflection of the night sky, but soon the pond's surface went still again, and the stars' closeness returned.

Nathan then remembered Sharon's ritual with the rocks. "What memory did you . . .," he started, but she quickly put her fingers to his lips.

"Some things," she explained lightheartedly, "a girl has to keep to herself." In the starlight, he could see her smile, and she slipped her hand gently behind his head and pulled herself up to kiss him.

To Sharon's surprise, she felt Nathan kiss her back. It was soft, barely noticeable, but she knew that he had responded in his forever-shy way. The boy reached down, his callused hand took hers, and they ambled back to Sharon's home.

Miriam sat in a rocking chair on the back porch, crocheting what looked to be a sweater for cooler months, pretending not to notice the young people's return.

"We're back, Mom," Sharon said sarcastically, not fooled by her mother's ruse of obliviousness.

"Oh! There you are!" Miriam said, acting surprised, but the shared gleam in their eyes between daughter and mother told of an uncommunicated joy between the two women.

Nathan again sensed something afoot, but what exactly, he couldn't be sure. "It's late, ma'am," he said. "It's best I head home."

"It is getting late." Miriam agreed. "Let us drive you home. It won't be any bother."

"That's alright, ma'am." Nathan thanked her. "But I can make my way home. It's barely a mile up the road."

"But it's dark!" Miriam exclaimed. "Aren't you even a little afraid to be walking all alone in the dark?"

Nathan looked honestly confused by the question. "No, ma'am. We hunt raccoon at night. I'm quite used to it," he explained.

"Oh!" Miriam said. She looked at the young man and then back again to Sharon. "Well, thank you again for taking Sharon to catch fireflies tonight. It's been awhile since she's had the opportunity."

"My pleasure, ma'am," Nathan replied and smiled. Then looking at Sharon, he said, "Good night."

"Good night, Nathan—and thank you." Sharon smiled back.

Mother and daughter watched Nathan turn and walk down their driveway. Soon, his image melted into nighttime's wall.

Sharon looked at Miriam, and they spontaneously laughed with joy. Mother and daughter stepped into the house with Sharon excitedly relaying to her mother the magical time that she'd spent with Nathan.

That night, long after Sharon had fallen asleep, Miriam said a prayer, thanking God that her little girl had finally started looking to a future instead of living in the past.

Chapter 9

Hunting Ain't About the Killin'

The next day, Saturday, the sun broke early without the promise of rain. After the morning routine, Jacob explained to Nathan and Mead the plan to make the old well safe.

They would attach their wagon to their tractor, load the wagon with rocks from a stone wall on their property, and then plug the well with the fill—finally ridding themselves of the potentially lethal hazard.

With Nathan's help, Jacob hooked up the wagon to the tractor's hitch and hauled it, with both boys riding inside, to the old fence. The relatively straight, gray line of carefully stacked stones, put in place generations ago, stretched for several hundred yards and had once marked a boundary line between two estates that were now partially consolidated as the Ernst farm.

While time and circumstance had subsumed the fence's original purpose, it now served as the domicile of field mice and chipmunks, which could be seen most days scurrying over the dilapidated structure. Those very rodents also naturally attracted predators such as fox and coyotes, but there was one additional hunter that Jacob reminded his sons still haunted these woods.

"Watch out for timber rattlers." Jacob reminded Nathan and Mead of one of the relatively few poisonous reptiles that made Upstate New

York its home. Seeing these shy snakes was always a thrill for the boys, but they understood that a painful, venomous bite was something to beware.

The morning sun climbed higher, and after nearly an hour of picking through the rocks, the three men had filled the wagon to capacity. With the boys sitting on top of the wagonload, Jacob drove slowly through the green fields and entered the forest, headed for the old farmstead.

Once Jacob had pulled to a stop, the man and his sons began throwing the stones into the well. The boys even made a game of the endeavor, seeing who could make the loudest splash. While the unloading of the wagon went quickly, the men stood dismayed after dropping the last stone with the well remaining unfilled.

"Just how deep is that thing, Mead?" Nathan turned to his sibling.

"It seemed that I dove pretty deep before I felt Storm's collar, and I never touched bottom!"

"Hmm," was all Jacob offered as he stared down into the well's dark, once-placid-again water.

"Pa," Mead said soberly as he relived the near-drowning incident of the day before, "I figure God must really care about us to help Nathan get the dogs and me out of that old well."

"God can be persistent that way," Jacob said, grinning at his growing boys. "And since the job isn't done, it looks like we'll need to make at least one more trip with another load of stone. We'll eat lunch first before we have at it again."

The boys jumped back into the empty wagon, and Jacob drove home. Once inside, he fixed the boys some sandwiches and soup.

"So, how'd your date go with Sharon?" Mead asked as he sunk his teeth into his sandwich.

"Who said it was a 'date'?" Nathan reacted defensively—too defensively, he realized.

"Hard to imagine what chores need to be done after the sun goes down is all," Mead observed.

"Mead," Jacob interjected with a tone signaling the need to change the subject.

Mead realized his teasing had stepped over the line, and he quickly said, "Sorry, Nathan."

While it was clear that Mead was sincere, Nathan took the upper hand and quickly swatted Mead's baseball cap off his head onto the kitchen floor with a loud, "Dah!"

The younger sibling laughed, knowing that the knocking-his-hat-off antic tacitly meant his brother was not angry with him.

With the meal finished, they stepped outside their home, when Jacob gave an unexpected command. "Turn the pups loose. We might as well get them some more time in the woods."

Nathan raced Mead to the pen. They released the four pups with Duke leading the pack out of their pen, all yipping excitedly. The young hounds naturally followed the slow-moving tractor, barking as they raced around.

Once at the fence, the men began the same pattern of picking up rocks, but now in the hot afternoon sun. Jacob had the foresight to bring a jug of water that all three drank from routinely to slake their thirst due to the grueling work.

The pups frolicked in the field and jumped up and down the stone fence, exploring the scents.

With the last stone loaded, the men took a much-needed breather and finished the last of the water. It was close to four o'clock in the afternoon now, and they still had to unload the rock. As they were about to return to the old well, a loud buzzing arose, akin to dozens of cicadas chirping at once. Justice began a long bawl and then proceeded to "face bark," which signaled that he was barking at something that was standing its ground or cornered.

At first, the boys shared a confused look, but their experienced father immediately began to move toward the barking pup, now joined by his siblings, near the fence about seventy-five yards away.

"Timber rattler," was all Jacob needed to say as he moved toward the commotion.

The boys looked excitedly at each other. They began to run, and at the point that they had almost passed Jacob in the short distance, their father held his hand up, indicating to his sons not to proceed.

There as predicted, on a large, flat rock atop the old fence, lie the multi-colored snake with its long body wrapped into a defensive coil. The snake's rattle, positioned above its body, shook a warning to the circling pups. The young hounds barked cautiously at the venomous reptile, giving it a wide berth.

"Pa, how do they know to stay away from it?" Mead observed the pup's behavior. "They're just pups who have never seen a rattlesnake before!"

"Instinct makes them wary," Jacob replied. As Mead proceeded closer to the spectacle, Jacob's hand suddenly caught Mead in the chest abruptly, halting the boy, and he added, "Something you might want to take note of."

Mead looked up at his tall father and nodded.

Jacob called the pups by name, and just as their innate wariness kept them from getting too close to the deadly snake, the canines likewise knew to obey Jacob. One by one, the pups abandoned the snake as its audible warning continued.

Only little Storm's curiosity caused her to hesitate, but another sharp command from Jacob bade the puppy fall in line with the rest of the pack. She abandoned the rattlesnake, quickly caught her littermates, now racing around the stationary tractor and wagon, seemingly forgetting any continued concerns about the peculiar reptile.

Jacob turned the ignition, the tractor's engine dutifully sputtered, and they began the ride to the well. After making the short trek, they tossed the rocks down the gaping hole again. When the wagon was only half-unloaded, Mead looked curiously into the well after dropping his latest load.

"Look, Pa! Look, Nate! I can see the last rock that I just threw in!" Mead exclaimed happily.

The other two men welcomed the news as they peered down the well at Mead's rock, partially protruding above the water's surface. With renewed excitement, they emptied the remaining wagonload even faster to the surprisingly welcomed, if harsh, sound of one rock landing on another.

Fifteen minutes later with the wagon unloaded, the trio had filled the hole with the last few rocks making a small mound akin to a grave marker. Jacob congratulated his sons on the task completed. The sun now hung low in the sky, telling of the time passed performing the arduous chore. Just as Jacob mounted the tractor to start their journey home, yet another dog-generated flurry sounded in the woods.

About two hundred yards away, the pups began howling, but the barking was different from the snake encounter and welcomingly familiar to the old coon hunter's ears.

"Another rattlesnake, Pa?" Mead asked.

"No." Jacob was clearly excited. "They're treed!"

Both boys gave an excited whoop.

Without hesitation, they headed to where the pups were barking even louder and faster now. When the Ernst men arrived, they found the hounds looking up one of the large apple trees.

Amongst the old tree's twisted limbs, covered with small green apples, were an old mother coon and five kitten raccoons. While typically nocturnal, raccoons at times forage during daylight. And today, this brood had unwittingly run into the young coonhounds.

"Pet 'em up! Let them know they did a good job!" Jacob told his sons.

Mead and Nathan raced to the hounds and praised the dogs on their first success in treeing not one but an entire family of woods bandits!

As the pups became louder, one of the unnerved kitten raccoon immediately above Jacob's head began to climb higher into the apple tree. However, the young woods bandit was an inexperienced climber and did not realize it had transferred its weight to a dead branch.

With an audible snap, the limb that the kitten sat on, broke, and the young coon hurtled toward the earth with four pairs of hound eyes staring in fascination.

With uncannily fast reflexes, Jacob grabbed the small raccoon in midair and held the critter aloft and above the possible fray of canine and unwitting prey. All eyes—the dogs, the boys, the kitten coon's siblings, and the mother raccoon—focused on the tiny creature in the coon hunter's hands. For those few moments, the forest seemed to hold its breath, waiting for the final drama to unfold.

The hunter took the raccoon in his hand and walked over to the trunk of the tree, positioning the animal so it could bury its claws into the soft bark. The young raccoon somehow understood the gesture, and once it found purchase, quickly climbed back high into the safety of the apple tree's upper branches.

For a moment, Jacob locked eyes with the mother coon, communicating a silent, mutual appreciation for this reprieve between hunter and hunted.

"Pa?" Mead almost shouted, which started the confused young hound barking again. "Why didn't you just let that coon fall to the ground and let the pups have a kill? I know it ain't huntin' season, but it wouldn't have been our fault if the dogs caught that coon on the ground."

The seasoned coon hunter spoke after a long pause, seeming to look right through his youngest son, trying hard to explain a deeper meaning. "Hunting ain't about the killin', son," Jacob murmured. Then, speaking louder to both Mead and Nathan, he said, "Gather up the pups. It's time to go home."

Jacob turned and headed back to the tractor and wagon with his sons and the young hounds dutifully following.

That night, as Jacob and the boys finished their evening meal, Nathan asked about the incident with the young ringtail.

"Pa?" Nathan asked. "Why do you suppose that kitten coon didn't try to bite you?"

It was a fair question, for even as young as that kitten raccoon was, the wild creature's instincts should have been to sink its teeth into the coon hunter.

"Hard sayin'," was the only response Jacob could offer.

With Sunday morning's chores finished, the Ernst family piled into their pickup truck and headed to Saint Catherine's. Once inside the quaint church, Jacob and Mead sat down in the pew. Nathan, still standing, looked at Jacob and gave his father a polite nod. The young man then proceeded to sit beside Sharon and Miriam, already seated a few pews in front of them, kneeling with their heads down in prayer.

Sharon grinned when she saw Nathan joining them.

Miriam glanced back at Jacob, and the two adults returned their own cordial and knowing smiles.

The Mass proceeded, and Nathan absorbed the peacefulness at both being in the church and his closeness to Sharon. At one point during Father Simmons' sermon, Sharon placed her hand to rest atop Nathan's hand. He turned to see her smiling at him, and he rotated his wrist to take her hand. To them, the chaste gesture seemed natural, an unspoken portent of things to come.

When the service concluded, the congregation emptied from the church with the late summer air still warm but hinting of the coming fall. Father Simmons stood at the back of the church, wishing the parishioners a blessed coming week.

Eventually, Mead walked up, right in line with Jacob, and reached out to shake the priest's hand.

"And how are we today, this beautiful Sunday morning, Mead?" Father Simmons asked in his gentle way.

"Well Father Simmons," Mead began. "It was the funniest thing yesterday. A kitten raccoon fell out of a tree, Pa caught it midair, and then put it right back in the tree! Doesn't that beat all, Father?"

"God certainly has a sense of humor." Father Simmons grinned at the young boy.

"Well, between you and me, Father Simmons," an ancient eleven-year-old boy looked straight back at the priest, "I think some folks are counting on it!" With that, Mead slapped his baseball cap on his head and marched out of the church.

Father Simmons genuflected following Mead's departure and then turned to the boy's father for an answer regarding Mead's behavior.

Jacob could only muster a dumbfounded look and shrugged his shoulders with palms up. "Well, Father, what I think my son meant was . . ."

"Jacob! How are you?" Stella Wharton asked, once again coming to Jacob's rescue by hooking his arm in hers and waving curtly at Father Simmons with the other hand as they walked into the parking lot.

When they were alone, Jacob thanked her. "It seems that you have saved me again, Stella."

Stella, her svelte body more than apparent in a stunning white dress, spoke so no one else could hear.

"Father Simmons wants your soul's salvation." Stella then leaned in even closer, raising on her tiptoes, and speaking into his ear in a sultry tone. "I want the rest."

Smiling at the tall widower with an unmistakably lewd look, Stella turned and sashayed to her shiny, expensive car.

Watching bewildered as Stella walked away, Jacob could not recall the last time that he had been left speechless twice in less than three minutes.

Chapter 10

Of Swamps and Smallmouth Bass

Mead came running into the house nearly out of breath. Nathan was finishing his breakfast but stopped to see what news his younger brother brought.

"Pa!" Mead shouted, entering the kitchen to find Jacob hidden behind the morning paper. "Butch got out again!" He explained, panting, "And he's nowhere in sight."

Folding the paper down to reveal his already-shaking head, Jacob got up and muttered, "Damn mule."

"Do you need any help getting Butch?" Nathan offered, standing up next to Mead, ready to assist their father in catching the persnickety creature.

"No, I'll get him. I think he's taking a liking to that pretty filly up the road a bit," Jacob said with no small measure of disappointment.

Mead couldn't resist as he grinned at Nathan. "He's talking about Jones's white pony, not you and Sharon."

Nathan struck his brother in the arm hard.

"Ouch!" Mead admitted the hurt from the well-delivered punch.

A few minutes later, with both boys still standing on the front porch watching Jacob walk down their driveway with bridle and rope in hand,

Nathan called out. "Pa, since it's the last week of summer vacation, do you mind if Mead and I go bass fishing in the river?"

"Are all your chores done?" Jacob stopped to ask.

"Yep!" both boys shouted enthusiastically.

"Then have at it," Jacob said, looking up at his sons as he resumed walking down the driveway to find the itinerant mule. He then shouted over his shoulder, "And I fully expect to be eating bass tonight!"

The boys laughed, knowing that their father had just playfully thrown down the challenge.

The late summer sun shone brightly in the midmorning, and the brothers were determined to have one more adventure before they were back to studying textbooks.

As the boys gathered their fishing gear, Nathan instructed Mead to retrieve a glass jar full of the nightcrawlers that they had captured the previous evening.

Fetching the bait placed out of the sun on the front porch, Mead heard their phone ring. He also heard Nathan answer the phone, but all the younger boy could make out was his brother saying an enthusiastic, "Sure!"

When Nathan emerged from the house, Mead quickly noticed his sibling carrying not two but three fishing poles and their large, blue metal tackle box.

"What's the other pole for, Nate? You can't but use one pole at a time when fishing for bass."

"You'll see," Nathan replied cryptically as he handed one of the poles to his sibling.

Mead knew to bide his time and wait for his brother to reveal the reason for the excess fishing gear.

"Let's go," Nathan said. The trip to the river was just slightly less than two miles, but dreams of catching some of the plentiful, hard-fighting smallmouth bass in the Tioga River mitigated any dismal thought of the long journey.

As they walked, the brothers spied a red maple with some of its leaves changing to the bright crimson color of its namesake, announcing a sure sign that fall was coming. Of course, the boys knew that meant coon hunting season was not far away.

"I think Moses would be proud of his pups," Mead said.

"I'm sure he would," Nathan agreed.

"Moses was a good hound, huh, Nate?"

"Yes, he was," Nathan confirmed, and Mead smiled.

They were coming up on the Helms' farm and saw Sharon standing in the roadway waiting for them.

Mead put the clues of the phone call and extra fishing pole together quickly. "Reckon we're having some company join us for fishing, eh?" he asked with a wry grin.

"Yep," Nathan finally managed to reply, knowing he was blushing uncontrollably again.

"Hah!" Mead laughed, seeing his brother's red face.

Sharon wore some old, torn blue jeans and a faded, yellow shirt. Her dark hair shone in the sun. She realized that Nathan was staring at her again and welcomed his attention. "I'm ready!" she said when the boys came closer.

"You ever been fishin' before?" Mead asked immediately with more than a little skepticism in his tone.

"Why yes, Mead," Sharon said, looking back and forth between the two brothers. "My largest smallmouth bass was over four pounds that I caught with my dad."

Mead whistled with newfound respect and said, "That's quite a fish." Ever the competitor, he quickly added, "Let's see who catches the biggest fish today! Twenty-five cents to the winner—what do you say?" Mead spat on his hand and then held it out for Sharon to seal the deal.

Nathan just shook his head, watching the exchange.

"You're on!" Sharon said, likewise spitting on her small palm, grasping Mead's hand, and shaking on the challenge.

"I'll scout out ahead and leave you two alone," Mead said sarcastically. Besides, he did not want to be the third wheel. The young boy set off at a quick pace, leaving Nathan and Sharon to themselves.

Nathan offered Sharon one of the fishing poles, which she gladly accepted. When he felt sure that Mead was far enough ahead to promise some privacy, Nathan motioned for them to begin walking.

"Ready for school?" Sharon asked.

"Ready as I'll ever be, I reckon," Nathan said, unable to hide his disappointment that the halcyon days of summer were soon ending.

"I want to try out for the cheerleading team," Sharon confided. "Do you think I'd be any good at it?"

"I think you would do very well," Nathan said, smiling.

"If I do make the team, would you come to watch me cheer?" she asked, biting her lower lip, awaiting his reply.

"Of course, I will," Nathan said with a smirk. "Besides, someone has to keep those football players away from you."

"Always my protector!" She grinned and tousled his nearly shoulder-length hair.

Mead was over one hundred yards ahead now, but the trio was still about half a mile from their destination as they walked along Ryland Creek Road's dusty, brown surface. The road's namesake creek ran parallel to the travelers and would ultimately empty into the river. The ancient rivulet, home to brook trout and crayfish, had for centuries cut its way into the hills, leaving the ravine's sides steep and difficult to navigate. Here the hardwood trees had ceded the hill's steep sides to eastern white pine and the flat-needled hemlocks.

High in the trees, the loud, shrill sound of a witch cackling filled the air.

"What in God's name was that?" Sharon looked alarmed, having never heard that sound before. Reflectively, she grabbed Nathan's arm and held it tightly.

Nathan started chuckling at her reaction to the sound, but Sharon was having none of it.

"Nathan, this isn't funny. What was that?"

The alarm in her voice snapped him out of his laughter, seeing that she was truly frightened. He silently admitted that the sound had caused the hairs to rise on the back of his neck when he had first heard it coon hunting with his father. "That's a porcupine calling," he explained.

Again, the shrill cackling filled the air.

"A porcupine? Really?" Sharon's fear instantaneously turned to wonder. She knew porcupines, when left alone, were harmless.

"Yep," Nathan said matter-of-factly.

"You remind me of my father in so many ways," Sharon said. "Daddy knew a lot about the woods, too."

She paused, and Nathan sensed that she wanted to say something else, but the young girl shook her head, thinking better of speaking her thoughts aloud. Instead, she slid her hand down his forearm and interlaced her fingers with his.

Sharon just smiled, and that sign was enough for Nathan. The two continued in silence, absorbing the forest's piney smells and sounds of songbirds. They finally reached the old, steel bridge that spanned this narrow section of the Tioga River.

They walked to the side of the bridge, and then down a narrow dirt path that threaded its way through the tall grass to the river's edge. They found Mead had finished baiting his hook and beginning to wade into the river.

Sharon sat down and reached to untie her shoelaces when Nathan gently put his hands on hers. "It's best you keep those old sneakers on. The rocks here can be sharp, and you never know if someone threw a glass bottle into the river where you could cut your feet."

"Thank you," she said and smiled softly at his thoughtfulness. However, when he offered to bait her hook with the live worm, she politely motioned to let her handle this task. Sharon was growing to be a lady, but she still had enough of the tomboy left in her to insist on her independence. When she expertly baited the worm on the hook, Nathan nodded with admiration of her skill.

With both their fishing poles ready, the young people entered the cool water and spread out about ten feet apart into the river, facing down current. Mead stayed closest to the shore, then Sharon, and finally Nathan, whose waist was submerged below the water. Each cast their bait downstream and gently jiggled the line back and forth to allow the slow current to present a tempting opportunity to a hungry bass.

Before the first fish was caught, they heard a car pull up on the bridge. The tires ground the surface gravel, and the vehicle finally came to a stop. The sound of a slamming car door told them the driver had parked and exited.

Less than two minutes later, Sheriff Sean Covington walked down and greeted them warmly. "Are the bass biting?" he asked.

"We just got our lines wet, Sheriff," Mead answered.

"Your father and I used to come here and fish when we were your age. Why—sometimes they were biting so hard that we had to hide the hook to bait it!" The police officer chuckled, stepping back in time, remembering his innocence.

"Spoken like a true fisherman, Sheriff," the old soul that was Mead said as he winked at his father's best friend.

Nathan just closed his eyes, shook his head slightly at his younger brother's response, wondering where Mead's words sometimes emanated.

Even Sheriff Covington had to laugh at Mead's candor. "Did your dad ever tell you how we first met?" he asked looking directly at the boys.

"I don't recollect he did, Sheriff," Mead responded.

"One of my favorite stories," Sean said, and now the young people smiled as the law officer's reputation for spinning yarns was as revered as much as J.P. Smith's ability.

"It happened when we were very young, about your age I'd guess, Mead," Sean began. "A gang of kids decided that they wanted to beat me up after school. There were five of them as I recall. Well, they jumped me when I went around a corner of the school where no one else could see. One of them sucker punched me, and I went down to the ground before I knew what was happening."

"Well, why'd they do that?" Mead asked, immediately enthralled with the tale.

"I don't know for sure. I suppose they didn't like the color of my skin." Sean paused and then continued. "Well, right as they were hitting me, your father appeared out of nowhere. I guess Jacob saw them following me, so he figured to follow them. And your father went right after their boss man and gave him a bloody nose with the first punch!"

"Who was that, Sheriff?" Mead asked.

"Why, I think you know him. It was John Allen."

Sean noticed Sharon and Nathan looking at each other and grinning at a shared secret.

"What happened next?" Mead asked eagerly.

"Well, your daddy wasn't satisfied with just taking out their ringleader, so he proceeded to stomp the living daylights out of the rest of them until they left us alone. You ever see your father in a fight?"

"Nope," Mead answered.

In unison, the brothers then added in a practiced monotone, "Pa says only fight if you have to."

"Well, he's right about that of course. But let me tell you, it's a sight to behold!" Sean said with a faraway look, peering into the past.

"So, I've been told," Mead said sarcastically, snapping Sean out of his reverie.

"When they left, I wondered why your pa had helped me. So, I asked him why come to the rescue of a black kid getting a butt whoopin? Know what he said?"

All three—including Sharon, who was following the officer's story just as intently as the brothers—stood, anxiously waiting to hear the answer.

"Your pa said, 'you don't judge a hound by how his hide looks.' Now doesn't that beat all?" Sean laughed hard, remembering those words spoken by Jacob Ernst over two decades ago.

"Pa still says that!" Mead joyfully confirmed.

"He does?" the lawman asked in feigned disbelief, cocking his head slightly.

"Yep. Why don't you ask him?" Mead suggested, and he motioned with his head for Sean to look behind him.

There on the riverbank, like he had been there all day, sat Jacob Ernst, listening to his best friend retell the story of their youth.

Although he should not have been surprised at his good friend's consummate stealth, the sheriff startled nonetheless. "You can still sneak up on me, Jacob, after all these years!"

"That means a lot coming from the toughest man in Steuben County," Jacob said as he laughed good-naturedly.

Jacob stood to his full height, and the police officer laughed loud and hard and gave his best friend a powerful hug.

"How'd you get here?" Sean asked. "I didn't hear your truck pull up."

"I rode him," Jacob said, hiking his thumb up the riverbank to where Butch was tied to a small sapling.

"Is that . . . no! That ain't old Butch, is it?" Sean asked incredulously.

"One and the same," Jacob said, the dismay in his voice blatant.

"Well, how are you doing, Butch? It's good to see you again!" Sean spoke to the mule.

The mule looked directly at Sean, hearing his name called, and *happily* brayed back at the police officer.

Both Mead and Nathan gawked at each other in amazement at the old long ear's apparent change in attitude.

"He always did like you better," Jacob said, sounding hurt.

"Don't worry, old friend." Sean tried to balm Jacob's wounded pride as he looked up the hill and smiled at Butch. "There's no accountin' for taste."

Again, Butch whinnied happily, seeming to agree with Sean.

"I see you're still tellin' stories." Jacob grinned, trying to change the subject.

"You're at the center of a lot of the stories I tell." Now it was Sean's turn to return the good-natured ribbing.

"Fair enough." Jacob laughed.

"How are your hounds?" Sheriff Sean Covington was good at many things, and chief among them was relating to the people whom he was sworn to protect.

"Good! This young litter holds a lot of promise."

"Lot of work raising a good coonhound," Sean acknowledged.

"You ought to come out hunting with us again," Jacob suggested.

"Who me?" Sean laughed again.

"Pa says you're one of the best hunters he knows," Mead offered without looking at them as the young boy was paying close attention to his fishing line.

"Well, maybe at hunting the bad guys," Sean said, and while the sheriff was among friends, no one doubted the veracity of his claim. Sean's long record of law enforcement remained spotless, and many criminals were behind jail bars because of this police officer's tenacity and talent for solving crimes.

"Got a minute?" Jacob asked, motioning for Sean to follow him up the bank.

"Sure," Sean said, knowing from their long friendship that Jacob wanted to speak privately.

The young people just looked at each other and shrugged as they watched the adults depart.

When they were at the top of the hill with Butch acting as a backdrop, Jacob leaned closer to Sean. "I read in the paper this morning that they closed the murder investigation of Bruce Gartner," Jacob said, referencing the horrific crime that he had first read about several months earlier in a Sunday newspaper.

"Yes," Sean confirmed but not without a touch of anger at the thought of the unsolved crime. "Whoever did it knew how to hide their tracks well. We're pretty sure it was drug related." Sean mentioned the growing criminal problem in the region.

"Any clues as to who did it?" Jacob persisted.

"Some folks recall seeing an expensive-looking town car with out-of-state license plates reading 'Illinois.' But you know people around here, Jacob. No one in these parts suspects someone is getting ready to perpetrate even a petty crime, let alone murder!

"It's a growing problem—this drug trade," Sean continued. "If it keeps expanding at the current rate, we're going to have a very big problem on our hands in twenty years or so."

"Do you think these hills will allow that?" Jacob asked and smiled, looking at the ring of hills that made up Painted Post.

"I hope not," Sean said knowingly and repeated softer, "I certainly hope not."

Suddenly, Mead's patience and attention paid off as he jerked his fishing pole into the air. "Gotcha!" he hollered.

Sean and Jacob rushed back down the bank to see what Mead had hooked.

"Bring him in, Mead!" Nathan encouraged as both he and Sharon reeled in their baited hooks so as not to tangle their lines with Mead's fish.

The large smallmouth bass broke the river's surface and tail danced across the water for several seconds in a futile attempt to dislodge the well-set hook in its mouth.

"Keep your pole up!" Jacob yelled, caught up in the excitement.

"Keep tension on the line!" Sean shouted.

"I am! I am!" Mead laughed and shouted as he continued to fight the fish.

Again, the bass broke the surface, and then it swam hard downstream. Mead's line screamed as the fish exceeded the tension setting on his reel. Mead pumped the pole and cranked in the line as Jacob had taught him.

Thus, the battle between boy and fish continued with more tail dances, Mead pumping the pole up, and the tension reel sporadically screaming. Slowly, the large bass began to tire. He continued to bring in the fishing line with everyone egging him on until he finally had the fish close to his side.

With a single, fluid movement, Mead reached into the water, pinched the bass's open mouth with his thumb, and scooped the large bass out of the water with its body flailing in the air.

Mead's audience clapped at the successful catch, and the boy bowed at the waist, his baseball cap's rim almost touching the water.

"I'd bet that bass goes three and a half pounds!" Sean Covington exclaimed.

Looking over his prize with an overly serious scrutiny and pursed lips, Mead turned to look at the police officer and said, "Why, Sheriff, the picture of this fish alone is gonna weigh all of four pounds!"

All laughed, but Sean would have the last word.

"Spoken like a true fisherman," Sheriff Covington said as his eyes narrowed and a devilish grin.

"Ha!" Mead bowed his head in deference at the well-timed riposte.

By day's end, long after the adults had departed, the young people landed a total of twelve bass that afternoon. When Mead and Sharon compared their take, Mead's first, huge bass won the day.

"I guess I owe you twenty-five cents, Mead," Sharon conceded and fished in her pocket to produce a shiny quarter.

Mead accepted the coin and smiled. "It's been nice fishing with you." While the rivalry was still present, the young boy was sincere.

After they had made the long walk back home, Nathan and Mead began preparing the bass for dinner. To their surprise, Sharon insisted on joining in the chore and proved herself to be more than up to the task.

"I'm sure glad that I didn't make a bet on whether or not you could fillet a fish!" Mead said with an appreciative glance at the superb job Sharon had accomplished with the boneless hunks of bass on their kitchen table.

The telephone rang, and Jacob answered. The children swelled with pride as they heard Jacob tell the caller of their successful fishing exploits. When he had finished, Jacob entered the kitchen. "That was your mother, Sharon. Miriam insisted that she come right over and prepare the fish for dinner tonight."

"My mother is an excellent cook!" Sharon exclaimed happily.

"We'll see about that," Mead said with reservation, causing all to chuckle.

Miriam, clad in an outfit similar to Sharon's, arrived less than fifteen minutes later. Once she had the lay of the kitchen, and the whereabouts of some ingredients and fresh vegetables from the garden, Miriam shooed the men away and asked Sharon to remain and lend her a hand.

The Ernst men walked out on their porch, watching the sun drop lower in the sky as they surveyed the forests.

"Be about another month before we cut the corn, Pa?" Nathan inquired about their twenty or so acres of standing corn.

"About that," Jacob confirmed.

"Do you think coon are eating our corn, Pa?" Mead asked.

"Without a doubt," Jacob responded. "It's just the way of things. Raccoon love corn, and will do what raccoons do, I suppose."

They continued talking about the upcoming hunting season when Sharon burst onto the porch. "Dinner is ready!" she announced.

The hungry men needed no further prompting and immediately followed her into the kitchen. The delicious smell was enticing from the bass, battered and fried, with a large bowl of boiled potatoes flanked by sweet peas and likewise fresh green beans.

Jacob sat down on one end of the table, with Miriam directly facing him at the other end. Mead sat by himself on one side of the table, while Sharon positioned herself close to Nathan.

There were several moments of awkward silence, but then Jacob asked Mead to say grace. The youngest Ernst dutifully obeyed his father, but both Nathan and Jacob noted that Mead said the prayer much faster than usual, and when finished, Mead began piling the fish and vegetables onto his plate.

"Pa, this fish tastes kind of different!" Mead proclaimed with his mouth full.

Miriam and Sharon held their breath, while Jacob and Nathan also froze, awaiting Mead's assessment of the meal.

"Well, it tastes different how, son?" Jacob finally asked after some tense moments.

"This fish tastes good, Pa! It's a whole lot better than your cookin'!" Mead explained in his usual candid manner.

They couldn't help but laugh again at Mead's honest assessment.

The children volunteered to clean the kitchen, and Jacob and Miriam happily welcomed the reprieve. They walked out the front door and sat on the porch steps. It was dusk now, and the stars were beginning to emerge in the waning tyranny of the sunlight.

"Do you miss them?" Miriam asked suddenly.

"Rose and Ken?" Jacob asked, mentioning each of their former spouses.

"Yes," Miriam clarified.

"I do miss them," Jacob admitted. "Ken was a good friend for a long time."

"You should have heard him talk about you, Jacob. Ken would tell everyone no one knew these hills better than you!" Miriam smiled, reminiscing.

Jacob nodded, returning her sentiment.

"Do you ever hear from Rose's parents anymore?" Miriam asked.

A pained look quickly replaced Jacob's smile.

"When they moved to New York City, just before Rose and I were married, they wanted us to follow them and live there. Rose knew that I couldn't leave these hills, and she quite frankly told her mother that we weren't leaving Painted Post."

Jacob searched his thoughts but continued.

"And when Rose died in childbirth, they blamed our rural hospital for not having the right doctors or facilities. Of course, they blamed me, too. They even wanted to sue the hospital, and I told them no.

"Ever since then, they may have only visited us once or twice, but they do send cards on the boys' birthdays and Christmas time."

"Oh, I'm so sorry, Jacob," Miriam offered sincerely.

"There's nothing to be sorry about," Jacob assured her politely. "For the relatively short time we had together in this world, I know that Rose was truly happy." There was a certainty in his voice that seemed to balm them both.

"Do you see much of Ken's mother?" Jacob asked, knowing that Ken's father had passed away years before due to a heart attack.

"My mother-in-law remarried some man in Syracuse, and he doesn't like children. She will make a trip down here three of four times a year, but she never stays for the night. Sharon is always happy to see her grandmother every so often, and I'm thankful for that, too. Sharon does get to see some of her cousins her age when my brother and his wife and kids make it back to town.

"My mother and father help out a lot, so I'm grateful for their support. My mother keeps nagging me to 'find another man' and to move on with my life. All things in time, I suppose, Jacob."

She paused as they both heard the children burst into laughter somewhere in the house. "Sounds like family," Miriam said, wistfully nodding her head toward the happy ruckus.

The pretty woman turned to look at Jacob, and their eyes met for a moment. Jacob turned his look to the ground. "There's magic in these hills, Miriam," he said.

Somehow, Miriam understood that Jacob was neither being philosophical nor changing the subject. But if this normally simple man was trying to convey his bond with the land, or perhaps hinting at a deeper insight of sorts, Miriam could not be sure. "It was good to cook a meal with men under the roof." She smiled and placed her small hand on the top of Jacob's muscular forearm.

"Thank you," Jacob said politely. "Mead was right—not only was the entire meal especially tasty, it certainly was a lot better than my cooking!"

They shared a soft laugh.

The new school year started with a rush of lessons and homework assignments. While Jacob insisted that his sons perform their daily chores, he also wanted to be sure that the boys studied hard. Jacob firmly believed a good education would elevate his sons' future possibilities, and he knew their mother would have likewise demanded diligent study.

Summer formally gave way to fall. The leaves of the maples and oaks soon followed suit, and the rolling hills of Painted Post burst into a myriad of colors. The older hounds knew that the change in foliage meant hunting season was not far off. Any sight of Jacob after sunset would cause the hounds to make a boisterous clamor in their expectation of going to the woods. Jacob could not bring himself to dampen their enthusiasm with a scolding, so he would let them carry on with their barking.

The opening night of coon season eventually arrived, and on that first Friday evening, the Ernst family headed to the woods in their old truck with the reliable Luke, as well as young Storm and Duke, on their first official hunt.

"Where we headed, Pa?" Mead asked as Jacob turned down a dirt road after driving what seemed like many miles.

"We're going to a place your grandfather took me a long time ago. I don't think I've hunted this place for nigh twenty years."

"Twenty years! Shoot, Pa, there ought to be plenty of raccoon in those woods after all that time."

"Should be, except for . . ." Jacob's voice drifted off.

"Except for what, Pa?" Mead sensed a story coming.

"Well, we're headed toward a place called 'Dead Man's Swamp.' Oh, there's raccoon there for sure," Jacob said as he turned down yet another old dirt road.

"Dead Man's Swamp? How'd it get that name?" Mead's imagination already had the best of him, and he was likewise affecting Nathan with the same inquisitiveness.

"Well, that's an interesting story," Jacob began, settling into his tall-tale-telling voice. "A long time ago, there was an old coon hunter named Joshua Pinkerton. They say he was a particularly crotchety old coot with no respect for his fellow man or the law. And if he had any active interest in getting to heaven, he hid it pretty well from everyone who knew him."

"Did he have any family, Pa?" Mead asked.

"Nope—not according to the stories. No woman would have him as he was so terribly miserable and all," Jacob said, grinning at his embellishment and continued.

"They say on one dark night that he decided to do a little coon hunting—out of season to boot! And he headed to this swamp 'cause he figured there would be plenty of coon coming there to eat the fish and frogs. Of course, that's pretty good reckoning for a pretty bad fellow.

"And sure enough, his dogs treed right smack in the middle of that swamp. Joshua was so determined to kill a ringtail that night that he waded into that black water without a lick of common sense to tell him otherwise. After about twenty minutes of going through that old swamp, he finally saw his hounds treed on a long-dead oak, and he could see the raccoon's eyes reflecting in his old lamp."

"Lamp, Pa?"

"Yep! This was a time long before the modern niceties like batteries and all. He carried an old carbide lantern, which burned with a flame, to see the raccoon."

"Sure must've been a long time ago." Mead ended with a long, drawn-out whistle through his teeth.

"Yep, sure was," Jacob confirmed before continuing. "But mean old Joshua was so obsessed with getting a raccoon that night that he didn't watch his step, and he went into a deep puddle of muck and subsequently began to sink. As he was getting sucked deeper into the depths of the swamp, he shouted for help, and as he looked up, there sat on a stump an old, ugly witch dressed in black, just looking at him!"

"Pa, are you saying witches are coon hunters, too?" Mead asked in sheer disbelief at the possibility.

"No, sir!" Jacob exclaimed. "I'm pretty sure she was just passing through with no intent to stay. This is Painted Post, after all."

"Oh! I see, Pa. That makes a lot of sense." Mead nodded and noticed Nathan listening on with growing amusement. "So, what happened next?"

"Well, recall that old Joshua wasn't much of a churchgoer, but he knew enough that the creature in front of him was there, just waiting for his demise. He cried out for help again, but the witch just ignored him, smiling as old Pinkerton sunk to his chest. Finally, Joshua said what the witch had wanted to hear, 'I'll do anything! Just save me!'

"Upon hearing those words, the witch said, 'I will save your life under one condition. You must never again leave this swamp, and you can only eat what dies within its boundaries. Do we have a deal?'

"Old Joshua agreed to her demands, never intending to honor the terms of their agreement, of course. She waved her arms, saying a spell, and the dark swamp spat him out onto solid ground.

"But when Joshua looked around, he was all alone, except for his hounds treeing. He told himself that he must have been seeing things, and the witch was simply a figment of his imagination. But when he went to the tree, the hounds took one look at him, and they ran away as fast as they could and clear out of the swamp!"

"Why did they do that, Pa?" Mead asked perplexed.

"That's what old Joshua wondered, too!" Jacob replied. "But when he looked down into the black water with the glow of his lamp going low, he saw his reflection and realized that the witch had changed him into a horrid ghoul! In sheer horror, understanding what the witch had transformed him into, Joshua let out the most wretched sound!

"In fact, the old folks say you can still hear him, moaning on moonless nights, or whenever he tries to leave that swamp, because his black-and-green skin will burst into fire until he retreats into the confines of the swamp—all the while crying out in pain.

"Over the years, several coon hunters who entered this swamp were never seen or heard from again. They would go in, but the only things ever to come out were the hunters' hounds. Supposedly, one young boy, picking blackberries along the swamp's edge one summer, came across a half-eaten body, but by the time he came back with the sheriff, there was no body to be found."

Jacob paused for effect. "So, that's how the swamp got its name." He ended the story abruptly, letting his words hang inside the truck cab while slowing the vehicle to a stop.

"And that's where we're hunting tonight?" Mead asked incredulously.

Jacob put the vehicle's transmission into park and smiled at his boys. "We're there now!"

As the men piled out of the truck onto the dark, dirt road, Mead made a quick quip. "Of course, Pa," he noted, "we would have to come to this swamp on a moonless night."

"It's just a story, boy." Jacob grinned from beneath his headlight that he'd already turned on.

"Uh huh," Mead said unconvinced, but he quickly snapped on his flashlight to add some comfort.

The warm, dank air above the swamp's water combined with the night's cooler air.

"And we've got a fog rolling in, too," Nathan observed.

"Only thing we're missing is a witch!" Mead moaned.

"Who says she's missing?" Nathan suggestively intoned, unable to resist playing into Mead's growing anxiety.

Mead punched his older brother in the arm in response.

Nathan just snickered as he turned on his flashlight.

Jacob released the hounds, and Luke immediately went to the task of finding a raccoon with the young pups, Duke and Storm, naturally following the older dog. They disappeared into the fog, and the men took an old game path that ran alongside the swamp's edge.

Mead, the last in line, gazed about as the night's fog began to thicken considerably. The young boy warily surveyed the swamp, wondering if any strange, misshapen figures would magically appear. The marsh's border was delineated by live, robust oaks and maples against much smaller, and mostly dead, gnarled trees and old stumps—a natural juxtaposition of arboreal life and death. Long tufts of swamp grass did flourish, their growth uninhibited by the lack of canopy in the swampy environs.

Luke's voice rang out into the night not more than one hundred yards ahead of the hunting party. Mead had been so focused on the swamp that the hound's loud voice startled him. Then Duke and Storm also began to sing along. Jacob suspected that the young coonhounds were just as likely barking at Luke versus trailing the raccoon, but they were learning and would soon associate the scent with the older dog's purpose.

The chase intensified as Luke's trailing bark became more rapid. This track was "hot," and the raccoon was likely not far ahead, already looking for a tree to climb. While Jacob and Nathan were delighted by the hunt's progression, Mead took a slightly different tack on the situation.

"Pa, I think the dogs are going deeper into the swamp!" Mead said, his voice thick with apprehension.

"Yep," Jacob noted, casting a sidelong grin at Nathan.

"Wonderful," was all Mead could manage to say.

At that moment, undoubtedly several hundred yards into the heart of the swamp, Luke switched over into a hard, chopping tree bark.

"Treed!" Nathan exclaimed.

"Let's go do what we came here for," Jacob said, looking at his sons as they heard the sweet sounds of Duke and Storm barking alongside the older hound. Duke was particularly melodious, and it delighted the hunters to listen to a canine so young with such a perfect voice. Not to be outdone, little Storm made up in enthusiasm with her quick, sharp barks for what she lacked in the baritone howls of the two larger males.

"Be careful!" Jacob said seriously. "The swamp is shallow in most parts, but it does have a few deeper pools toward the center where we're headed."

"Lovely," Mead moaned. Lovely indeed, he thought, as an old hoot owl called out repeatedly in the foggy night.

Jacob and Nathan quickly headed toward the baying hounds.

Mead was still reluctant to enter the swamp until he realized the fog was quickly obscuring the lights of his father and brother. If he didn't get moving soon, they would be out of sight. Even if Mead knew that they were relatively close, the thought offered little comfort in the eeriness of a potentially ghoul-inhabited swamp. His first step into the smelly liquid brought some relief as he discovered the water was barely a half-inch deep, just as his father had foretold. Shaking his head, still unconvinced that his wariness was not unwarranted, Mead followed his family deeper into the old swamp.

While Mead was happy that the water was shallow, the thickening fog was not helping the situation. The gnarled trees seemed to appear suddenly, and his imagination on more than one occasion portrayed these dead husks as sinister beings reaching for him. Still, the young boy could tell that he was closing on the hounds. If there was one sense of familiarity this night, it was the sound of Luke accompanied by the chorus of the young pups.

Mead had to negotiate several huge, fallen trees. Being smaller, he took longer to climb over the obstacles, and now the fog had wholly absorbed Jacob and Nathan. Offering some relief, he could hear his brother and father talking, perhaps fifty yards ahead. Although Mead could not make out their words, the mutually pleased tone indicated that they were underneath the tree with the hounds and could likely see the raccoon.

Mead quickly came upon one more natural barrier—a tangle of old trees and briars. While confident his brother, father, and the hounds were just on the other side, he could not tell which side of the obstruction Jacob and Nathan had taken to circumvent the sharp thorns. A broad pool of water to his left seemed the easiest route to take. With quick abandon, the youngster stepped into the water with the hopes of being reunited with his family—human and canine.

However, the expectation of joy quickly yielded to sheer terror when his first step found no shallow bottom, and the young boy plunged into the dark water. Mead held on to his flashlight and splashed loudly in the black swamp.

Thankfully, a large tree had fallen across the pool, and Mead latched on to its decaying trunk. Only his pride stopped him from calling for help. He kicked himself mentally for making such a foolish mistake— the reason there had been an absence of vegetation springing from the pool should have alerted him to its potential depth.

Well, Mead reasoned in traditional Ernst fashion, he'd gotten himself into this mess, now he would have to get himself out.

Maintaining his hold on the trunk, Mead pulled himself partially out of the water and began slowly shimmying down the large tree. Almost to the pool's edge, he felt his foot kick something. He could tell it wasn't the bottom of the swamp, and it moved slightly, but he figured dry, or at least swampy, land must be close by now.

Mead's horror returned when, directly in front of him, a black, skeletal hand, covered with the green slime of the swamp, rose out of the water and began arcing through the air directly at him. With the easy-to-imagine intent of pulling him beneath the water, the boy was sure that Joshua Pinkerton had just found his next feast!

"Ahhh! Ahhh! Ahhh!" Mead screamed as his family's traditional stoicism abandoned him altogether.

Suddenly, a second hand grabbed him by the scruff of the neck, and Mead gasped, resigned that his young life was over. A powerful, upward jerk pulled the boy onto the log, and his light came to rest not on a ghoul but the smiling face of his brother. Right beside his older sibling stood the young pup Storm, looking on with considerable interest.

"The hand! The hand!" Mead frantically pointed to the ghostly appendage in front of them.

"You mean this?" Nathan grabbed the "skeleton" and quickly snapped in half an old tree branch that Mead's foot had stepped on to raise it out of the water. Mead gasped a sigh of relief as Nathan turned the branch over several times as proof of its true identity and then threw it toward the middle of the pool.

"I thought old Joshua Pinkerton had me for sure!" Mead exclaimed.

Nathan shook his head, laughing, as he extracted Mead from the pool. "It's just an ol' branch, and besides, I suspect you don't taste very good. Joshua would have to have been mighty hungry to want to eat you!" Nathan grinned and turned to rejoin their father and the hounds.

"How do you know when he ate last?" Mead shouted.

Looking into the wide pool of water, Storm suddenly and uncharacteristically growled.

"What's gotten into her?" Nathan wondered. "C'mon Storm, let's go!" Reluctantly, the young hound obeyed and fell alongside Nathan as they turned to rejoin Jacob and the other dogs.

A noise caught Mead's ear, and he turned to see something large swirl the water in the middle of the dark pool. He then quickly ran to catch up with Nathan.

When Mead presented himself, soaking wet, to his father, Jacob asked if the cold was bothering him.

"I'll be all right, Pa," Mead said bravely, happy to find a means to restore at least some of his pride.

That night, the men, coupled with the trio of hounds, would tree four large raccoons in the dark swamp, all the while with Mead looking over his shoulder. After the last raccoon had been taken, they stood with their hounds at the edge of the swamp.

"Let's call it a night, boys," Jacob recommended.

Then, emanating from the middle of the swamp, a loud, eerie groan filled the air and a subsequent loud splash in what must have been one of the swamp's deeper pools.

Had it been a large, old tree finally plummeting into the marsh? Had it fallen in its own time?

Or had it been something else, perhaps something evil, thrashing in that fetid water?

"What was *that*?" Mead put a voice to what both Jacob and Nathan were thinking.

Jacob looked into the swamp for a long moment with no pretense of hiding his bewilderment at the mysterious sound. When he finally turned his pale look back to his sons, he could muster one simple response.

"Hard sayin'," was all the seasoned coon hunter offered.

When the hunters returned to the truck to head home, Mead took one last glance out into the expanse that was Dead Man's Swamp. He imagined old Joshua Pinkerton, sitting on a black stump within his swampy confinement and cursing the missed opportunity for a good meal.

Who was to say the young boy was wrong?

It was Painted Post, after all.

———— • ————

When the truck's headlights had faded into the distance—the darkness filling the void of the light and the sounds of the coon hunters but a memory— an ancient evil again moaned, its voice haunting the motionless swamp air.

The hounds! The evil thing cursed the night. It could never penetrate the protective aura of the hounds! It was not allowed to get close to any dog. Perhaps that constraint had been the cruelest part of the witch's spell.

Its constant, gnawing hunger not sated, the ghoul slid beneath the dark swamp water once more.

It would have to wait another night for a meal.

Chapter 11

Relationships

1980

S haron wore her green-and-white cheerleader uniform as she stood on the Ernst front porch alongside Nathan and Mead. The spectacle playing out transfixed all three of the young people.

"Taking bets?" Mead asked, turning to look at his brother.

"Nope," Nathan responded, looking back at Mead, who was now as tall as he was. The early fall air of Nathan's junior year felt cool, with the trees in Painted Post just beginning to show off their bright fall foliage.

When the three teenagers had made it to the Ernst farm after their walk from the bus stop this afternoon, they quickly espied the unfolding standoff.

Butch had again escaped the confines of his stall. The mule snorted loudly as it looked into the steady eyes of Jacob Ernst. Animal and man were only about twenty-five feet apart and stood motionless, trying to assess the other's strategy.

"What is going on?" Sharon asked.

"It's sort of hard to explain," Nathan said, grinning. "These two have somethin' of a sordid history."

"Oh, yes," Sharon said as she nodded, recalling the strained relationship between Jacob and the ornery animal.

"Butch!" Jacob commanded as he began waving his arms gently with one hand holding a bridle. "Now stay steady, boy."

Jacob took a step forward while Butch took a step back, maintaining the distance between them. Jacob shook his head, frustrated by his lack of progress in catching the mule.

"He's a stubborn one," Sharon observed.

"Pa or the mule?" Mead retorted.

Sharon raised her eyebrows and tilted her head slightly but let the question go unanswered.

Butch put his head down and began grazing on the tall grass in the yard.

Jacob saw his chance. "Atta boy," he softly cooed. "That grass tastes good, doesn't it?" He stepped lightly and quickly to close the distance between him and the willful creature.

Jacob came alongside Butch and slowly began to slip the halter over the animal's head. But as soon as his hands touched the animal, Butch threw his head, catching Jacob in the midsection, throwing the man several feet in the air. Jacob landed ungracefully on the hard ground in a heap. Butch snorted at him, then ran down the driveway, turned onto Ryland Creek Road, and disappeared.

"Damn mule," Jacob muttered angrily as he stood.

"Oh my!" Sharon exclaimed, starting to walk over to help. Nathan quickly grabbed her arm, and with an alarmed look, silently shook his head, indicating that she should not approach his father at this moment.

"Pa, do you need any help?" Mead asked.

"No, boy," Jacob responded as he began walking in the wake of the mischievous mule, "I know where he's headed. I'll get him . . . eventually."

The young people watched as Jacob turned onto Ryland Creek, and like Butch, escaped their sight.

"Can we see the hounds?" Sharon asked Nathan.

"Sure," Nathan said, but he sensed that she wanted to speak with him privately.

"I'll leave you two lovebirds alone," Mead said, smirking as he disappeared into the house.

As Nathan and Sharon approached the cages, the dogs barked and happily wagged their tails.

"You truly love these hounds and the forests, don't you?" Sharon asked, watching one of the hounds approach her.

"Yes," Nathan admitted and quickly added, "I guess it's all I've ever known in a way."

"It is who you are. I know this." Sharon's voice drifted off.

Nathan sensed that she was talking more to herself than him. "Is everything okay?"

She turned and smiled. Sharon counted herself blessed to have a boyfriend who intrinsically knew her thoughts and emotions.

"Sometimes," Sharon started, "the other girls at school tease me, but I know they're just mean. They talk about how you're rarely at the sporting events when I'm cheering. I know it's usually the weekend, and it's hunting season, and how you're with your brother and father, running behind your dogs in these woods. Their boyfriends are either on the sports field playing or in the stands watching." Her voice faded, but she smiled mysteriously.

"How do you feel about that?" Nathan asked a bit apprehensively.

"I feel proud, Nathan Ernst," Sharon said, now looking into his eyes, the warmth of her look unmistakable. "You are who you are, and that's what I love about you. There's no pretending to be somebody else in you."

"Who else could I be?" Nathan asked innocently, causing her to laugh aloud.

"That's what I mean," Sharon said as she closed the short gap between them and took his hands in hers. The imp in her suddenly returned, and she grinned. "Besides, if you're in the woods chasing raccoon with your family, I know you're not chasing other girls."

"I suppose there's always a bright side," Nathan said, returning her grin.

Butch's loud snort broke them from their reverie. They looked down the road to see Jacob leading the old mule down their driveway headed toward the barn.

"I see he captured that stubborn old thing." She laughed.

"Yeah," Nathan mused, "looks like Butch has everything under control."

"Oh stop!" Sharon protested with a laugh, coming to Jacob's defense.

"Come," Nathan said. "I have something to show you."

"Where are we headed?"

"Up there." Nathan motioned with his head up the hill into the forest.

Sharon looked past the field, which now held browning, eight-foot tall cornstalks. "In this?" she asked, indicating her cheerleading outfit.

Nathan turned to her, exposing his back. "Jump on!"

Sharon grinned, remembering their familiar routine, and quickly jumped on Nathan to ride piggyback.

With Sharon now hugging his back tightly, Nathan then began the long walk up the hill alongside the cornfield.

They said nothing, as Sharon marveled at the changing leaves. The bright gold dressing of the sugar maples and orange foliage of the shagbark hickory trees enchanted her. The earthy odor of the forest, and the sweet smell of the corn, combined to overwhelm her senses.

She loved all of it.

They finally came to the edge of the pond, its watery surface darker now with the sun low in the sky; still, the reflection of the trees and their colors in the pool continued to hold Sharon's awe.

Nathan set her down gently on the ground.

"It's beautiful," Sharon said barely above a whisper. A light wind kicked up tousling her hair as she turned to him. "I choose you, Nathan Ernst," she said.

"Choose me over what?" he asked.

"Over everything," she said. "Over the silliness of the other girls' games, their jockeying over who's the most popular, over their shallowness, their. . ." She stopped, shaking her head. "You're blushing." She laughed again.

"I am?" Nathan asked, but he already knew her statement to be true.

"Yes, you are!" Sharon loved to tease him.

Nathan looked momentarily past her, then gently wrapped his arms around her and slowly spun her around. "Shhh," he said as his hand softly cupped her chin and turned her head to look at the opposite end of the pond.

Sharon gasped.

There, a mother bear with two of her cubs, each weighing about seventy-five pounds, now explored the far side of the water's edge. The wind was in the young people's favor, as the mother bear had not yet caught their scent to expose their presence.

The young bears began to romp about, one rising slightly on its back feet to cuff the other on the head with its front paw. The other cub charged the would-be attacker, and both young bears tumbled around on the bank, playfully biting each other.

The old sow walked to the pond's edge to drink the water, ignoring her offspring's commotion. After the long draw, water dripping from her muzzle, the adult bear looked up directly at Nathan and Sharon.

The bear did not startle, as nearly all other forest denizens would, but instead moved her head laterally back and forth. The old female bruin then quickly gave a sharp grunt, and the obedient cubs immediately stopped their horseplay. Their mother's warning issued, the young bears turned and soon followed her back over the pond's levee and disappeared into the barrage of the forest's colors.

But seconds later, one of the cubs, a male, re-emerged to look directly at Nathan. Both hunter and bear locked eyes.

"Perhaps we will meet again," Nathan murmured, conversing directly with the overly curious cub. Another sharp grunt from the sow bear somewhere in the forest demanded the cub follow, and with one last glance at Nathan, the small bear finally turned and vanished into the forest.

"That was incredible," Sharon said. "Were you scared?"

"No, because we weren't between her and her cubs," Nathan explained. "If we had somehow ended up in that predicament, then she would have likely attacked to defend her little ones. That would certainly have been a fight that I could not win."

"As any mother ought!" Sharon agreed. "And thank you."

Nathan laughed and began, "It's my pleasure. I'm glad you enjoyed—"

"No," she interrupted him. "I mean, yes—thank you for taking me to these special places. I so love this forest! But I meant, thank you—for not fighting. You've kept your promise, and that means so much to me."

Nathan nodded silently, reaffirming that vow.

———— ❖ ————

The next afternoon in the high school's large gymnasium, the sweat rolled down Sharon's cheeks as she went through the cheerleading routine for what felt like the umpteenth time. When they finished, their coach, once again, displayed her disappointment.

"Not good enough, girls!" Ms. Benton yelled. "You have to kick higher!" Normally, Ms. Benton, a new teacher and not all that much older than the girls she coached, would begin pointing out individual flaws. But thankfully, she only shook her head in exaggerated disgust.

"Take a five-minute break, and then we'll get right back to it," Benton said and added insult to injury, "And then we'll see if you girls can actually *cheer.*"

Sharon plopped down on the wooden bleacher. Moments later, her self-proclaimed rival, Kim Bateman, flanked on either side by some of her friends, decided to poke fun at Sharon once again.

"Well, well," the flaxen-haired Kim began. "It looks like your boyfriend finally decided to come out of the woods."

Confused, Sharon followed Kim's look into the upper parts of the bleacher, and true to her observation, Nathan sat alone. Not far from away, but clearly segregated, were some boys wearing their school sports jerseys with large numbers on the front and back. When Nathan made eye contact with Sharon, he waved to her.

Sharon immediately left Kim and her entourage to walk up the bleachers and sit with Nathan.

"You came to watch me cheer?" Sharon asked happily.

"Well, Pa has to work late tonight, so I thought I'd watch you. It's a lot better than watching Mead, let me tell you." Nathan laughed.

"Well, thank you," Sharon said with a touch of sarcasm. But truthfully, she was relieved since she would not have to listen to Kim's incessant carping.

Or so she thought.

Not to be snubbed for any reason, Kim and her friends climbed the bleachers to stand in front of Sharon and Nathan.

"You're Nathan Ernst?" the antagonist began. Not truly waiting for an answer, she added, "I'm Kim Bateman."

"I know who you are," Nathan responded. How could he not? Kim was considered by many to be the most popular girl in school.

"So, you run 'round the woods at night with your ol' coon dogs?" Kim affected a backwoods drawl.

"Yes, ma'am," Nathan answered before Sharon, familiar with the other girl's wiles, could intervene. "Do you go coon hunting?" he continued naively.

"You wouldn't catch me dead in the woods!" Kim sneered, returning to her normal voice. She hated to admit it, but Helm's boyfriend was handsome. Still, she wouldn't concede anything to Sharon Helm—not a thing.

"Everything okay, honey?" Jack Robertson, the captain of the football team, came up and put his hand on Kim's shoulders.

"Nothing I can't handle, sweetie," Kim replied, although it was obvious their affections were superficial at best. Perhaps the popular girl tacitly understood that the feelings Nathan and Sharon held for one another were real, and thus entered jealousy.

"How can you look at those defenseless, cute raccoons and kill them in cold blood?" Kim asked in a nasty, accusatorial tone.

"Well, I guess that I never really thought about it," Nathan said as he shrugged. "I suppose it's the same as someone passing by a field full of cows and still being able to eat steak."

"Girls!" Coach Benton yelled, looking up at the bleachers at the small congregation of teenagers. "We don't have all day, ladies! Let's get to it!"

Sharon sighed relief and felt unusually thankful that Benton was calling them back to the grueling practice. "I'll see you in a bit." She promised Nathan. She ran down the bleachers, fell into her place in line, and the exercises began again.

Jack Robertson looked at Nathan as the young coon hunter stared directly back at him. He only vaguely knew Ernst and did not consider Nathan a formidable challenge. The football player scoffed, knowing his friends were near, then turned and walked back to their spot in the bleachers.

As the routine dragged on, Nathan looked at the far side of the gym to see Larry Allen surrounded by several other boys. They wore dingy-looking hooded sweaters, and as they huddled around each other, they kept looking around to ensure no adults espied their activities. Nathan's keen eyesight noticed some of them passing small, plastic bags amongst themselves. Larry even accepted some money from one of the boys.

Illegal drugs, Nathan knew as he shook his head. He thought for a moment about Larry's father, John, known to be a substance abuser, and could only imagine that the son was unfortunately destined to share the same fate as the father. After the not-so-covert exchanges, the group broke up, and they left the gym by different exits.

After forty-five minutes of constant haranguing, Benton finally called for the team to cease. "You girls are hopeless!" Benton yelled at the group. "Why do I waste my time? Why? Okay, let's call it a night, but plan on a Saturday practice!" The entire team collectively moaned, but none of the girls dared challenge this coach.

Nathan walked down the bleachers to join Sharon just as the relentless Bateman began her nagging anew.

"Well, you just have yourself a good ol' time in the woods tonight, Nathan dear," Kim mocked him. Jack Robertson and his friends joined Kim on the floor and stood close to her in a show of solidarity.

"Thank you," Nathan said, his perfect manners irking the popular girl.

Sharon picked up her school bag and motioned for Nathan to leave.

"Tell me, Sharon, how does it feel to be one of his dogs?" Kim asked, the wickedness of her tone encouraged her sycophant friends to snicker.

Sharon stopped and silently handed her tote bag to Nathan, who immediately accepted it with a puzzled look.

Nathan watched in sheer amazement as Sharon walked up to Kim, and with no warning, punched the other girl in the face. Unprepared for the physical assault, the school's most popular girl folded to the floor with blood dripping from her nose.

"I am no dog!" Sharon shouted as she turned about and took her tote bag back from Nathan. "We can go now," she said, as if nothing out of the ordinary had just happened.

Together, the young couple started to walk away.

"Are you going to let them do that to me?" Kim cried to Robertson, holding her hand over her nose.

Robertson looked down at Kim and then to the departing Nathan and Sharon. Jack may have been the captain of the football team, but he feared Kim's anger more than anything. Robertson knew that he could not harm Sharon. But Nathan was fair game and beating him would sate his girlfriend's desire for revenge. He motioned for his closest friend to follow him, and they both began darting after Nathan.

But just as they were several feet behind the unsuspecting Nathan Ernst, both boys' forward momentum was not only suddenly stopped, but a violent, powerful force flung them backward so that both boys landed hard on the gym floor.

The "force" that had foiled their plans to exact vengeance slowly turned around.

"Anything else, boys?" asked the growing giant Mead Ernst, simultaneously daring his brother's would-be assailants.

Robertson and his friend quickly scrambled to their feet. But another of Jack's friends, who had witnessed the effortlessness that Mead had just displayed in stopping them, grabbed Robertson's shoulder and shook his head silently, cautioning against further action.

"How could you?" Kim screamed at Jack, seeing his inaction, as she ran toward the other end of the gym. Flummoxed, Robertson threw his arms up in the air and conceded defeat.

Just as Nathan and Sharon were about to board their school bus, Ms. Benton caught up with them.

"Helm! You are off my team!" Benton bellowed.

Sharon looked directly at her former coach. "Good," she said and walked onto the school bus.

Benton was livid, as she had expected the young girl to plead for the coach to reconsider the decision. How could she—how could anyone—not want to be on the cheerleading team? Mouth agape, the cheerleading coach looked at Nathan.

"Have a nice day, Miss Benton," Nathan said with a smile as he climbed the bus's short steps.

Benton stood motionless, trying to catch sight of Sharon, as the bus driver closed the door and drove away from the schoolground.

Nathan sat beside Sharon near the back of the bus, staring ahead but saying nothing. There were only a few other kids on the bus situated toward the front.

Nathan cleared his throat. "That part about how it's not good to fight—"

"Let's just not talk about it, okay?" Sharon interrupted.

"All right," Nathan said and nodded sagaciously. Still, he could not resist adding, "But that was a pretty good punch you threw back there."

"Thanks." Sharon laughed, shaking her head.

———— • ————

"Jacob!"

"Yeah, Mike?" Jacob responded to his boss.

"Would you mind getting some chicken feed for Ms. Rosen? She's out front in the red pickup truck," Mike, the diminutive, gray-haired store owner called out.

"Sure, no problem," Jacob said. He moved along the old wooden dock as he had for many years. The local feed store had been his place of employment since he'd been a young boy. The work was hard, but it paid the bills, for which he was grateful.

Jacob found the eighty-pound sack of feed near the back of the store's dimly lit warehouse and easily hoisted the bulky burlap sack over his shoulder. Walking to the dock, Jacob located the elderly Ms. Rosen, whom he had known for many years, waiting patiently in her truck.

"Hello, Jacob! How are you?" Ms. Rosen was always a cheerful person.

"I'm fine, ma'am, and you?"

"Oh, these old bones creak and ache most days," Ms. Rosen complained. She quickly added with a grin, "But I keep going! Are you getting ready for coon season?"

"Yes, ma'am—season opens this week come Saturday," Jacob said, smiling at the thought.

"My Abel was a coon hunter." Ms. Rosen referenced her deceased husband of many years. "Do you remember him?"

"Oh yes, ma'am! I hunted with him and my pa when I was a boy. Abel was a hard hunter and a good judge of dogs. Pa and I were always proud to call him a friend."

"I've had trouble with some coon getting into my henhouse of late. Would you and your boys mind hunting on my farm a few nights to clear some of those critters out? How are those strapping young men of yours doing anyway?"

"It would be our pleasure, Ms. Rosen. And Nathan and Mead are doing well—growing like weeds!" Jacob exclaimed.

Ms. Rosen thanked Jacob again, climbed into her vehicle, and started the engine. Rosen's truck moved away to reveal Miriam Helm, standing there smiling at Jacob.

"Miriam! How have you been, and how can I help you?" Jacob asked.

The pretty, petite woman, clad in blue jeans and plaid flannel shirt, walked up to Jacob and handed him a receipt for some pre-paid items. "Oh, I just need a few things—getting the house ready for winter and all. You know the seasons here in Painted Post," Miriam said.

Jacob readily agreed as he read the list and noted the location of each item. "I'll need to get the keys for some of these items."

"Jacob!" Mike yelled and threw a set of keys directly at the tall man.

With his famously quick reflexes, Jacob snatched the keys out of the air.

"Thanks, Mike," he said.

Mike disappeared back into the store to serve more customers.

"He threw those keys at you pretty hard!" Miriam exclaimed, always amazed at the abilities of Jacob Ernst.

"He's been doing that for years," he explained. "Thank goodness you didn't ask for an ax!" Jacob added with a wink.

Miriam laughed.

Well, I'll be," Jacob said before he could turn to get the merchandise.

Miriam could see Jacob looking over her shoulder, so she turned to see Sharon in her cheerleading uniform with Nathan walking toward them in the distance. Even far away, the affectionate bond between the two teenagers was apparent. "I think our children have fallen in love, Jacob," Miriam said with a happy and wistful smile. And then she quickly added, "What about us, Jacob? Is there hope for us?"

If there was any sense that Jacob understood the double entendre, he didn't show it. The tall man looked back to Miriam and smiled. "There's always hope, Miriam," Jacob said politely and disappeared into the warehouse to get her merchandise.

Miriam softly sighed as Jacob left. For a moment, she felt a kinship with Stella Wharton, understanding the frustration of trying to find a way into the heart of Jacob Ernst.

"Mom!" Sharon shouted, surprised to find her mother. Miriam's maternal instincts took over even before the young girl broke into tears as she explained the events leading to her expulsion from the cheerleading squad.

"Kim Bateman, you say?" Miriam asked when Sharon had completed her story, and she wiped away her daughter's tears. She then added in a show of solidarity, "I always wanted to smack her mother when we were in school."

Nathan and Sharon chuckled at the thought.

Chapter 12

Proms and Porcupines

1981

Today, a Saturday in late May, was the day of the high school senior prom. Of course, Nathan, grown tall and strong, had formally asked Sharon to join him on this special night.

Sharon had been charmed, watching the country bumpkin stumble through the formality of his request; but what she found ever endearing was that Nathan did not take her acceptance for granted.

Nathan Ernst was forever the gentleman.

This morning, Nathan had asked her to go for a walk to another special place, but he had refused to provide any detail, only beckoning her to come to the farm. Having been friends for so long, Sharon's curiosity piqued at the something new that he wanted to reveal. She arrived at the Ernst homestead early that morning dressed in jeans and hiking boots as requested.

When Sharon walked up the front steps, Nathan smiled. "Come with me. I have something to show you," he said, his stare affixed on her.

Nathan took Sharon's hand and led her silently through the forest, following the stream near his home. After nearly thirty minutes of walking, they finally stopped.

"What is this place?" Sharon asked, taking in the natural beauty surrounding her on this late spring day.

In the ravine lined with ancient hemlocks, Nathan and Sharon stood below an eight-foot waterfall. The gushing water rapidly fell over the falls' top, cascading on several uneven stone steps to a gray slate bottom, and rapidly decelerating to form a small pool at its base.

Green moss covered the waterfalls' banks and nearby decaying logs. Small purple-and-white woodland flowers dotted the sides of the ravine, with Black-eyed Susans clustered where the sunlight could poke through the conifer's dense foliage.

"We just call it the Falls," Nathan felt obliged to answer.

Like the Ernst family, Sharon became enamored with the small enclave. "This place is amazing!" she exclaimed.

Nathan wondered if she was talking to him or the hidden waterfalls.

"Well, we are on Ryland Creek, after all," Nathan quipped, and Sharon's smirk relayed that she understood. "Pa said that he and Ma used to come here often. It was her favorite place—a long time ago," he said, looking away as his voice became distant while trying hard to remember his caring mother.

"Can this be our place as well?" Sharon asked, looking at him, and biting her lip. For a moment, she feared to have trespassed into a part of Nathan's heart where she had no right to be.

"Yes, I would like that very much," Nathan answered sincerely, quelling her angst.

Sharon's countenance morphed into her impish grin as she quickly sat down on a large rock and doffed her footwear. She haphazardly stuffed her socks into her hiking boots and then took her first tentative step into the cold stream. Sharon could feel more than the cold slate bottom against her bare feet. The magic of the place surged through her, and she giggled.

"Be careful," Nathan warned with years of chasing raccoon across many creeks quickly coming to the forefront of his thoughts. "The algae on the rocks can make them slippery."

"Always my guardian angel, aren't you, Nathan Ernst?" she teased. Sharon continued to step into the stream, the bottom of the creek still smooth and soft, as the cold water's depth rose to her mid-calf.

Nathan warily watched her.

"C'mon, chicken!" Sharon taunted. "Big, tough coon hunter ain't scared of a little cold water, are you?"

"I'd rather watch you," he replied.

She rolled her eyes and shook her head in make-believe derision. Her brown eyes narrowed, as she was wont to do, which Nathan knew to be a harbinger for her playful antics. Not disappointingly, Sharon suddenly swung her right leg, splashing him with a stream of water.

"Ah!" Now Nathan acted in fake terror, but in truth, the young man who had run through these hills for years was no stranger to frigid creek water.

Sharon laughed, thrashing in the water, kicking her legs higher and higher and continuing to douse Nathan. He offered but a feeble defense by holding his arms up against the spray.

Sharon became intoxicated by the surroundings, and she turned around to watch the rushing flow. She continued to kick streams of water back at the Falls, believing her efforts could defy gravity and cause the water to reverse its course. Sharon began to bounce to gain more momentum, but upon achieving her highest kick, her planted leg slipped.

Without firm footing, her entire body wheeled in the air, her head rapidly descending toward one of the few large rocks hidden below the surface of the pooled stream. Helpless, Sharon screamed and closed her eyes while her entire body went rigid, bracing for the pain of the impending impact.

And then she felt . . . nothing.

Floating there in the air below the Falls, her confused thoughts flooded back to the enchanted feel of this place. Did some ephemeral spirit hold her aloft midair to prevent her from harm? She slowly opened her eyes to discern what mystery had averted calamity.

Nathan stared at her as his strong arms cradled her against him. He shook his head slowly, not reprimanding her, but merely forgiving her innocence regarding the nature of things that he knew by heart. "You have to be careful," he repeated softly.

Sharon's amazement stole any possibility of an immediate response.

She looked down for a moment and placed her hand on his shirt, dampened by her earlier frolicking.

The rushing water was the only sound that filled their ears.

She looked back up at the young man who stood stolidly there, her forever protector, frozen in time. "You're always there, aren't you?" she spoke after a momentary eternity, her wonderment coming out as a whisper above the noise of the waterfall's constant inundation.

The forever-boyish grin crossing his handsome face, and a slight nod, was all the confirmation that she needed.

Nathan turned slowly, and following his own advice, carefully traversed the short distance back to the pool's edge, carrying her effortlessly. He gently dipped his left shoulder to set her feet safely back on the creek's slate. He kept his right arm wrapped firmly but gently across her small shoulders to ensure she was steady. Satisfied she would not slip, Nathan released her as she stepped back.

Sharon kept her eyes on him for a moment as she slowly took several steps backward away from him. She then knelt, searching the water's edge, finally finding a small, round rock. Grasping it in her right hand, she closed her eyes, reflecting carefully for a moment, and then threw it into the center of the deep pool.

Kerplunk!

When she turned, Nathan became unsettled at first. The girl there moments before had vanished, and a woman stood before him. She held a serene look—her character suddenly aging decades. With the simple tossing of a small stone, some burden had fallen away, and wisdom quickly moved in to fill the void.

"A-a-are you okay?" Nathan stammered, unable to suppress what he had witnessed in her startling transformation.

Sharon moved to close the short distance between them. She hugged him, putting the side of her head against his chest.

"Never better," she reassured him. And then she repeated, "Never better."

Nathan's arms wrapped around her as he looked up at the large conifers' branches high above that silently reaffirmed his belief in the magic found in these hills.

The Helms' old truck pulled up with Miriam coming to a full stop not far from the Ernsts' front porch. The passenger door opened, and Sharon stepped out gingerly.

The girl, who had been barefoot and clad in jeans below a hidden waterfall but a few short hours earlier, now wore a bright, pink-and-white, full-length gown. Her hair was feathered and fell softly about her bare shoulders.

Sharon looked angelic.

Jacob Ernst appeared from inside the homestead, looking from Miriam to Sharon. The kind man smiled broadly. "Well aren't you the prettiest picture, Miss Helm."

"Thank you, Mr. Ernst," Sharon replied gratefully.

"Nathan is inside. He's almost ready," Jacob informed the ladies.

"May I go inside and get him?" Sharon asked.

"Sure, he's in the kitchen," Jacob said.

Miriam, dressed much like Jacob in jeans, watched her daughter run into the house. "Our children are growing up, Jacob."

"Some days, it doesn't seem that long ago when we were that age," he replied.

"And other days?" Miriam asked.

"Other days, it feels like a very, very long time ago," the old coon hunter admitted, and the two adults shared a good laugh.

"By the way, do you have an open-ended wrench?" Miriam asked.

Jacob nodded, cocking an eyebrow at the strange request.

As Sharon made it through the living room headed for the kitchen, Mead suddenly popped out from around the corner. Mead, forever wearing the ratty baseball cap, had grown tall now, even taller than Nathan. He held out his arms to block the short brunette.

"Mead Ernst!" she said, clearly surprised. "I'm looking for your brother!"

"Don't you know that it's bad luck to see your date before the prom?" Mead teased, grinning from ear-to-ear.

"That's when it's a wedding, blockhead," Nathan said as his strong arm pushed aside his younger brother, and with a quick, practiced motion with the same hand, knocked Mead's hat off.

Mead chuckled as he picked up the cap from the floor and slapped it back on his head.

Nathan stepped outside the kitchen dressed in a black tuxedo, keeping one hand behind his back. Like Sharon, the young man dressed in jeans and boots but hours before now stood transformed.

They stood there, taking in the sight of each other.

"I think that I'm going to be sick," Mead smirked. Nathan punched him in the arm as he departed, and Mead grasped his injured arm, only partially pretending to be in great pain.

When Mead and his buffoonery had left the room, Nathan turned to Sharon. "I have something for you," he said, bringing his hand forward to reveal a magnificent white rose corsage.

"Nathan, that's gorgeous," Sharon said softly with her entire gaze on the genuinely beautiful flower.

"May I?" Nathan asked, motioning for Sharon to raise her hand.

The young girl extended her small hand, and Nathan gently

threaded her fingers through the white lace band until it came to rest lightly on her wrist. She brought the flower closer to her face so she could smell its fragrance. She stared at Nathan but then looked past him as something caught her eye.

"She was beautiful," Sharon said, quickly sidestepping Nathan to stand in front of the framed picture hanging prominently on the wall.

Nathan turned to see her admiring the treasured photograph of his mother with her long, brown hair framing her face. Rose's eyes seemed to follow them.

"Yes, she was," Jacob Ernst readily agreed, startling the young couple as they turned to see the tall man smiling.

Miriam stepped from behind Jacob and approached the teenagers with her arms hidden behind her.

"Thanks for letting me take Sharon to the prom, Mrs. Helm," Nathan said formally with a slight quiver in his voice.

"You are a fine young man, Nathan Ernst, but there is one rule that you must obey." From behind her back, Miriam produced a large, eighteen-inch long, box end wrench. She put one end of the tool almost touching Nathan's tuxedo, and with her other hand, she scooted Sharon forward, so her pink dress nearly touched the wrench's other end.

"And that rule is this!" Miriam continued, "Tonight, the two of you are not allowed to get any closer than the length of this wrench!"

"Mother!" Sharon screamed, mortified, turning several shades darker pink than her dress.

The entire room, to include Mead who had reentered unannounced, joined in the hilarity with Sharon feeling pressured to join in.

Nathan had passed his driver's license exam a few months before. Jacob, Miriam, and even Mead waved them goodbye from the porch as the couple drove down the driveway in an old pickup truck. Nathan drove several miles to their high school, where many of their friends greeted the couple warmly.

In the school's gymnasium, the night became filled with laughter and dancing to a live band playing the latest and classic rock and roll tunes. Discotheque lights bounced a spectrum of colors around the young people. Boys and girls without formal dates asked one another to the dance floor.

During the night, Nathan spotted Larry Allen, often looking at Sharon. The jealousy in Larry's eyes was met by a hard look from Nathan, indicating that their long rivalry remained, and Sharon was off-limits as far as Larry was concerned.

Once Sharon caught the two males with their eyes locked, and she gently leaned into Nathan to distract him.

Several times that night, other boys would approach Larry and whisper into his ear. Larry would look around for the adult chaperones, and once sure they were not being watched, he and his "clients" would disappear into the locker room.

Nathan watched this pattern, knowing from oft-spoken rumor what was going on.

Larry was gaining a reputation as the high school's most prominent drug dealer. The local authorities had even questioned him several times, but Larry was nothing if not clever and always seemed to be one step ahead of the police.

"I see you watching him," Sharon commented at one point during a slow dance with her arms wrapped around Nathan's neck.

"Just a habit, I suppose, to keep an eye on him whenever you're around," Nathan replied, refocusing his attention on the pretty girl.

"He's led a hard life in many ways," Sharon said. She knew Nathan's animosity had waned little through the years, and his wariness of Allen would never entirely dissipate.

Nathan was amazed but admired her empathy toward the other boy, who would have done her harm on more than one occasion. "You reap what you sow," he said with the slightest edge to his voice.

Suddenly, the prom's crowd hushed while the band did its utmost not to miss a beat. On the far side of the gym, his uniform ever immaculately pressed, stood Sheriff Sean Covington. Nathan noticed the officer speaking to a teacher who pointed to where Larry Allen had been just minutes before. The crowd cleared a path as Sean walked slowly but determinedly toward the locker room. With just a slight pause, Sheriff Covington disappeared behind the locker room's door.

"Busted," remarked one girl, who'd been dancing with her date close to Sharon and Nathan.

Moments later, several of Larry's "customers" hastily evacuated the locker room, but it would be several minutes more before Sheriff Covington walked out, looking grim. However, the lawman was alone, and Larry Allen was not in tow in handcuffs, as many of the prom-goers had expected.

Nathan looked at Sharon, and she nodded, understanding his unspoken request. He then moved to intercept his father's longtime best friend just before Sean exited the building. "Is everything okay, Sheriff?" he asked.

In a daze, the tall man looked hard at Nathan for a moment. But then Sean shook his head as he recognized the young man that he'd watched grow from a child.

"You sure do clean up pretty, Nathan." Sean smiled as he laughed.

"Is everything okay?" Nathan repeated politely.

Sean looked around to ensure no one was within earshot. "Larry Allen's father, John, died in a one-car accident tonight near Savona." The sheriff mentioned the small hamlet up the highway about ten miles. "I told him what happened. His stepmom is coming to get him to take him home."

"Is Larry all right? How did he take the news?"

"I'm not sure," Sean admitted. "I told him what had happened— even repeated myself—but Larry just kept staring at me never saying a word. When I asked if he understood, he only nodded. When I offered to wait until his stepmother got here, he just shook his head.

"Most people bring their grief onto themselves," the Sheriff imparted wisdom gained through many years of police work. "John Allen had an uncanny talent in that respect. It's a tragic ending to a sad life."

Nathan remained quiet, wondering how he would react if learning that his father had just died.

"Listen," Sheriff Covington began. "I well know there's no love lost between the Ernst and Allen families, but would you do me a favor and make sure his stepmother finds him?"

"Sure, Sheriff, I can do that. I know Ms. Allen, and I'll recognize her when I see her."

"Thanks, son," Sean said as he patted Nathan on the arm. "Tell your pa I said hello." With that, he walked to his police cruiser, the vehicle as spotless as his uniform, and drove off into the night.

Nathan stayed by the door entrance awhile longer, but then he thought it best to locate Larry. He reentered the large gymnasium to find the other couples formed into several groups. They were talking, but no one was dancing, although the band continued to play.

Sharon spotted him and walked hurriedly over, her face showing a dire concern. "Oh, Nathan! I just heard that Larry Allen's father was killed."

"I know," Nathan said, trying to calm her. "Sheriff Covington asked me to make sure his stepmother found him when she arrives. Do you know where he's at?"

"He hasn't come out of the locker room yet."

"I'm going to see how he's doing," Nathan said, but as he began to walk to Larry's purported location, Sharon tugged on his arm.

"Nathan," Sharon said, but her former look of empathy for Larry's plight now showed admiration. "I'm proud of you—you always do the right thing."

"Well, I'll try." Nathan smirked.

When Nathan found Larry in the locker room, he could only see Larry's back as the other boy gripped the sides of a sink below a small mirror. He could not see Allen's face in the reflection, as his head hung down. "Larry, are you all right?" he asked, stumbling on the words.

"Nathan Ernst," Larry said in recognition, shaking his head without looking up.

"I'm sorry about what happened to your father," Nathan offered sincerely.

Larry stood up straight and turned. His eyes were bloodshot but not from tears. Rather, the belabored effort to focus on Nathan just a short distance away signaled that Larry was quite intoxicated. "Don't be sorry, man. He wasn't much of a father," he said, almost laughing.

Nathan stood silently unsure of how to respond.

"Not like you!" Larry continued as his voice turned accusatorial. "You have the perfect father, the perfect family. All nice and cozy there on your little farm raising your little coon dogs!" Larry tried to step forward, but in his impaired state, he lacked coordination. But for stumbling back into the sink for support, the teenager would have fallen onto the hard floor.

Nathan remained silent, knowing there could be no coherent discourse this night.

"And of course, you have the perfect girlfriend too!" Larry was sneering now, and he continued shouting, "Sharon should be my girl!"

Larry lunged at Nathan, but in his debilitation, faltered again. To Larry's dimwitted brain, he was falling slowly toward the floor and then seemed suspended.

Nathan's strong arms jerked Larry into an upright position such that their faces were close. If Larry felt any gratitude in not hitting the floor hard, his momentary relief dissipated as his eyes met Nathan's grim look.

"I am here at Sheriff Covington's request," Nathan spoke in a low voice. "I promised him that I would get you to your stepmother, and so I will."

And there it was. Nathan felt the anger welling within him once again. His hands began to tremble with the flowing adrenaline. Even with the solemn oath that he had made to a young girl once on a dusty road called Ryland Creek, it took all his will to control the rage.

"If you ever touch Sharon again," Nathan's voice strained, "I'll forget the promise that I made to her a long time ago."

Larry did not understand what Nathan referred to; nor was that insight necessary, for he could see in his rival's eyes that the words were no idle threat.

"Larry! Larry Allen! Are you in there?" A woman's hoarse voice was shouting just outside the locker room.

"Mom," Larry said with his head lolling forward.

Nathan stepped to the side and tucked his neck underneath Larry's arm. He walked Larry, whose head now sagged to his chest, outside the locker room.

"Oh, my God!" Larry's stepmother, Jill, snapped harshly. "You're drunk or high, aren't you?"

Larry had just enough strength to raise his head and say, "It's just you and me now, Mom." His head fell forward again.

"Nathan, can you help me get him to my car?" Jill Allen asked without mentioning her stepson directly by name.

"Yes, ma'am," Nathan replied.

Another large boy in a tuxedo offered to support Larry's other shoulder, and between the two young men, they walked Larry to the parking lot and poured the nearly unconscious teenager into the back seat of Jill's old station wagon.

"Thank you, Nathan," Jill said, truly grateful, but if there was any hint of remorse over the news of John Allen's death, Nathan could not detect it. Motioning with her head toward Larry's unmoving form in the back seat, she added, "I'll get this piece of work back to the house."

Once Larry and his stepmother had driven away, Nathan proceeded back to the school feeling a bit guilty about not being able to spend every moment with Sharon. But the pretty girl allayed his fears as she met him at the door.

"Let's go home," Sharon suggested. "I'm tired, and it's been a long day."

"It's only nine thirty. Are you sure?" Nathan asked.

"I'm sure."

"Okay," he relented. "We'll call it a night."

"It's kind of early in the evening for you, huh, coon hunter?" She grinned, taking his arm and draping it over her shoulders.

"You never know—sometimes the raccoon run early." Nathan smiled, and he courteously opened the door to his old truck and helped her in.

As they drove home, Sharon said sadly, "Our senior prom night will be forever remembered for the death of one of our classmates' father. I remember when we lost my dad. Larry must feel so awful right now."

Nathan said nothing, recalling Larry's expressed sentiment, deciding not to relay to Sharon anything that had occurred between himself and Larry this night.

Nathan turned onto the Ryland Creek Road. There was no moon tonight, and the darkness seemed somehow closer, almost palpable, as the young couple traversed the darkened hollow. They passed the small bridge, and the truck climbed to the top of the steep hill with ease.

"Are you afraid to die?" Sharon asked suddenly, and it was her intensity more than the actual query that caught him by surprise.

"No—not really, I suppose. I hope when it does happen, I face it bravely," Nathan replied.

"I imagine you will," Sharon said, never doubting for a moment that Nathan had told her the complete truth.

"Pa says we'll meet our Maker when we die and see all our loved ones who have gone before us. It just makes a lot of sense that this life is not the end—that there has to be something more."

Sharon just nodded her understanding.

"Are you afraid to die?" Nathan asked, returning her question. He then started to drive by his home but noticed something unusual. He brought the vehicle to a stop and backed up on the dirt road.

"What's the matter?" Sharon asked confused.

"There's a light in the barn. Mead may have forgotten to turn it off. Mind if we take a look?"

"Sure—my mother isn't expecting me home this early anyway," Sharon said.

As the truck's headlights illuminated the dirt driveway, Mead appeared from the barn. Despite the darkness, both the young teenagers could see Mead's hands covered in blood.

Nathan threw his truck into park, opened the door, and jumped out to meet his tall sibling. "What happened?"

"Storm got out of her pen, and she got into a porcupine," Mead explained.

"How bad?" Nathan asked, fearing the worst.

"Pa thinks she's got close to six hundred quills in her," Mead said. "And we're having a hard time holding her still."

The porcupine was the bane of many a coon hunter in Upstate New York. With thousands of sharp needles ready to impale an attacker, the process of extracting quills from a hound was never easy. Unfortunately, the barbed needles hurt as much coming out as they did going in. In the past, Nathan had occasionally been pricked while attempting to remove the stickers from a hound. A single quill was painful—six hundred quills had to be utterly excruciating! It was little wonder that Storm was putting up such a fuss.

"I'll take Sharon home, and I'll get back here to help you and Pa."

"No," Sharon spoke up. "Go ahead and get changed so you can help. I can wait, Nathan. It's no problem."

Just then, Storm's frantic, pained yelp came from inside the barn, and the young people could hear Jacob's raised voice cursing all porcupines everywhere.

"I best get back there to help Pa hold her," Mead noted.

"I'll be there in less than ten minutes," Nathan told Mead. Then he said to his date, "Thanks, Sharon. I'm sorry this had to happen."

"It's okay, really," Sharon reassured him.

"Mead!" Nathan shouted just before Mead had reentered the barn to help Jacob with the ongoing melee. "Tell Pa that John Allen died in a car accident tonight."

"This has been one bad night," Mead replied.

"I'll be right back," Nathan promised Sharon.

Nathan ran inside the farmhouse and then up the stairs to his bedroom where he stripped out of the tuxedo and lay it haphazardly on his bed. Just as quickly, he donned a pair of blue jeans, an old, light flannel shirt, and his boots. He ran down the stairs expecting to see Sharon waiting for him, but she was nowhere in sight.

Nathan exited the house, hoping to see Sharon waiting in her lovely prom dress, but again, he could not find her. Nathan hurried toward the barn, but as he neared the lit barn door, instead of the canine's painful yelp, the young man heard the soft murmur of voices.

What's going on? Nathan wondered. Upon entering the barn, he had a difficult time believing his eyes.

Jacob, wearing his old, brown fedora, held a pair of stainless steel medical clamps, and with a quick yank, Nathan saw his father extract four or five quills from the hound's snout. Storm, for her part, looked like she had sprouted white whiskers on her muzzle. Jacob dipped the implement into a nearby pail of water to remove the blood and proceeded to repeat the task to remove more quills.

Mead held the young hound calmly by the back legs.

Incredibly, the hound that had been fighting so hard against the very efforts attempting to help her was neither squirming nor fighting them.

Nathan quickly discerned the reason for Storm's calm. On the hay-covered barn floor knelt a girl in a prom dress, gently holding the hound's front shoulders and attention.

Sharon spoke calmly, and the dog seemed to understand and sat, withstanding the extrication process without tribulation. Tiny rivulets of blood trickled down Sharon's forearms, but if the gore was bothering the young lady, she gave no indication.

Nathan walked over to them, almost feeling that his presence was unwarranted, and asked, "Need any help?"

"Your girlfriend has everything under control," Mead chided.

"So I see," Nathan agreed.

Sharon looked up briefly to smile at Nathan but then returned her attention to the wounded hound. Ten minutes later, without Storm making more than an occasional whimper, the process that should have taken much longer was complete.

Jacob directed Mead to wash the dog's wounds with water and to return her to her kennel. Mead snapped a leash onto the hound's collar and walked out of the barn with Storm.

Looking at the now bloody Sharon, Jacob said, "We can't let you go home looking like that. Your mother would have a heart attack the moment she saw you before we could explain what happened! If you don't mind wearing some of Nathan's old clothes, you can clean up, and we'll get you home shortly."

"Thank you, Mr. Ernst, I'd appreciate that," Sharon said, looking down at the bloodied dress.

"I think your dress is ruined," Nathan lamented.

Rising to her feet, Sharon walked over to Nathan and took his hands in hers. "It's only a dress." She gave him a quick peck on the cheek, smiled, and said, "I know where the shower is." She then left the barn and proceeded to the house.

"You ever see anything like that, Pa?" Nathan asked. The two men, both veterans of many quill removal episodes, knew that Sharon's calming effect on the hound was far from ordinary.

"In all my years," Jacob began, "I've only seen one other person who could do what that young lady just did in keeping an animal so calm simply by talking to it."

"Would that be Grandpa Ernst?" Nathan inquired.

"No," Jacob said as he took an old rag and removed the blood from his hands and forearms. "The only other person I ever knew who could do that was your mother."

The old coon hunter smiled, and it was evident, if unsaid, that Jacob was giving Sharon the highest of compliments. His father then quietly walked away, leaving Nathan, having accomplished little during the quill extraction, alone in the barn.

It certainly had been a day of tragedy and miracles, Nathan mused.

In the farmhouse, Nathan found an old pair of jeans and a small, soft shirt that no longer fit him. As he came to the bathroom door, he could hear the shower going, and he knocked rapidly.

"Yes?" Sharon called out above the noise of the shower's running water.

"I have some clothes for you! Where should I put them?" Nathan shouted so she could hear.

"Just put them on the sink, please," Sharon responded.

Nathan entered the steamy room. Sharon had placed her soiled dress neatly to the side of the vanity, and he put the clean jeans and shirt on the bathroom sink.

"Thank you," she said, sticking just her head out from behind the green, opaque shower curtain to smile at him.

"You're most welcome," Nathan replied to the wet-haired girl. With that, he exited the bathroom and went downstairs to sit on the couch to wait for her. To his surprise, he heard his father talking on the telephone, and Nathan quickly deduced that Jacob had called Miriam Helm to explain the situation.

For the second time that night, Nathan looked at the wall to see his mother's picture, and he recalled his father's words.

The only other person I ever knew who could do that was your mother.

Ten minutes later, Sharon came down the wooden steps stepping lightly with her bare feet making hardly a sound. The old pants and shirt she wore, although they had once fit Nathan as a youth, hung loosely on her tiny frame. Her wet hair draped around her shoulders, and while perhaps Sharon was no longer dressed as a prom debutante, Nathan was convinced that he had never seen a prettier girl in his life.

"I love the way you do that," she said, breaking his reverie.

"Do what?" Nathan asked.

"The way you look at me," Sharon said softly.

"Miss Sharon," Jacob said as he entered the room from the kitchen.

154

"I spoke with your mother to tell her what happened. She said you may spend the night here if you like."

"That would be great!" Sharon smiled.

"That's what she said you'd say." Jacob grinned. "I'm going to bed—the sun rises early, and there's church in the morning."

Jacob paused at the bottom of the stairs before leaving the young couple alone. "And Nathan?" he beckoned his son.

"Yeah, Pa?" Nathan responded, turning his attention from Sharon to his father.

"Mrs. Helm had some words for you, too," Jacob said suddenly formal.

"What'd she say, Pa?" Nathan asked befuddled.

"I seem to recall she said to 'remember the wrench,' or something such," Jacob informed his son.

"That was my mom, all right!" Sharon laughed, validating the message conveyed.

Nathan blushed silently.

"It's good advice," Jacob added before he climbed the stairs for the night.

Alone now, Sharon lie down on the couch in a fetal position, resting her head upon Nathan's leg as a pillow. Nathan placed his hand on her upper arm, and Sharon likewise put her hand over his fingers.

They were quiet for many minutes.

"I'm not afraid," Sharon said, her voice heavy with exhaustion on the brink of falling asleep, but she managed to crane her neck to make eye contact with Nathan.

"Not afraid of what?" Nathan asked, caught off guard by her sudden pronouncement.

"I'm not afraid of dying—not if I'm with you," she said.

He nodded that he understood, and Sharon nestled her head on his leg again. Less than a minute later, Nathan could tell by her breathing that she had fallen into a deep slumber.

The next morning, more than a few parishioners at Saint Catherine's noticed the attire Sharon wore to church. Although Sharon saw the gawkers, the young girl ignored them.

To Nathan, Sharon looked quite natural with her hair pulled into a ponytail, jeans, and his shirt.

Nathan and Sharon found Miriam, already sitting in her usual pew. Mother and daughter smiled and hugged one another at their reunion. Nathan sat quietly next to Sharon and hung his head to pray.

That Sunday morning, Father Simmons gave a rousing sermon on the blessing of reconciliation, the forgiveness of God, and the need to forgive one another. As he heard the priest's words, Nathan could not help but think of Larry Allen and the loss of his father, and the young man offered a silent prayer that Larry would find solace.

Per their familiar routine at the end of the church service, the parishioners piled out of the church to greet the kindly Father Simmons at the exit. As he shook hands, Mead walked up, and with his height, could now look Father Simmons directly in the eye.

"You're growing tall, Mead!" the priest exclaimed. "And do you have any coonhound stories for me this morning?"

Almost reflexively now, Jacob, who was but two feet behind Mead and witnessing the beginning of the exchange, winced.

"Well, Father Simmons," Mead began, "last night our little coonhound Storm got into a porcupine. We had to pull close to six hundred quills out of her, I reckon. That makes for a long night, Father, let me tell you. She's a good hound, but all dogs have their faults."

"We all do!" The priest saw the chance to teach a lesson and continued, "Just like people, we all have our faults, too! But unlike people, God doesn't expect the animals to go to confession to expiate their sins."

"Agreed, Father!" Mead smiled.

"And confession is good for *everyone*." Father Simmons let the suggestion hang in the air.

Mead did not miss the not-so-subtle hint. "Oh, I'll go to confession, Father. Just let me know when you have a long, long time," Mead said with a wink, shook Father Simmons' hand, slapped his old baseball cap on, and walked out of the church.

Despite himself, Father Simmons could not help but laugh heartily as he once again found himself genuflecting in Mead Ernst's wake. As Jacob approached the priest with an is-everything-okay look, the priest was still smiling, shook Jacob's hand, and waved the good parent on with best wishes for the coming week.

Chapter 13

Lessons Revisited

1983

Ten years hence . . .

Its stealth had been perfect. The hounds had not picked up its scent, as it had been careful to maintain a downwind path toward them. Although its vision was not as sharp as canine eyesight, visual acuity was unnecessary now as the coonhounds were busy loudly treeing beneath an ancient oak—giving away their exact location.

It was appropriate, after all, as many things begin and end beneath oak trees.

The black and tan hounds were only 25 yards away, and by its keen olfactory sense, it judged that the man was nearing too—just over beyond the creek's bank it estimated, and thus, only seconds before the Enemy arrived.

Instincts took over as it charged the hounds.

It would kill the dogs instantly.

And then it would be just it and the Enemy.

———•◦•———

The present . . .

At 20 years old, Nathan Ernst was lean and muscular. The young man drove his truck into Painted Post as it was nearing lunchtime, and he had acquired a new favorite place to eat.

Nathan pulled his truck up alongside the local pub, not far from J.P. Smith's General Merchandise & Hardware Store. He noted a few sleek, black town cars in the parking lot with out-of-state license plates. These vehicles certainly stood apart from the local trucks and more modest automobiles parked nearby. Nathan thought the increased patronage would be good for business—even if they were only passing through.

As he entered the small eatery, and Nathan's eyes quickly adjusted to the dimmer light while the jukebox played a contemporary rock song. He found the ever-present and still quite corpulent hardware storeowner, J.P. Smith, sitting alone at one of the dining room tables. J.P. was making short work of a large, tasty-looking steak, a sizeable baked potato so covered with sour cream that it looked like a man-made volcano, and a mound of green peas.

The young man noticed there were many patrons today, notably six strangers in what seemed some expensive, dark business suits. Recalling the vehicles he'd seen in the parking lot, Nathan quickly associated these well-dressed men with the high-end transportation. They sat around two tables and had positioned themselves to view all who entered the restaurant while remaining strategically close to the bar. Considering how loud they were getting, it was obvious they had begun partaking of the restaurant's harder liquor offerings.

Something else caught the hunter's eye. Talking to who seemed to be the largest man amongst the suits was none other than Larry Allen.

Larry was now well known as the local "medicine man" and purveyed all manner of illegal street drugs. To see Larry chumming it up with these strangers raised Nathan's suspicions that these men were in Painted Post for less-than-honorable reasons.

A welcomed sight quickly stole his attention as Nathan sat down at an open table. A beautiful, dark-haired woman walked out from behind the bar and came straight over to him with her order sheet in hand. He knew the charm of her smile and the gleam of those stunning eyes.

"So, what will it be, handsome?" she asked in a sultry voice, leaning closer as her brown eyes narrowed slightly.

"What do you recommend?" Nathan asked, pretending this visit was his first time eating at the establishment.

"Well, the steak burger is on special today and the odds-on favorite," she replied while leaning in very close such that their faces were only an inch apart. "You may only get one better offer today." Saying no more, she closed the distance and kissed him on the lips.

While the world seemed to hold only these two young lovers, the catcalling of the well-dressed men in the corner snapped Sharon out of her reverie. Surprised or not, she continued to smile unapologetically at Nathan.

"Let me get their order," Sharon whispered to Nathan. "I'll be right back." As the pretty woman walked over to the men, she gave them a hearty, "What'll it be, boys?"

Nathan turned around, smiling and thinking how lucky he was to have Sharon's affection. Suddenly, a mountain of a man sat down beside him and slapped Nathan painfully hard on the back.

"Are you off work today, little brother?" Nathan asked Mead. Looking at the huge man whom Mead had become, Nathan knew his "little" reference seemed inappropriate.

"Nope!" Mead said. "Just came by to have some grub before I head back to the grind. You feelin' rich enough to buy me lunch?"

"Sure." Nathan laughed. "Get whatever you want off the menu."

"Well shoot!" Mead exclaimed, smiling. "I just might get something to go as well!"

Sharon returned to the bar to turn the order from the gaggle of well-to-do strangers into the kitchen and began wiping some glasses clean. She looked squarely at Nathan, only a few yards away, as she went about her work.

Nathan cast an eye back to the men who seemed determined to get more boisterous with each passing minute. The two out-of-towners closest to the bar were egging one another on until finally, one found the courage to walk up to Sharon. He gave a couple of sidelong glances back to his friends, who urged him on.

The man was not physically big by any stretch of the imagination, but if his body had been sized to his narcissistic ego, he would have been larger than Mead.

"Hey, honey," the man finally spoke, attempting to sound suave. "My name is Reginald. I'm not from this hick town, but I thought that maybe we could have dinner tonight. It's on me," the man said as he produced a one-hundred-dollar bill from a suit pocket.

"And perhaps, later on, we could find our way to my motel room," Reginald continued, ending with a lewd look crossing his not overly handsome mug.

Sharon leaned over the bar. "Reginald?" she asked innocently.

"Yes, darling?" Reginald smiled to show several gold teeth in his maw.

"May I call you Reggie?" Sharon smiled prettily, and batted her eyes slowly, affecting a thick woodsy drawl while speaking so loudly that both Nathan and Mead could easily hear every word.

The brothers winced, knowing what was coming next.

"You can call me anything you want, sweetheart!" Reggie looked behind him to his friends, saying the words loud enough for them to hear. The suited men were focused on their friend, continuing to shout their approval for Reggie's apparently succeeding advances on the naïve rural girl.

"Reggie," Sharon began. "This 'hick' town? Well, this is *my home.* And as far as dinner with you and going to your room tonight." She spoke loud enough for each patron in the diner to hear every syllable. "Buy yourself a real nice meal and eat it all by your lonesome, because I'd never be seen with the likes of you!"

Crestfallen at the public shaming, Reggie's toothy smile immediately transformed to an odious look as he heard his friends mocking him. Two of the outsiders even asked Reggie if he was going to allow Sharon's insolent behavior to stand unpunished.

Before Sharon could get out of reach, the hot-tempered man grabbed her forearm, and with some surprising strength, pulled her halfway over the wooden bar and kissed her hard on the lips.

With her free hand, Sharon clawed her aggressor, who screamed as her fingernails drew blood across his face. With his other hand, he brought his fist back to strike this insolent wench and teach her a lesson in humility.

Reggie willed his arm to move, but a firm grip on his bicep

161

effortlessly withheld any forward momentum. He looked back to see Nathan Ernst.

"I strongly suggest that you let the young lady go if you want what's best," Nathan said evenly.

"What are you asking me to do?" Reggie sneered. There was no fear in his eyes as he could see over Nathan's shoulder that his compatriots were already beginning to rise from the table and come to his defense.

"Mister, I'm not *asking* you to do anything—I'm *telling* you: let go of her—*now!*" Nathan warned.

"Who is she to you, anyway?" Reggie demanded.

"She would be," Nathan said but then paused. Looking at her, he then asked, "Sharon Helm, will you marry me?"

While perhaps not the idyllic scenario that she had often dreamt, Sharon was stunned by the words that she had waited so long to hear.

"Yes! Yes! Yes!" Sharon shouted, and the entire Painted Post crowd let loose a resounding cheer, as now all eyes were on her.

Turning his attention back to Reggie, who still had not relinquished his grip on Sharon's forearm, Nathan said sternly, "This young lady would be my fiancée."

"Bah!" Reggie sneered, thinking the entire wordplay between Sharon and Nathan a simple ruse. "Get lost, punk!"

No more banter was necessary in Nathan's view, and he whipsawed the rude man around to face him. As Reggie started to move forward, Nathan used his leg to sweep the other man's foot from the floor, leaving Reggie off balance, and with a forceful shove, drove the man half-falling backward. Reggie's shoulder blades painfully caught the bar top's edge, and his eyes now turned wide with fear as Nathan drew his arm back with his hand balled into a tight fist.

Nathan looked up into Sharon's eyes, which silently pleaded for him not to strike the stranger, and to keep a promise made long ago.

While his rage seethed, Nathan honored his word and grabbed Reggie by both expensive lapels. Yanking the other to within inches of his face, saying nothing but communicating clearly, Nathan propelled Reggie into the bar again. This time, the back of the man's head caught the bar's edge, and the now unconscious Reggie slid to the floor in a shameful heap.

Nathan heard a commotion just in time to see the first of Reggie's companions rushing toward him but a few feet away. However, the avenger's eyes went wide when his forward momentum abruptly halted as Mead grabbed the stranger by the shoulder. Instead of spinning the man around, Mead punched him at the base of his skull. The man's eyes rolled upwards, and the would-be avenger landed next to Reggie on the floor, similarly unconscious.

The third attacker, slightly larger than Nathan, rushed Mead now, and for what he lacked in savvy, he made up in viciousness. However, the stranger was caught by surprise as he had imagined the large man to be a slow oaf. The man's lack of anticipation was rewarded by a lightning-fast punch from Mead that ended in a spray of blood. The other fell to his knees, howling in pain, with his eyes already swelling shut with what was assuredly a broken nose.

The fourth man, learning vicariously from his companions' egregious mistakes, approached Mead cautiously and threw a solid punch into Mead's cheek. While his fist hit its intended mark, the desired effect was something else. Mead looked at the stranger and just shook his head like a teacher supremely disappointed with a student's best efforts falling short of the mark.

Desperate now, the out-of-towner struck Mead in the face again, but there remained no evidence of harm from the assault. The man prepared to strike once more, but the giant landed two solid punches: first to the torso, then to the head. The man's body lurched under the punishing blows, and he, too, found himself on the floor, albeit moderately aware of his surroundings.

The fifth man came at the brothers while reaching for something inside his suit. But before he could pull any form of weapon out, Nathan grabbed the assailant's arm and pinned it against the man's chest. Over Nathan's shoulder, Mead threw a powerful jab with his right hand, hitting this latest assailant, and snapping his head back.

With Nathan's free hand, he grabbed the man's nape and hurled him directly, if unintentionally, at J.P. Smith, who had been enjoying his meal throughout the melee. Without even looking up, and with seemingly practiced effort, J.P. grabbed either side of his plate and lifted it just as the man crashed into the table. Over went human and furniture, but J.P., without flinching, never spilled a single pea as he lifted his meal above the fray. The storeowner just turned around in his chair, set his plate on the nearest table, and resumed eating.

Mead and Nathan looked at the last of the suited men, still sitting at the table in conversation with Larry Allen. He held up a finger to his lips to hush Larry from further discussion and looked nonchalantly at the two brothers, assessing the spectacle before him.

The man in the perfectly tailored black suit, with both manicured beard and hands, stood gracefully to his full height, which was a full inch taller than Mead. In a slow, deliberate manner, the man removed his suit coat to display a well-muscled upper torso beneath a pressed white shirt. He then removed a red silk tie but kept his eyes on the brothers' exact location. Even a casual observer could feel the lethality seeping into the room.

The man sauntered toward Nathan and Mead, surveying his fallen comrades littering the eatery's floor. His comrade with the broken nose had his hands cupped around his face, blood streaming between his clenched fingers as he rocked slightly back and forth on his knees. The other men who were conscious were only barely moving or softly moaning.

It was apparent to the large man that he could expect no assistance from his friends. Nonetheless, he continued to close the gap between himself and the Ernst brothers, shaking his head with a resigned look as once again he had to clean up a mess that others could not. He stopped a few feet in front of the brothers, who stood confidently in front of the large man.

"My name is Carlos."

Unpredictably, the man struck Mead with two quick, brutal strikes to the torso. This assault was not like before, for Carlos was a seasoned fighter as well as physically powerful, and Mead showed none of his previous bravado as the attack knocked him off balance.

While Carlos had seemed oblivious to the fight between the brothers and his companions, he had studied it all and already assessed how Nathan and Mead fought. He quickly turned on Nathan, who was moving forward to assist his brother. The large man's fists struck the eldest Ernst sibling hard and continuously from the midsection to the head.

Nathan heard Sharon gasp as she watched her fiancé's frame shudder with each punishing hit. He glanced at her, trying to calm her fears, but Carlos continued his harsh assault until one final, powerful punch knocked Nathan to the floor at the foot of J.P. Smith's newly found table.

Mead, recovering from Carlos's assault, was almost upon the big man. He had hoped to have the element of surprise, but Carlos was too experienced to be caught off guard so easily.

Once again, the larger man surgically landed heavy blows on Mead, who offered only a weak defense.

With the final blow from Carlos, Mead went crashing into J.P.'s table, with the corpulent storeowner again flawlessly lifting his plate just in time, ensuring no loss of food. As fate had it, there was still another table nearby, and J.P. only moved his chair slightly to set his plate down, as if the ensuing battle was just part of the daily routine in Painted Post.

Carlos walked over to gaze down, smiling at the two local men sprawled on the floor.

In the far corner of the bar, sitting at the opposite end of the room, an older, tall and lanky man stood. He wore an old, beaten, gray fedora beneath which showed his short-cropped, salt-and-pepper hair. The man walked slowly while Carlos, the practiced predator, watched the older man's approach with amusement.

Before he was within striking distance, the old man slowly removed his hat and set it down on J.P.'s table as he walked by. He then closed the gap and stood looking evenly into Carlos's dark eyes.

"Are you looking for trouble, old man?" Carlos taunted.

"Not exactly," came the simple reply.

"I suppose you're going to tell me that you're the big, bad man in this town," Carlos said smugly, almost spitting in the man's face. "Well, friend, I'm not from around here."

With his short prelude complete, Carlos suddenly threw a powerful strike directly at the older man's head, determined to teach these bumpkins who indeed was the top dog.

However, now it was the younger man's turn to be completely

surprised when the old man reached out with inhumanly fast reflexes and caught Carlos's hand in midair—stopping his fist as if the outsider had attempted to punch a concrete wall.

But more than the spectacular physical feat, it was the older man's icy response that caused Carlos to blanch.

"That would've been my guess," Jacob Ernst responded.

Carlos felt Jacob's first punch and knew immediately that he had made the most fundamental error: underestimating one's opponent. The thug was no stranger to fighting; in fact, he was paid well—very well—by his employers to intimidate, and, if necessary, physically beat, anyone who stood in the way of their interests.

However, in all his life, this consummate henchman had never been hit as hard. The older man dealt crushing blow after crushing blow. At one point, Carlos's knees buckled as he felt his head snap back from a strike to the chin, and he began to fall backward.

Unfortunately for Carlos, the punishing ordeal wasn't over as Jacob quickly grabbed him beneath the arm and pulled him nearly fully upright again to receive yet another incredibly hard punch to the face. The room spun now, and Carlos prayed for the relief of unconsciousness. One last time, Jacob's strong arm lifted the younger man's considerable bulk upright, and Carlos felt not one, not two, but three consecutive hits.

The world disappeared for Carlos, and he dropped to the cold floor.

The man of few words went over to J.P. Smith's table, retrieved his well-worn hat, and placed it on his head. He took a few more steps to stand in the bar's dim light to gaze down at Mead and Nathan, both of whom, propped up on their elbows, had witnessed Carlos's final demise.

"Pa?" Mead uttered, staring up at Jacob in sheer disbelief.

Jacob Ernst looked at his sons, snapped his right arm out, punching an imaginary foe while catching his right inner elbow in the web of his left hand.

"You gotta punch through," Jacob instructed. Nodding once and smiling, satisfied that the lesson was understood, the old coon hunter turned to the still-supping storeowner and said, "Have a good day, J.P."

With no further ado, Jacob walked out of the restaurant.

"Same to you, Jacob!" J.P. shouted joyfully as he placed the last forkful of food into his mouth. When he finished chewing that final piece of delicious steak, J.P. turned to Mead and Nathan, who had just managed their way to their feet and said, "I told you watching your pa in a fight was a sight to behold!"

After what they had just seen with their own eyes, neither brother was in a position to deny J.P.'s long-held and often-said assertion.

Larry Allen rushed over to Carlos, who was now shaking his head and fighting his way back to consciousness. Larry looked at Mead and then at Nathan in both fear and disgust.

Carlos pushed away Larry's attempts to help him up. He leapt to his feet looking around spoiling for a second attempt at Jacob. The thug would not be caught unaware a second time!

But another tall, lean figure approached Carlos, who immediately recognized the uniform and espied a gold badge on the man's chest.

"Think we've had enough excitement around here for one day, don't you, *Carlos?*" Sheriff Sean Covington looked at Carlos, the tall, black man's stance almost daring the younger man to say something contrary.

"I don't want any trouble, officer," Carlos said with his palms up defensively, regaining some measure of composure.

"Seems you've had your fill of that already today, eh?" Sean goaded the stranger on by adding insult to actual injury.

A defeated look came across Carlos's countenance as he retreated and regrouped with his likewise beaten friends who began to file out of the bar.

"Ahem," Sean Covington said, watching the strangers, "don't forget the tab."

Carlos walked between Nathan and Mead and over to Sharon, who was still behind the bar. With an arrogant look, the big man threw four, crisp, one-hundred-dollar bills on the bar in front of her. "Keep the change!" he sneered.

"Nice tip," Sharon said, unable to hide a smirk.

Larry Allen followed the strangers out of the diner and to their cars, but Carlos waved him off with a dark look as the large man entered his automobile.

"I'm sorry, man!" Larry offered apologetically.

"Don't be," Carlos replied, having regained his composure as he entered one of the town cars, "I promise you, we will be back," he smiled wickedly just before he shut the car door.

Larry knew these men, and a shiver ran up his spine.

The black cars' engines started one by one, and they filed out of the parking lot and left Painted Post in their wake.

———————

One week later, a very well-dressed man looked out the windows of his penthouse across the night skyline of his hometown of Chicago. He smiled. The city was his hunting ground, and he stood as its apex predator.

"I understand we had some trouble in some Podunk town in Upstate New York?" Ronnie's voice was conversational as he continued to look out across the multitude of urban lights.

"Yes, sir," replied the only other man present in Ronnie's luxurious home.

Ronnie pursed his lips slightly as he turned to look at the large man who stood before his large, dark mahogany desk. Physically, this man was intimidating, but there was no question between them about who was the master and who the servant. The man had his arms in front of him, with his hands folded as if praying, and held his head at a lowered attitude. The man had been with Ronnie a long time, and the crime lord always insisted on knowing the whereabouts of the hands of anyone in his presence.

"You see, my friend," Ronnie, who went by many aliases, paused slightly. "That simply won't do, now will it?"

"No, sir," the man replied, knowing well there was no other acceptable response.

Ronnie sat down in an elegant leather chair and began drumming his fingers on the lustrous wooden desk. The boss was trying to keep his anger in check, the other man knew from long experience.

"We have to expand our territory. You know this, correct?" Ronnie asked.

"Yes, sir."

"Trust me, my friend! In twenty years, that market in Upstate New

York is going to be robust. We have to think long-term and get in on the ground floor to keep our competitors out."

The other man just nodded while Ronnie stared directly at him.

"But now we have a *problem*," Ronnie continued.

There it was, just as the man had expected—the hint in Ronnie's voice of disappointment, and the promise of his infamously volatile temper about to erupt.

"When others learn that my men get their backsides handed to them by some local punks—well, what kind of message does that send about me as an employer?"

"It's not good, sir," the man dutifully replied.

"Not good!" Ronnie slammed his fist hard into the wooden desk, causing a cavernous boom throughout the room. "When *my men*, are defeated, then I am defeated. You know this, correct?"

"Yes, sir, of course." The fear that crept naturally into the man's voice pleased Ronnie. Much of the crime lord's business approach relied on fear and servile obedience.

"So, we have some loose ends to tie up, don't we, my friend?" Ronnie asked.

"Yes, sir. Would you like me to see to it?" the man asked.

"You would certainly seem to be qualified for the task at hand," Ronnie said sarcastically. "Send a message—I know that you know how to do just that.

"This incident occurred in a small town called Painted Post, eh? Why does that name sound so familiar?" Ronnie asked.

"You and I were there some time ago to teach a lesson," the man explained, the euphemism understood between them.

"Ah yes, Painted Post, I remember that place now. It seems we must teach that lesson again, eh?" Ronnie grinned, recalling the event of years past.

"It would seem so, sir."

"I understand our local associate knows these men who caused us such an inconvenience very well?"

"Yes, sir," the subordinate said, not surprised that his boss had inside knowledge of the incident. Ronnie did not get to his position in life without keeping his ear to the ground.

"Lean on him for the information we need," Ronnie advised, to which the other man readily nodded.

Ronnie then opened a drawer in his desk, pulled out some papers, and began to read, signaling that the conversation was finished. The man turned and walked across the finely carpeted floor and reached the door.

"And I understand that there was a girl involved, too?" Ronnie asked, still perusing the papers on his desk, which caused the man to stop and turn his head slightly to listen further. "No loose ends, my friend," Ronnie said, providing his final instructions.

The man nodded at his boss's inference and vacated the posh living arrangements. By the time he reached the elevator and hit the button to take him to the ground level, he had already begun to plan a strategy to accomplish his mission.

Chapter 14

Passages

Kerplunk!

Sharon watched the spout of water erupt and subside due to the small stone that she had just thrown. Nathan sat at the edge of the pool below the Falls next to her habitually doffed sneakers with socks stuffed inside them. The day before their wedding, Sharon had asked to take one final walk to their favorite forest hideaway before they became officially husband and wife.

Nathan, as he had learned long ago, did not question her routine, and that is why her next question came as a surprise.

"Do you know why I throw stones in the water?" she asked.

"Because you're letting go of something," Nathan repeated what he understood.

Her eyes narrowed as her sly grin emerged. "Do you want to know why I threw *that* rock?" she egged him further.

"Only if you're willing to share," he responded.

"Then c'mon, chicken!" A barefoot Sharon stood ankle deep in the cold creek water, playfully taunting her fiancé to join her.

Nathan removed his boots and likewise put his socks into his footwear. "Sheesh, that's cold!" he admitted, sliding his foot into the frigid water. He moved slowly, adapting to the creek water pooling below the waterfall. Although the air was warm this early fall day, if it had any effect on warming the water, he could not tell. When close,

Nathan reached out to grab Sharon. But just as he was about to put his hands around her waist, she scooted back into deeper water up to her knees. Now it was his turn to return the grin as he attempted to move closer.

Again, just as he was about to catch her, she quickly retreated into deeper water until it came up to her waist. Tantalized by her beauty, Nathan moved toward her, but once the water hit his belt line, the tough woodsman could not help himself.

"Oh, my goodness, that's cold!" he repeated. "We're never going to have children now!" Nathan moaned.

At that remark, Sharon surged toward him, taking his contorted face in her hands and kissed him long and hard. "You had better give me children!" she exclaimed.

Then, as quickly as she had grabbed him, she moved away, just out of reach again. She turned in the water and proceeded to climb the Falls' natural slate steps until she stood just before the white falling cascade. Looking over her shoulder, smiling sweetly at the young man following her every movement, she stepped into the raging water and disappeared behind the flowing, white veil.

Nathan was still staring at her disappearance when he saw Sharon's forearm emerge from the watery curtain. Palm up, fingers rolling closed, ending with her index finger wagging—she gestured for him to join her. Sharon's hand slowly withdrew and disappeared behind the falling water once more.

He moved to climb the creek's natural steps as she had. The slimy algae almost caused him to slip and fall back into the pool. But Nathan recovered his balance awkwardly, somewhat grateful that Sharon had not seen his uncharacteristic clumsiness. Standing before the falling water, he stepped into the downpour.

Nathan was amazed at how easily he had moved through the frigid wall of water. Now beneath the Falls' rocky overhang, in front of him sitting on the cold rock with her hair wet from the passage, Sharon smiled. He was also pleasantly surprised to note that there was plenty of light to see clearly, and the sound of the falling water behind him seemed muted. She patted the ground next to her, although Nathan needed no encouragement to be near her. When he did sit down, Sharon quickly nestled up against him, a silent testament that she, too, felt the cold and needed his warmth.

They shared the tranquility, as these longtime friends were wont to do. Nathan knew from experience that she was gathering her thoughts.

"Do you remember the night we caught those fireflies in the field those many years ago?" Sharon began, still watching the mesmerizing waterfall in front of them.

"Yes, I do," Nathan said, easily recollecting that night.

"Do you also remember that I threw a rock into the pond that night?" She turned and looked deeply into his eyes, praying that he would remember.

"Yes, I recall that," he confirmed.

"I threw that stone to let go of the pain of losing my dad. My mother told me that up to that day, she thought that she'd lost both of us—Daddy and me. I didn't realize that I was living my life looking back and feeling sorry for myself, even though I knew my father would want me to be happy. That night, I quit looking back. It was the first time I had been truly free since he died." Sharon's voice drifted off, remembering that poignant moment with crystal clarity.

Nathan nodded, and he could see in the flickering light that the water welling in her eyes was not solely from their immediate surroundings but from within.

Sharon shook her head to ward off a bad feeling trying to wedge its way into her head, but then she continued. "Do you remember the first time you brought me here to the Falls?"

"Yes, I do. You threw a stone that time, too." Nathan's memory caused her to smile as he had, like so many times before, anticipated her question.

"That rock, that time—I let go of being afraid to be hurt if you would not love me back," Sharon explained.

"You needn't have worried about that," Nathan reassured her.

She quickly put her hand up and gently placed her small fingers on his lips. "I know that now, but I didn't know it then." She spoke softly and moved her face closer.

"And what of the stone you threw today?" Nathan asked curiously.

"Some things a girl has to keep to herself," she teased.

"Walked right into that one." Nathan laughed, shaking his head. But he added more seriously, "You've thrown many rocks along the way."

A simple but powerful observation that Sharon had to admit was correct, but her response came even more forceful. "The only times throwing all those stones ever seemed to work and erase the pain that I felt—the only times it ever mattered—is when I was with you."

That night, the man slipped silently into the Helms' darkened driveway. He was thankful that the mother and daughter had no dogs, unlike the Ernst family up the road. Dogs were his age-old nemesis and would have alerted the women to his presence, thus making his task that much harder.

The man was big, but he glided through the night with perfected stealth. He came up alongside the small, blue car that he knew to be Sharon's vehicle and then lie down on the ground to crawl beneath the car. With a pen light, he located the brake lines. From his front pocket, the man produced a small wire that had two rings on either end. Placing his thumbs in the wire saw, he slowly and methodically worked the rings back and forth, readily cutting into the metal brake lines until he saw the smallest drop of fluid emerge from the now-damaged lines.

Perfect, he thought as a wicked smile crossed his lips.

He slipped from beneath the vehicle, stood slowly, and looked up at the darkened house, confident that its inhabitants were oblivious to his presence, and the wrong just committed.

The evil slithered down the dirt driveway and faded into the night.

Sharon sat before the mirror, wearing her white wedding dress. The morning sun shone through the window behind her, and the glowing image reflected in the mirror of the bride and her admiring mother.

"You are beautiful, my daughter." Miriam's voice was soft but also beamed with pride.

"Thank you, Mom." Sharon looked down at the pair of shoes on the ground that she had not yet donned. "Nathan is a good man. I've waited so long for this day."

"Nathan is the finest young man that I've ever met. In many ways, he reminds me of your father—handsome and always gallant, always protective. And I know how long you've waited. You told Nathan that you planned on marrying him when you were about twelve, as I recall." Miriam's eyes twinkled with insight.

"Mom! You were eavesdropping on us!" Sharon was shocked and could not help but blush.

"You were my only daughter—of course, I was listening in!" Miriam laughed without apology. "Besides, my dear, you and Nathan eventually marrying has been the talk of this little town for a very long time."

Sharon spun in her chair to look at her mother directly and said in mock disbelief, "Oh really?" Then mother and daughter burst into laughter. They stopped their mirth when they heard a loud knock at the front door.

"Who could that be?" Sharon asked. "It had better not be Nathan! He can't see me on our wedding day before the ceremony—it's bad luck!"

"Oh, I don't think it's Nathan." Miriam's voice belied that she knew who it was, but she rose and left the bedroom without revealing her secret.

Sharon heard her mother greet the visitor, assuring whoever it was that it was okay to enter, and welcomed the guest into their home. Just as Sharon was about to stand and see for herself who had come on her wedding day, Miriam reappeared in her bedroom doorway with Jacob Ernst.

Sharon's soon-to-be father-in-law wore a black tuxedo, and with his hair combed neatly, Jacob cut quite a dashing figure. The young woman could not help but notice her mother's approving eyes on Jacob as he stood there in the doorway with one hand behind his back.

After a few awkward moments of silence, Miriam prompted him into action. "Go on, Jacob! We don't want to miss our children's wedding, do we?" Miriam laughed.

Jacob snapped out of his bashfulness and brought his hand forward to reveal a magnificent white-laced bridal veil. He offered it to Sharon, who took the garment, all the while mesmerized by its beauty.

"This was the veil Nathan's mother wore on our wedding day. You're about the same height as she was, so I figured it would fit. I would be honored if you'd wear it today." Jacob somewhat surprised himself at how smoothly the words flowed.

Sharon burst into tears and shouted, "Yes! Yes!" She got up and hugged him.

The tall, graying man smiled as he returned the hug of his future daughter-in-law.

Miriam came over and gently pulled her daughter away, thanking him for the thoughtful gift.

"I'll see you in a bit," Jacob said, smiling at both ladies as he departed.

Jacob walked down the driveway to his old truck. As he passed by Sharon's car, the old coon hunter saw a strange, single footprint in the dirt. A large man had made the track and not the Helm women. Jacob dismissed it though as probably a delivery driver for the many things a wedding entailed.

Jacob made the short ride back to his farm. Stepping out of his old truck, he found both of his sons, dressed in tuxedos similar to his own, talking on the front porch.

True to form, even while formally dressed, Mead could not help but wear his baseball cap, making for a disjointed wardrobe. "Where'd you go, Pa?" he asked as their father joined them.

"I had to make a special delivery," Jacob said, grinning as he walked past his boys and into the house. Both Nathan and Mead looked at each other but knew that trying to pry the information from their father would have been pointless.

"I think Pa wants to raise another litter of pups soon," Mead said, motioning with his chin toward the kennels.

While Nathan now rented an apartment in nearby Corning, he nodded, indicating that he was aware of Jacob's plans for a new litter of coonhounds.

"So, you're going to do this?" Mead kidded his older brother as he changed the subject to the pending event.

Nathan smiled—he most certainly was going through with the wedding.

"She's a good woman," Mead said uncharacteristically serious.

"Yes, she is," Nathan spoke aloud in full confirmation. "And with Sarah Findley as the bridesmaid, perhaps we can arrange for Father Simmons to perform a double marriage?" Now it was Nathan's turn to return a verbal jab.

"Me? Marry Sarah?" Mead said in feigned horror, although as sure as the local townsfolk had been about Nathan and Sharon's pending nuptials, they were equally confident of the eventual union of Sarah and Mead.

Nathan chuckled at his brother's overreaction.

"Uncle Mead," the big man said wistfully. "I kinda like the sound of that."

"All things in time, brother," Nathan said, thinking of a future with children of his own.

The sound of a car coming down the driveway caught their attention, and they saw Sharon's car heading toward them.

Mead immediately grabbed Nathan by the shoulders, and with little physical effort on his part, turned his brother around like a child's top, pushing him through the open front door. Even if Nathan had wanted to offer any resistance, it would have been futile against the giant's strength. Mead grabbed the door and shut it quickly, then yelling so Nathan could hear him, "It's bad luck for the groom to see the bride before the wedding ceremony!"

Behind Sharon's car, two more vehicles arrived driven by Miriam Helm and Sarah Findley. All parked on the green grass. The women stepped out of their autos; each dressed beautifully. Mead noticed that Sharon's vehicle stopped a little clumsily, but he assumed the bride was having difficulty navigating the car's pedals due to the bulky wedding attire and her fancy shoes.

The coonhounds barked loudly—curiously joyous sounding and somehow knowing a special union was about to take place.

Mead stepped off the porch to meet the ladies. "And to what do we owe this unexpected pleasure?" he asked graciously, unable to take his eyes off the yellow-haired bridesmaid, Sarah, who was quite aware of his attention and smiled back.

"Just making sure Nathan wasn't heading for the Pennsylvania border!" Sarah wisecracked, only to receive a playful hit in the arm from the bride herself. "We have something old, something new, and something borrowed—but we need something blue," Sarah explained.

"I suppose a bluetick coonhound won't do?" Mead asked, and his tone sounded so serious that none of the ladies could tell if he was joking or not.

"No!" Miriam finally exclaimed.

They laughed, sharing a mental image of Sharon with a leash in hand, walking a hound down the center aisle of Saint Catherine's church!

Jacob appeared from inside the front porch with a long, blue ribbon in his hand. He walked down the wooden steps to the ladies, and for the second time in nearly an hour, Jacob again presented his soon-to-be daughter-in-law with a gift.

"This ribbon also belonged to Nathan's mother," Jacob explained. "Rose used to pull her hair back, tying it up with this whenever we walked in the woods."

Like before, Sharon's eyes began to well with tears, and she tenderly accepted the gift. Knowing the heirloom's pedigree, she immediately dipped her head forward and tied her hair back with the bow.

"Thank you, Jacob."

The old coon hunter was visibly shaken, for he had not heard Sharon speak, but rather the voice of his lost wife. The sun's brilliant light shone in Jacob's eyes, but through the glare, for a moment as Sharon looked up, her visage transformed into the very likeness of the beautiful Rose Ernst.

"All things in time, Jacob. Remember that everything happens for a reason." Rose's voice sounded clearly in his mind, but the vision then disappeared, and Jacob stood with his mouth agape.

"Is everything okay, Jacob?" Miriam asked, reflecting the same confused stare of all three women trying to discern the reason behind his suddenly ashen look.

Jacob Ernst had witnessed the magic of Ryland Creek on bright, moon-filled nights, but never before in broad daylight nor in the presence of others!

"What d-did you say?" Jacob directed his question to Sharon with his unusual stammering only adding to the growing confusion of those around him.

"I said thank you, Mr. Ernst," Sharon repeated.

"Oh . . . uhm . . . please call me 'Pa.' No need for such formality after today," Jacob said, recovering with his usual aplomb.

Sharon smiled anew and moved forward to give him a firm hug. He looked up to see Miriam's eyes now filling with tears. Jacob nodded, hugged the young woman back, and without another word, he turned and went back up the steps and into the house.

"It's time for us to go now," Miriam announced.

"I'll go to the church," Sharon said. "Father Simmons said I could hide down in the basement until Nathan arrives. And Mead—you make sure Nathan gets to the church!" Sharon giggled, which was so contagious that Sarah joined in.

"Sarah, I need to pick up a few more things from the caterer. Can you help me?" Miriam asked and then looked at her daughter. "We won't be late, dear, I promise."

Sharon smiled as she walked away and got into her little blue car. She started the engine, put the car in reverse to turn around on the green lawn, then headed back down the driveway and turned down the road.

As soon as Sharon's car was out of sight, Nathan emerged from the house and quickly walked up to Miriam as she entered her old truck on the side of the driveway.

"So today is the day you're finally going to marry my little girl." Miriam beamed at the dapper young groom as she leaned out the open truck window.

"Yes, Mrs. Helm, that is my intent," Nathan said, looking at the ground, still shy after all these years. *"All things in time, Miriam— everything happens for a reason,"* the voice said.

Miriam stared, visibly shaken, because the baritone voice that she heard did not belong to Nathan Ernst. As Miriam blinked quickly in the bright sunlight, the image staring back at her was that of her deceased husband, Kenneth Helm. Like Jacob earlier, now Miriam stood frozen by an apparition from the past.

"Is everything okay, Mrs. Helm?" Nathan asked, clearly concerned. The vision had dissipated to reveal once again the handsome, young groom staring at her.

"Oh . . . uhm . . . please call me, 'Ma.' No need for such formality after today." Miriam shook her head slightly to clear the ghostly image in her mind. She turned the ignition of her truck while Sarah, already in her vehicle and just ending a private conversation with Mead, also started her car.

Nathan stepped back and kneeled to touch something in the otherwise dry, dirt driveway. "I stepped in something," he said, more worried about it possibly staining his wedding attire than anything else.

"Hope it ain't dog you-know-what!" Mead joked.

Nathan's curiosity was piqued, his fingers feeling the smooth viscosity of the red-colored liquid. "That's brake fluid," he deduced.

"That's where Sharon's car was parked," Mead noted.

Ryland Creek's ravines could often channel sounds over long distances. As the brothers stood looking at each other, a loud, crashing noise carried on the wind.

Alarm quickly covered Nathan's face as he mentally connected the fluid on his fingers and the sound. He sprinted to his truck and jumped in, the engine immediately roaring to life. The groom spun the pickup around in the driveway in a cloud of dust and turned onto Ryland Creek Road before a now-confused Miriam or Sarah could leave.

Dread filled him as it never had. Rounding the first bend that began the road's descent, Nathan breathed a sigh of relief at not seeing Sharon's car. Had her brakes failed at that juncture, she would have gone straight over the steep edge of the ravine. There was only one more curve to make, and after that, Ryland Creek became relatively flat.

As he negotiated that final curve, Nathan realized his worst fears, for there was Sharon's car smashed into the side of the small bridge. The car's front end was terribly crumpled, indicating the considerable speed the vehicle must have been going when it finally hit the bridge's solid steel guide rail.

As he pulled his truck to a rapid stop behind the wrecked car, the scene Nathan beheld would stay in his memory for the remainder of his life.

Sharon had somehow managed to crawl away from the vehicle, and she now lie on her back less than ten feet from the opened car door. The long, white wedding dress with its laced train flowed over the green grass with her upper torso slightly propped up by the hilly attitude of the bank.

Nathan jumped out of his truck. "No! No!" He screamed as he ran and fell to his knees beside her.

Sharon stared up, but her gaze seemed to look through him, and Nathan noticed blood trickling from the corner of her mouth. His arms gently cradled her as he brought her closer, afraid to move her much due to the apparent internal injuries that she'd suffered.

"Oh, my beautiful Nathan," Sharon murmured as her hands went gently to his cheek. For even now, she was brushing aside his tears. "It hurts, Nathan."

Nathan heard a car pull up behind him but could not take his eyes from her.

"You must live your life. Promise me you will do that," she said softly, her voice weakening now.

"No!" Nathan screamed again, trying to will away her injuries.

Sharon dropped one of her hands to the ground, searching for something. Blood now began to flow from one of her ears, and in her soul, she sensed her life force ebbing. Reaching around the ground blindly, she finally found that which she sought, and her small hand cupped over something that she brought to her mouth and kissed.

The small rock she held to her lips became covered with blood. With what little energy she had left, Sharon pressed the stone into Nathan's free hand.

"You know what you must do with this. You *must* do it," Sharon said as she coughed hard and sprayed him with more blood.

Sharon stared beyond and smiled serenely. "Your mother is so beautiful," she said cryptically. Then she looked back at him with an impossible grin, and she made a soft, airplane engine noise, her finger corkscrewing through the air, gently poking his chest.

For the briefest of moments, Nathan saw Sharon transformed into the laughing, wet-haired young girl at the swimming hole those many years earlier. Her hand slid down the white shirt of his tuxedo, leaving a wake of bright red.

"I am not afraid." Sharon gasped suddenly, and then much softer, she spoke, barely above a whisper, "Hold me."

Tears flooded Nathan's eyes.

As Sharon's eyes closed for the final time, Nathan's head sunk to his chest as he cried aloud, "I love you." Her tiny form slumped into his arms as he cradled her next to him and slowly rocked back and forth.

For a moment, the wildlife in the surrounding hills stopped to listen to the sound of Nathan's wailing. The birds stopped singing, and some say that even the evil souls trapped in the Black Oaks felt sorrow for something other than themselves for those long moments.

On the Ernst farm, the oldest hound Duke let out a long, mournful cry, and the other hounds hung their heads low.

Another voice behind Nathan began shouting. He recognized Miriam's shattered cry, screaming her daughter's name repeatedly. He could also hear his father saying something, and then a steady hand placed on his shoulder. Then came the sound of other cars arriving, people shouting, some crying, and still others calling for someone to get an ambulance.

None of that mattered now.

For Nathan Ernst, the entire world had ended, and his future had dissipated into the forested air of Ryland Creek.

<hr/>

It seemed that nearly all of Painted Post attended Sharon's funeral. People flooded into the chapel paying their last respects, coming up to Miriam, telling her what a beautiful daughter she had raised, and how heartbroken they were at her loss.

Pictures of Sharon's smiling face took up an entire wall near her casket. Some of the photographs were recent, even one of her making a silly expression behind the bar where she had worked, while other images showed her as a child standing with her father in a pretty dress in front of their farmhouse. The long bench, normally meant for people to sit on, was nearly full with a myriad of beautiful flower bouquets that mourners had provided to pay their last respects.

There was room for one person on that bench beneath a picture of teenage Sharon staring intently into a glass jar full of fireflies, and there sat Nathan Ernst, dressed entirely in black. His head bowed forward, his hands folded as he crouched with his forearms resting on his upper legs. When people came up to him, well aware of the tragedy that had befallen the would-be groom, they tried to offer their deepest condolences. Sometimes Nathan would look up and provide a short, polite thank you to the consoling individuals, while other times he only kept his head down, and nodded slightly in acknowledgment.

In the church where Sharon had prayed since she was a little girl, Father Simmons presided over the funeral Mass. The priest told of his heart breaking while standing at the altar, waiting to marry her and Nathan, when he had learned of the tragic news. The good Father tried to console the many sobbing parishioners by explaining that God had a plan. And while perhaps humanity was never meant to understand that scheme completely, all would see Sharon again, for surely Heaven had welcomed its newest angel.

Nathan sat near the front of the church, motionless, except for occasionally wiping away the tears that flowed. When the pallbearers rose at the end of the Mass to take the casket to the black vehicle waiting just outside the church, the entire crowd hushed as Nathan stood.

Walking up to the front pallbearer, Sheriff Covington, Nathan touched him lightly on the sleeve. The police officer looked up surprised. "Are you sure that you want to do this, son?" Sean asked, his voice low and surprisingly tender.

Nathan did not respond but shut his eyes and nodded quickly.

Sean stepped aside, guiding the young man's hand until Nathan made contact and grasped the casket's handle. But the local lawman would not shirk this final responsibility to the little girl whom he had watched grow to become a beautiful woman. He tapped the shoulder of one of the other men performing the solemn duty, and the police officer took up his new position immediately behind Nathan.

As one, the pallbearers lifted the casket and slowly carried it to the back of the church. The congregation watched in a continued hushed awe at the scene of the heartbroken young man taking his bride to her final resting place.

At the gravesite, the sun shone brightly. Father Simmons said the final rites with dozens of mourners present. As the casket was lowered into the cold ground and out of sight, Miriam Helm again cried aloud, her pain palpable as her loss filled the air. Jacob Ernst gently put his arm around Miriam, looked up to see Nathan staring at the emptiness, and then the older man escorted the bereaved mother away from the cemetery.

For a long time, Nathan stood there, alone with his thoughts. A large hand landed on his shoulder, and he looked up to see Mead.

"Are you going to be all right, brother?" Mead asked, his tone more solemn than any other time in his life.

"I want to be with her for a little bit longer," Nathan replied, turning his eyes back to the open grave.

Mead hesitated, wondering if he should stay or say something else, but then figured it would be best to leave his brother alone with Sharon this one, last time.

Again, time seemed to stop for Nathan, its passage only betrayed by the setting of the sun.

Knowing what had been lost, the three cemetery personnel assigned to fill in the open grave waited patiently.

At some point, Nathan sensed another standing beside him in the dusk. How long the individual had been there, he was uncertain, and Nathan looked up to see the red, swollen eyes of Larry Allen.

Larry had dressed respectfully; perhaps the cleanest anyone could ever remember him looking. "I'm sorry for your loss, man," he said, and sincerity hung in the air between the lifelong rivals.

"Thank you," Nathan said, returning the sentiment.

The two men stood there for a long moment when Larry confessed. "I loved her, too," he said, his voice breaking barely above a whisper.

"I know," Nathan replied and placed a hand on Larry's shoulder. He turned back to the open grave and repeated, "I know."

Larry nodded several times, and after a few more minutes of silence, left the gravesite.

After another hour, with all the world dark, Nathan reached into his front pants pocket to feel the small stone that he had put there. He knelt on one knee, said another silent prayer, then stood and slowly walked away.

In that simple prayer, Nathan Ernst could not bring himself to think the word "goodbye."

Chapter 15

Rediscovery

The entire world turned gray for Nathan Ernst. Even the fall colors of Painted Post seemed prosaic as the days became weeks, and the weeks became months, following Sharon's death. Nathan moved back into the Ernst family homestead. He could not live in his small apartment; the dreams that he had once held for Sharon and starting their family weighed too heavily upon him in that place.

The leaves fell, and winter came once. Jacob would often take his latest batch of hounds to the woods. The old coon hunter would try to coax his grieving son into the familiar routine of chasing ringtails once more, but Nathan would only respond with a promise to join him "next time."

But that next time never seemed to happen, and Jacob would go out into the forest alone with his dogs except for the few times that Mead would accompany him.

Nathan's hair and beard grew long—his disheveled appearance contrasted sharply with his former clean image. Several young ladies would attempt to engage Nathan in conversation whenever they would see him in town. However, his responses to their queries, while polite, were never more than a superficial courtesy.

Stella Wharton once witnessed two young and quite attractive women attempting to elicit a response from Nathan when they ran across the young man in town. With a simple, curt greeting, Nathan hurriedly moved past and disappeared into J.P. Smith's General Merchandise & Hardware Store. They complained to one another at the young man's apparent lack of interest in the opposite sex.

"Ladies," Stella Wharton, ever-dressed expensively, interrupted the jilted young women. "That was an Ernst who lost his one true love." She motioned her head with a sidelong look at J.P.'s store, continuing wistfully and with a knowing tone of experience, "Even if somehow you could get close to him, you would be fighting a memory for the rest of your life."

Mead worked many long hours as a carpenter each week, but he tried to make it over at least once during the weekend to see his brother and father. The sallow look on his brother's face told Mead that he was speaking to the husk of the former man. Nathan's replies to his attempts at banter were often single word acknowledgments or denials.

Nathan was losing the one battle that he could not fight his way out. And worse, it seemed like he did not want to win.

"What can we do about Nathan?" Mead asked his father once when he was sure they were alone. The seasonal "January thaw" hard arrived in Upstate New York, and temperatures slightly above freezing had melted the majority of the previous month's snowfall.

Jacob looked at his youngest son, shaking his head. "There's nothing we can do at this point. There will come a time when your brother will move back into the light, but he's the only one that can take that first step."

"Perhaps he should see a doctor, or maybe Father Simmons?" Mead suggested.

"The good Father Simmons has been here quite often," Jacob informed his son. "Nathan is always cordial, but even Father Simmons told me that he feels like he's talking to someone at a faraway distance."

Mead nodded his head, slowly understanding. "Any sign he's hitting the bottle?" he asked. Although he'd never known Nathan to drink to excess, the query was fair, particularly considering the stark transformation of his brother's appearance.

"No indication that he's gone to drinking, and I wouldn't expect he would," Jacob said with a sigh. When he saw Mead's expression begging for further explanation, the older man continued.

"He doesn't want to numb the pain. At this point, Nathan feels that he must suffer. To do anything less would seem disloyal to Sharon's memory. And here's the thing—it won't be any of us that pushes him out of his depression." Jacob paused.

Mead could tell that his father was speaking from experience.

"It will have to be Nathan who finds something to latch on to, so he can pull himself back into this world," Jacob concluded.

The two men sat contemplating Nathan's dilemma of not wanting to let go of the very thing causing his pain.

"Are we meant to suffer in this life, Pa?" Mead inquired.

"No, son," Jacob said slowly, looking in the direction where he knew Nathan to be. "We're meant to learn from whatever life throws at us. And nearly always, that means working through your pain, and not running from it."

Mead nodded, and again they paused. He then changed the subject. "How's coon hunting going?"

"We're having a good season. And Grace should be having pups in two weeks or so." Jacob mentioned the impending birth of the next litter of coonhounds.

"It's always good to have pups on the ground." Mead paused and then added, "Pa?"

"Yes, son?"

"I'm thinking of asking Sarah Findley to marry me," Mead announced. "But with Nathan in such a state, and with Sarah having been Sharon's bridesmaid, it doesn't seem right to ask her right now."

Jacob smiled broadly at the thought of pending nuptials for his youngest son. "First, Sarah is a good girl, and I think you two would make a fine husband and wife. And while your concern for your brother is honorable, you must follow your path in the same way Nathan must find his way again. Rest assured, your brother will be happy to hear that you'll be getting married. When do you plan to ask her proper?"

"I've worked hard these past six months to save up enough for an engagement ring," Mead said, beaming at his father's encouragement.

Jacob had noticed the long hours that Mead had been working lately, and now knowing his son's purpose, all seemed to fit in place.

Mead continued. "Sarah's birthday is the middle of next month, so I thought I'd ask her then. Besides, if she says no, there will still be cake and ice cream," he joked, and both father and son shared a laugh. "Any advice, Pa?" he asked, serious again.

"Well," Jacob began, looking at the floor, "the old saw goes that a man marries a woman thinking she'll never change, and a woman marries a man thinking he will change. Turns out—both are wrong. So, I guess I'd add that you need to see the woman that Sarah can become, and likewise make sure that what she sees in you likely won't change anytime soon—if ever."

After a pause, Mead grinned at his father. "You learn that while you were coon hunting with Grandpa Ernst?"

"No," Jacob said, returning the smile. "That bit of wisdom came from your mother."

Mead said a grateful goodbye to his father, and he stopped by to see Nathan, who was sitting in a rocking chair, below the favorite picture of their mother.

Nathan stared outside at the bleak winter landscape, rocking gently. In his hand, he rolled a small rock back and forth repeatedly between his fingers.

"I'm going now, Nate. I'll see you soon," Mead said.

"Be good."

His brother's reply was short, but Mead also sensed it was heartfelt.

Nathan Ernst might have been willing to accept the suffering for his own, but he would not stoop to cause his family similar pain.

Two weeks later, Jacob predicting it to the day, Grace gave birth to some beautiful coonhound puppies.

"Grace had her pups!" Jacob announced when he found Nathan at the breakfast table. "Four females and one male. The male is the largest, too, and what a pretty litter!"

"She had five pups, eh?" Nathan responded.

But there was something different in his voice—interest—the first time the grieving young man had shown a concern for anything in many months.

"Why don't you come see them?" Jacob suggested, not wanting to lose the moment.

"Sure, Pa," Nathan said.

That simple affirmative lit hope within Jacob. The old coon hunter had been already dressed to go outside in the cold, early February morning, but he waited patiently as Nathan donned his winter gear

The sun was just now rising, and its light reflected in the ground's icy glaze. The men's boots noisily crunched the frozen earth, and the adult hounds came out of their coops to bark happily at their masters.

When they entered Grace's pen, Nathan peered into the whelping box Jacob had constructed long ago. Jacob had rigged a single lightbulb inside the coop to help maintain the warmth, but it also served to allow Nathan to see the squirming bodies. The little balls of fur squealed as they instinctively moved to the familiar comfort of their mother.

The heavily bearded Nathan reached out and grasped the nearest puppy, lifting it up. This pup was different. While its siblings' coloration was the traditional walker's mottled white, brown, and black like their mother, the color of this animal was the jet black of a cur.

"It's okay, Grace," Nathan said to gently reassure the mother who moved her muzzle to touch the squealing puppy in midair.

"That's the male," Jacob informed his son.

The younger man unconsciously smiled as he turned the pup around in the air, inspecting it. Jacob had not exaggerated when he spoke of the litter's comeliness. Nathan carefully returned the lively pup to his mother's side.

"I have to go, Pa," Nathan said suddenly, but he had caught himself smiling, which somehow felt prohibited.

"I'll need help naming them," Jacob called out as his son was leaving.

Nathan stopped and said over his shoulder, "Sure, Pa. I'll give it some thought." He hurried back to the house, fumbling with the rock that had found its way back into his hand.

His response still gave Jacob some hope, though.

"Thanks, Grace," Jacob said, and the hound, hearing her name from her beloved master, wagged her tail amidst the commotion of the feeding pups.

Perhaps, the old coon hunter mused, it would be the magic of puppies that would begin Nathan's path to recovery—that special something to latch on to in this world.

◆ ◆

At three-weeks old, the puppies, eyes wide open, moved about on wobbly legs in their kennel. Jacob picked up the closest puppy and presented it to Nathan.

"Ethel," Nathan suggested.

"Ethel?" Jacob repeated, a little skeptical at the pup's suggested name.

Nathan laughed, and Jacob noted it was the first time he had heard his son laugh in a very long time.

"Just kidding, Pa," Nathan said, smiling.

"Good!" Jacob said in exaggerated relief. "I was having a hard time imagining the thought of traipsing the woods at night shouting, 'Ethel!' A man has got to have some pride."

Nathan smirked at his father's forever backwoods sense of humor. "We'll call her Sky," he said, now serious.

"A good name!" Jacob agreed and set the female pup down on the ground.

Nathan proceeded to name the other three females, one by one, as Jacob presented them: Cilla, Suzie, and Song.

Jacob searched for the male pup, who had managed to amble to the far side of the coop. The old coon hunter stood, walked over to pick him up, and then handed the young cur to Nathan.

Nathan accepted the ebony pup and lifted him into the air. He inspected the dog with a professional eye and noted how perfectly colored and the exceptional handsomeness of this dog. Unlike the others, this puppy looked directly back into Nathan's eyes, displaying no fear of the giant who held it aloft.

"We'll call him Seth." Nathan brought the pup into a cradled position next to his chest and patted him on the head.

"Another good name," Jacob confirmed.

Nathan smiled and set the male on the ground, and the newly dubbed Seth wobbled his way back to Grace where his littermates had decided that it was feeding time.

The two men walked silently out of the kennel. Nathan closed the coop door halfheartedly. He reached into his front pants pocket to feel the ever-present rock—the tactile sensation of the object against his fingers provided a needed sense of loyalty to Sharon's memory.

With every pace to the front porch, Nathan's depression likewise crept back to the forefront of his mind. He finally planted himself on the uppermost porch step. While it was nearly spring, and even a comfortably tepid, early-March morning, Nathan's thoughts became again as dreary as the gray-brown and still leafless landscape that surrounded their farm.

Jacob sat beside Nathan and produced his hunting knife, which he used to begin whittling an old stick. The razor-sharp blade produced long shavings of wood on the lower porch steps. In five minutes of silence between the two men, the pile of shavings grew considerably.

"Pa, you don't have to stay." Nathan sought to break the silence, hoping to reassure his father that it would be okay to leave him alone with his thoughts.

"I remember when your ma left this life," Jacob started while still focused on the task of flaying the wooden stick. "I was pretty sure the world—or leastways my world—had ended. One moment she was there as I held her hand when Mead was born, and the next thing I seem to remember was the doctor telling me that they had lost her." Jacob paused and then added in a hushed tone, "We never really had the chance to say goodbye."

"Doesn't seem fair." Nathan's angry tone rang clear.

"Doesn't really work that way, does it?" Jacob carried on. "Life isn't about fair—it's about livin'—most people don't understand that. Life happens, and it is what it is. An airplane crashes, or a ship sinks. Innocent lives, good people, are lost. These are all tragedies. You then grieve your losses, and when possible, you learn from them. Then you move on, *just as those we've lost would have wanted us to.*

"When your ma died, I wanted to take my life, so I could be with her—right then and there. For a while, it didn't seem like I could bear her loss for another hour, but then an hour would pass." Jacob paused, and his constant whittling slowed a bit, and then he continued. "But I had two boys to look after, and I know your mother would have wanted me to raise you to have families of your own someday."

"Weren't you mad at God that day when Ma died?" Nathan asked.

"Son, it was that day, more than any other before or since, that I leaned on Him the most," Jacob confessed, looking directly at Nathan.

"It just doesn't seem like God should have let it happen," Nathan began. "Sharon was a good person! If anyone should have died that day, it should have been me!" Nathan's voice trembled in the nether region between sorrow and anger.

"When a young child dies of cancer, do you think that child is anything but innocent? Do you think the child's parents are somehow being punished? I'm fairly certain that's *not* how it works.

"And as pretty as Painted Post is, I'm likewise sure that Heaven is infinitely more beautiful. In the end, you realize it wasn't God who necessarily put you in a bad situation, as much as it's Him who pulls you through it."

Nathan reflected a long while on his father's words. "Pa—the legends about Ryland Creek—about sometimes seeing your loved ones who have died in the moonlight mist. Do you think they're true?"

Jacob stopped whittling and looked Nathan in the eye with a happy gleam. "I know they're true, son," he said, looking up at the sky for a moment and then back. "I know they're true."

The old coon hunter did not elaborate further—nor did he have to—as Nathan understood.

"Where'd you learn all that fancy thinking, Pa?" Nathan somehow found it in him to poke fun at his father. "Did Grampa Ernst tell you all this when you and he were coon hunting?"

"Oh, it was your Grandpa Ernst who explained it to me all right, but not when we were hunting," Jacob said with a smile. "He told me all that right after your mother died." Motioning with his head at Nathan, Jacob added, "Pretty much where you're sitting now."

Nathan was speechless.

Jacob looked up to finally stop whittling the branch and uttered, "Well, I'll be damned."

At first, Nathan was confused, but when he turned his head, the younger man understood his father's awestruck moment. In front of them, having traversed an incredible distance for such small legs, stood Seth. With the humans' full attention now, the little hound let out a long, incredibly loud bawl to announce his presence.

"Well, I'll be damned," Jacob repeated. "In over forty years of raising pups, I've never seen one so young make it so far, and then bark like that!"

"Sorry, Pa, I must not have closed the pen completely."

"Nothing to be sorry about, son."

Nathan rose from the steps and walked to the infant hound as Seth was undoubtedly waiting for him—and perhaps just for him. Seth bawled aloud and pranced about joyously as Nathan reached down to scoop up the young pup into his arms.

Nathan hid his countenance from his father as tears, pent up for many reasons and many months, began to flow. Again, Seth's tiny voice crowed in excitement, wagging his tail rapidly.

"Let's get you back to your mama and your sisters," Nathan said, his voice strong and steady as the flooding relief poured into his soul. As he began to walk away, still not wanting to reveal his face to his father, Nathan said louder over his shoulder, "I think that he will make an exceptional hound."

Jacob watched his son take the pup back to the kennel. The old coon hunter looked up briefly to the sky, remitting both a response and a thankful prayer.

"He already is," Jacob muttered.

Chapter 16

An Exceptional Hound

Seth grew large and strong, and wherever Nathan would go, there his hound would be. Never on the Ernst farm had there been a hound such as Seth. At five months old, the ebony cur could run inexplicably fast. Not only could he easily run circles around his sibling sisters, who were but half his size, but even the most mature of the Ernst hounds could not catch him.

Seth's voice sounded extraordinary as well. Not even Jacob's prize coonhound, Radar, who at five years old was in his prime, could match the volume of Seth's deep bawl.

Jacob Ernst, a man who had known many hounds in his decades of chasing raccoon, had never seen anything like the young Seth. "He truly is an exceptional hound," the coon hunter would say on more than one occasion.

Nathan, now clean-shaven, spent many of his waking hours taking Seth and his siblings for long walks around their land. Not surprisingly, Seth's sisters stumbled repeatedly as all puppies do when first learning their way through the woods.

But it was not that way for Seth. The young hound raced through the forest with a natural ease—as if practiced for many years.

On one particular mid-August day, Seth ran around, barking joyfully at his sisters, taunting them as always. And chase him they did, but never to any avail, as Seth's seemingly effortless bursts of speed easily outfoxed their clumsy maneuvers.

As man and hounds happened deeper into the woods, they came upon a massive oak felled by the fury of a violent summer storm the night before. The tree's branches still held bright green leaves. Again, Seth barked at his littermates—challenging them to follow. Off they went, chasing Seth as the young dog ran headlong at the fallen oak.

Nathan's heart skipped a beat. Jacob had told many stories of hounds becoming fatally impaled on branches as they ran through the woods. Unlike his sisters, whose pace rationally slowed as they neared the entanglement of broken limbs, Seth's speed *increased*.

As he neared the edge of the tree's branches, and with incredible agility, Seth stretched his forepaws directly ahead. In sheer amazement, Nathan watched the puppy negotiate the smallest of gaps as the young hound's body sailed through the maze of branches, without disturbing a single leaf, to disappear behind thick, still-verdant foliage.

And then—silence.

Nathan held his breath.

Seth's sisters pranced about bewildered at their only brother's whereabouts.

Nathan took a step forward after what seemed an eternity, but soothing reassurance flooded over him as Seth's triumphant booming voice came from behind the green wall. Seconds later, the young, seemingly tireless hound sprinted around the tree's crown. Instead of rejoining his siblings, Seth ran to Nathan and leapt into the air, landing his two paws onto the man's chest, confirming that all was well.

Nathan stroked the young hound's head and acknowledged what his father had already confirmed. "You truly are amazing."

Seth roared again in delight, sensing his master's approval, and with that, sprang off Nathan's body to once again harass his sisters into a game of chase.

The summer was long with these experiences as the young hound pups explored the forest, learning its scents and sounds.

Jacob Ernst watched over the waning summer months as the bond between Nathan and Seth grew stronger. While the old coon hunter was sure beyond doubt that Seth would make an incredible coonhound, the real gift the hound brought to the Ernst household was the resurrection of his son's soul. Jacob was not so foolish to believe that Nathan's hurt would ever be entirely expiated, for the older Ernst knew deeply of loss. But this young dog's zest for life was contagious, and Nathan was finally looking to the future.

Whenever Nathan would leave the farm, the young man would open Seth's kennel, and the hound would jump into the front seat of his truck, barking and looking forward to the long rides through the country and into the nearby small towns. With the vehicle's passenger window rolled down slightly, Seth would stick his nose out the window, always sampling the wondrous scents, and always learning.

October arrived. One Saturday morning, with the tree leaves showing off their bright colors, Nathan took Seth into Painted Post to fetch some hardware. Once in town, Nathan snapped a leash onto Seth, and man and dog proceeded into the hardware store.

"What have we here?" J.P. Smith, the ever-large storeowner, beamed as he saw Nathan walk through the front door with the handsome, jet-black hound.

"This is Seth, J.P.," Nathan said, making formal introductions. "And Seth, this is J.P."

"So, this is the hound whose potential I've heard so much about!" J.P. smiled, and for his part, wagging his tail and clearly happy, Seth let out a roar. Other customers in the store looked up to see what had made such a booming noise. Most of the folks smiled politely and waved at J.P. and Nathan.

Most anyway . . .

"I've known your pa for many, many years, Nathan. He's not one to brag about anything—it's just not in your father's nature. But the way Jacob speaks about what this hound might do one day borders on such boastful talk!" J.P. winked at Nathan as he finished.

"He's yet to tree his first raccoon, but we're hopeful," Nathan said as he looked at Seth.

"How old is he now?"

Nathan thought for a moment and then replied, "Why, he's a little over eight months old now."

"And when does coon season start?" J.P. continued.

"Why, uhm, the season opens two weeks from today—exactly." Nathan had not thought of the coincidence.

"Are you going to take Seth out the first night?"

"Hadn't thought about it," Nathan admitted, "but it's not a bad idea!"

Seth roared again, appearing to agree with the idea of his first coon hunt.

J.P. could only laugh at the young hound's reaction.

"I need to get some hardware," Nathan informed J.P.

"I'm sure you know where it is. Nice to see you again, young man!" J.P. then turned his attention to a customer who had arrived at the register.

Nathan knew where the parts were, and he would have paid for the goods a full ten minutes earlier, but the sight of Seth had many people stopping to talk excitedly to the young man and his magnificent hound.

When Nathan proceeded to the store's front to make his purchase, at the counter stood Larry Allen. Larry looked haggard, as today it seemed that the illicit drug dealer had been sampling his wares again. As Nathan approached, it was also clear from J.P.'s annoyed look that he was repeating the total of the purchase as Larry's befuddled mind tried to count out the correct amount of money.

"*Forty-four dollars and fifty-eight cents,*" J.P. said, his voice bordering on exasperation.

It was not like Larry didn't have the money to pay for the purchase. The thick wad of twenty-dollar bills that he held in his hand displayed for all to see would have paid for the purchase many times over. But Larry's muddled mental state would not allow him to focus.

"Forty-four dollars and fifty-eight cents," Larry repeated in a slow, slurred speech.

As Nathan approached Larry, Seth did something that he had never heard his dog do previously. The young hound let out a loud, low growl as the canine's eyes locked on the drug dealer.

Dogs can be good judges of character that way.

The hound's threatening voice seemed to snap Larry into the present. His eyes flashed in alarm as the ebony dog came into focus. Reflexively, Larry raised his right hand high over his head to strike.

Nathan immediately stepped between the hound and Larry, and with a tone that was part command and part threat, offering a simple warning.

"You will *not* harm him." Nathan's voice held an edge far too familiar.

Larry then looked up, gasping as his body reflexively recoiled in fear when he recognized the form of Nathan Ernst standing before him. Quickly turning to J.P., he threw half the wad of money in his hand onto the countertop. "Keep the change!" Larry said, stumbling to the front door.

"You think you should be driving in your condition?" J.P. asked Larry.

"I'm not driving," Larry replied with a cryptic, crooked smile as he found the door handle.

Seth then stuck his head out from behind his master's protective stance, and with his eyes still on Larry, again let out a menacing growl.

Without further delay, the drug dealer fumbled with the latch, swung the door open, and scrambled out of the store.

Picking up the money left on the counter, J.P. looked at Nathan and then to Seth, still staring at the spot that Larry had but moments before occupied. "I like that hound even more!" J.P. grinned as he waved Larry's tendered payment in the air.

"I've never seen Seth do that before," Nathan said in a matter-of-fact and likewise non-apologetic tone.

"There's no accounting for taste," the sultry voice of Stella Wharton said as she breezed by J.P., Nathan, and Seth. Fashionably dressed as always, the attractive woman's high-heeled shoes clicked on the floor as she moved to the store front window to watch Larry stumble through the parking lot.

True to his word, the drug dealer walked over to a waiting, black town car. Stella watched the back door open, but she could not see who allowed Larry entry into the expensive conveyance. She readily imagined the vehicle's owner was either one of Larry's clients or his supplier. Once the door closed, the car left the parking lot and sped out of sight.

Nathan put the hardware on the countertop and reached for his wallet to purchase the goods, but J.P. Smith waved him off.

"No need to pay for that today," J.P. said as he smiled broadly and tucked Larry's tendered cash into the register. "That hardware is on the house on account of your wonderful hound."

Seth barked happily.

"Thanks, J.P.," Nathan said.

"He truly is an exceptional hound," J.P. said, wholeheartedly agreeing with his good friend Jacob's assessment of the young dog.

As Nathan reached into his pocket to pull out his truck keys, the sound of something hitting the hardwood floors rang out. He immediately fell to his hands and knees, searching for that which was so precious to him.

"Did you lose something?" J.P. asked as he leaned over the counter to see the young man looking frantically to find something.

"I dropped a stone," Nathan said with a hint of desperation in his voice.

"Oh, don't worry about that," J.P. said, completely oblivious to younger man's concern. "I sweep the floors every night before I go home. I'm sure that I'll find it."

"I have to have it!" Nathan nearly screamed.

As Nathan continued to search for the stone, J.P. looked at Seth, who returned the storeowner's gaze, cocking his head to one side puppy-like, apparently confused by his master's erratic behavior

"There!" Nathan exclaimed, finally locating the strangely colored stone. "There it is!" He took several steps, quickly grasped the stone, and this time, placed it securely in his shirt pocket.

"All okay, young man?" J.P. asked still, perplexed by the strange scene that had just played out before his eyes.

"All's well," Nathan confirmed, the consolation evident in his voice. He then added calmly, "All is fine—now."

J.P. nodded at Nathan's reassurance but was still confused by the young man's eccentric behavior.

"Thanks again, J.P. Come on, Seth," Nathan said and led the dog outside to his truck.

As the door shut, Stella and J.P. took one long look at one another and simultaneously shrugged, knowing neither could explain what they had just witnessed.

Larry Allen stepped outside the vehicle, holding three times the amount of cash that he had less than an hour before in J.P.'s General Merchandise & Hardware Store.

But this was an unusual transaction since it was normally Larry paying the car's occupants a large wad of cash for his illicit merchandise to sell retail on the streets. This instance, there was no exchange of any sort, except for an answer to a strange query, with Larry's solemn promise not to reveal anything about the conversation.

Luckily, Larry had known the information that the occupants—one individual in particular—had sought. He also knew that if he were ever to break his pledged vow of silence, he would pay for the breach of trust with his life.

These were dangerous men.

Still, Larry wondered as he watched the car drive off into the distance, why would anyone want to know where Jacob, Nathan, and Mead Ernst hunted raccoon?

It was the first night of coon hunting season.

Nathan yearned to take Seth to allow the older hound, Radar, to show the younger dog how to chase ringtails. Radar was a superb coonhound, without any bad habits to pass along, so he was an excellent candidate as a mentor.

Jacob agreed with Nathan's desire, not just because Jacob also wanted to see Seth properly trained, but also because his eldest son was taking a renewed interest in life.

Jacob knew coon hunting could have that effect.

With Jacob's truck loaded with the hunting gear and the hounds, father and son proceeded to a nearby public game management area. Driving to a pond where the raccoon would undoubtedly come to forage, they released the hounds, which immediately ran off into the shadowy woods beyond the hunters' headlights.

The men walked nearly one hundred yards from the parking area to the pond. Before they could get to the water's edge, Seth's voice rang loud in the night. Both men looked at each other but did not react to hearing a young hound on his first hunt. Many times, young hounds simply barked to bark, not truly indicating that they had located a coon's trail.

What mildly surprised the men several seconds later was the sound of the seasoned hound Radar's voice opening on a trail. From the locations of their bawls, the men could readily discern that the dogs were not together. The men took the meaning that the young hound was nonsensically barking, while the mature hound was doing the actual work of tracking the raccoon.

Seth's voice filled the night again several times, and when Radar next barked, it seemed that the older dog was following Seth's trail and not vice versa!

"Pa, you don't think . . ." Nathan's words hung in the air as Jacob showed a deep concentration, listening as both hounds were trail barking loud and fast.

"Nathan, I think Seth struck that coon before Radar, as hard to believe as that sounds."

Then, sounding practiced a thousand times over, Seth's voice switched over from a long trail bark to a loud, ringing chop bark. Less than thirty seconds later, Radar also began barking on the same tree.

Jacob verbalized what both were thinking. "Son, your nine-month-old pup just out struck and out treed the best hound we own."

"Beginner's luck, Pa?" Nathan suggested, although there was still an unmistakable hint of pride in the younger man's voice.

"Hard sayin'," was all Jacob could offer.

That night, the hounds would tree five times with five raccoon taken.

The theme that would capture the excitement of an entire village over the next week or so was neither the taking of the raccoons in that place nor the number.

Instead, the news that set tongues to wagging and wagers placed in small diners throughout Painted Post was that a nearly nine-month-old pup named Seth had outperformed a decent, five-year-old coonhound four out of five of those occasions.

In a single season, Seth's famed reputation as a top coonhound, "who could invent raccoon," grew. Out-of-town hunters would call upon the Ernst family household, asking to hunt with the young, fast-becoming-legend hound. Many of those "requests" were truly "challenges," all of which were accepted.

And without exception, Seth won every hunt.

At the end of one particular chase, a very well-to-do hunter from Ohio—his top hounds thoroughly beaten trailing and treeing coon behind Seth—made an offer.

"I'll give you ten thousand dollars in cash, right now, for that dog," the out-of-towner offered.

Both Jacob and Nathan looked at each other over the generous bid, and then Nathan spoke up.

"Seth is not for sale," Nathan informed the hunter. "Not now, not ever, not for any price."

"I can get another hunter to go in with me on the purchase, and we'll give you twelve thousand dollars for that hound!" the other hunter persisted.

"Not now, not ever, not for any price," Nathan repeated firmly, and the other hunter knew there was no sense in pursuing the purchase of the amazing hound.

Seth was born and would die on the Ernst farm as far as Nathan was concerned.

The next morning, Mead arrived on the farm with his fiancée, Sarah.

"Twelve thousand dollars!" Mead exclaimed as he sat at the kitchen table and let out a sheer whistle in disbelief. "You can do a lot with that kind of money!"

Both Jacob and Nathan nodded in agreement with their steaming cups of coffee in front of them.

"He's an exceptional hound," Jacob confirmed.

"I want to go coon hunting with this hound!" Sarah blurted out, shocking all three men, for none of them, Mead included, had ever heard Sarah mention hunting of any sort.

"Well, honey," Mead began somewhat sarcastically, "coon hunting is at night—in the woods."

"Don't you try to frighten me, Mead Ernst! I don't scare easy. Why I'm marrying you, aren't I?" Sarah smirked.

"She makes a good point." Nathan grinned at Jacob, who was also chuckling.

"I'm not afraid of these hills—especially not the ones I grew up in!" the feisty blonde continued.

"Okay," Mead said, teasing, "but don't expect me to hold your hand if you get scared!"

"Bah!" Sarah said, laughing, and with a short hop and a quick swipe of her hand, she swatted Mead's omnipresent and dingy baseball cap from his head. His hat landed on the floor in front of him.

"Why does everyone do that?" Mead asked, retrieving his hat from the floor for the umpteenth time.

That night, with the quartet of hunters, Seth proved worthy of this reputation and struck a raccoon's trail not more than fifty yards from their truck. Nathan had decided to hunt Seth alone tonight, and Jacob had agreed.

Nathan knew this decision was out of pure pride—to prove to Mead this hound could do it all—and by himself.

Jacob was happy for several reasons. This hunt was the first this season that he had both of his sons coon hunting with him again. Further, his someday daughter-in-law Sarah had shown an interest to see this amazing hound called Seth. The old coon hunter wanted to ensure that she had a good hunt, and he felt confident this young dog would deliver as promised.

Besides, if Sarah were to be the mother of his grandchildren someday, he hoped that she would approve of keeping the Ernst family coon hunting for another generation. Jacob often thought about such things.

When Seth did tree a short time later, his tree bark confused the seasoned coon hunters.

"Is he treed?" Mead asked, noting that there seemed to be a slight dislocation in the hound's voice from one minute to the next, although he appeared to repeat the pattern.

"I think so," Nathan said, admittedly bemused, also noting the slight changing locations of the hound's voice. He felt embarrassed that he could not explain Seth's behavior.

When both sons looked to their father for an explanation, even Jacob was forced to shrug.

They proceeded toward the treeing hound. The men were more than a little surprised not only to have Sarah keep up with them, but she led the way to the tree.

The mystery of why Seth's voice seemed to move from one place to another only grew deeper as they made their way closer to the coonhound. When they finally arrived at the hound's location, the hunting party watched as Seth ran nonsensically in circles, barking but not indicating which of the many trees nearby might contain the raccoon.

"I think your dog has gone plumb crazy!" Mead laughed, poking fun at his brother as the youngest Ernst bent over to plant his hand, and then chin, on top of his walking stick.

"What in the world is he doing, Pa?" Nathan looked at Jacob for help in trying to explain Seth's odd behavior.

"Son, I have no idea," Jacob said, baffled, as he, too, felt a bit mortified at this point, perhaps more so because of this being Sarah's first hunt.

"You might have wanted to take that offer of twelve thousand dollars!" Mead continued his goading.

Inexplicably, Seth roared and charged at Nathan and leaped into the air placing his huge front paws on his master's chest.

"What's the matter, boy?" Nathan asked his hound.

Slowly, Seth looked over at a tree to his right, and when Nathan's light followed the hound's eyes, there was a raccoon in the tree, staring at the commotion.

"There's the coon!" Sarah said delightedly.

Then Seth roared again, demanding the humans' attention, but this time, Seth looked to a tree to his left. When all turned their lights to search the tree, there in the branches was yet another raccoon looking at them.

"It can't be!" Mead first spoke, his teasing replaced with awe.

Satisfied that the quartet had located the second raccoon, Seth barked a third time, but this time, the hound leaned somewhat backward to look up yet another tree.

"Nah!" Mead said in disbelief but still added his headlight with the others to shine a third tree where not one, but two, sets of raccoon eyes reflected in their lights.

Seth, the growing legend, had treed four raccoons at once.

"Good boy, Seth!" Nathan's shouted, heard loud and clear throughout the forest.

Mead let out a loud whistle. "That dog simply isn't right in the head," the baffled, gentle giant said in sincere admiration.

———————•◦•———————

One week later, Nathan poured a hot cup of coffee in the kitchen. The sun had set, and thoughts of chasing ringtails with Seth were in the forefront of his mind. The moon was already out, and a light fog covered the ground as the warmer air battled the coming night's cold.

"Pa?" Nathan called out. The young man had not heard his father stirring in the house for a while. He knew Jacob would want to go coon hunting this night, so the silence in the house puzzled him.

With the warm cup in hand, Nathan left the kitchen, moved to the living room, and glanced out the front windows. He took a long sip of coffee, pleased to locate his father outside in the moonlight, but soon stood with mouth agape as he took in the complete scene.

In the moonlit mist, there was the ethereal form of a woman next to Jacob. Nathan could readily tell that the two were communicating, although he could not be sure from inside if Jacob was speaking aloud. The shorter form of the woman, so strange yet so familiar to Nathan, seemed to reach forward to take Jacob's hands. She looked up into his face, and even at this distance, her profound sadness filled Nathan's senses.

Jacob did not flinch as the ghostly figure reached out, but instead, the old coon hunter only looked at the ground and slowly nodded his head, acknowledging some mutual understanding.

The specter then stared directly at Nathan, and he swore the figure smiled at him; and with that smile, a sense of destiny manifested.

A breeze whipped up out of nowhere, and the ghostly figure of the woman dissipated in the fall air. Jacob stood, unmoving for several moments, and then he looked up at the bright moonlight.

Even at this distance, Nathan could feel his father sigh.

As Jacob turned, the old coon hunter made eye contact with his son. He seemed to stop for just a moment but then proceeded to the porch.

"Pa," Nathan, the younger man's voice incredulous, stopped Jacob at the doorway. "What did I just see?"

"I have to go coon hunting tonight," Jacob said, not addressing Nathan's query. The old coon hunter seemed distant and spoke like a man finishing a race.

"Well, Seth and I will go with you," Nathan offered.

Jacob looked up, his eyes were moist, but his voice was firm. "Not tonight, son. I need to go hunting alone—just to think," he said, managing a smile.

Nathan was baffled by his father's unusual response. "Are you sure, Pa?" He sensed at this point that it was useless arguing.

"God promises the destination, but the path itself isn't always of our own choosing; we only control the willingness to make the journey," Jacob said cryptically.

Jacob then put his still-strong hand on his son's shoulder. "There are some hunts where we have to go it alone, son," he explained somberly.

Jacob turned, and Nathan watched him put Cilla and Radar into the truck, both barking excitedly for they knew the routine. Seth bellowed his desire to join them, but Jacob calmed the anxious hound with some soft words. He started the engine and turned on the headlights. Nathan ran up to the truck, and Jacob, seeing his son approaching, slowly rolled down the vehicle's window.

"Where are you going hunting tonight, Pa?" Nathan hoped to get at least that much information from his father.

"Ryland Creek—where else?" Jacob tried to say with some muster in a joking manner, but he could tell that his son sensed that something still wasn't right. "Tell Mead . . .," His voice drifted off, and he seemed to stare through the younger man.

"Tell Mead what, Pa?" Nathan asked.

"Tell him I love him, and I love you too, boy," Jacob said as he put his hand over Nathan's hand that rested on the truck door.

"I will, Pa," Nathan promised. While his sense of alarm remained, he just repeated, "I will. I love you, too."

Butch snorted unusually long and loudly from the barn, apparently upset by something.

"What's gotten into Butch?" Nathan wondered.

"Hard sayin'," Jacob laughed, looking down and shaking his head. But he added with a much softer and oddly reminiscent tone, "Damn mule."

There was a long pause between the two men.

"There's a beautiful moon out tonight," Jacob finally said as he looked up at the silvery orb hanging above them. Nodding goodbye to Nathan, the old coon hunter rolled up his window and drove slowly down the road. Nathan watched as the night absorbed the vehicle's headlights.

That would be the last time that Nathan would see his father Jacob alive.

Chapter 17

Transitions

But nine years hence . . .

The last coon hunter pulled the trigger again to hear the sickening sound of the firing pin. His rifle was out of ammunition, and there was no time to reload. While he knew his last few shots had been true, and that it was moving blind and sluggishly now, the beast still moved toward the wounded hound. And, rather than run, the brave coonhound refused to back down.

The monstrous creature was feet now from the dog, and it felt a renewed sense of the purpose in these final moments.

One more deadly lunge, and this saga would be over.

The present . . .

S heriff Sean Covington pulled his police cruiser up to the side of the dusty back road, but he was not alone this night. The normally peaceful forest was lit up with the myriad flashing red lights of no less than ten official police and emergency vehicles and accompanying personnel that had arrived before him.

Steuben was Covington's county, and he knew every landmark intimately. He had seen many accidents and tragedies on these old, winding country roads. Tonight, however, Sean was responding to a call on his police radio, and the initial information that he had received from his deputy had been short and dreadful.

"Sheriff," the call from his deputy, John Cassady, had begun. "You better come out to Ryland Creek near the small bridge." There had been a long pause on the radio. Moreover, the next words that came from his veteran deputy came across choked.

"It's Jacob Ernst," Cassady had said. After another long pause, the deputy finally added, "And it's not good."

Fifteen minutes later, Sean opened the door and stepped out of his police cruiser. While he had not escaped the passage of time, the aging man was still lean and intimidating as he stood to his full height. Reaching into the car and placing his gray, wide-brimmed hat on his head, there was little doubt who was in charge whenever Covington entered a crime scene.

Deputy Cassady walked up to Sean. The wise, old sheriff smelled the vomitus on his subordinate's shirt, and the broken look on Cassady's face told Sean that the stain on that usually spotless uniform had been self-inflicted. Sean's suspicions were piqued, as he knew his deputy had witnessed many gruesome sights during his tenure on the police force. If this incident had shaken the veteran police officer's courage, what lie ahead could only be harrowing.

"Sean, it's Jacob," Cassady said, his voice still shaking. "He's been . . . and it wasn't . . .," the younger man's voice trailed off, unable to finish. Looking down at the ground, and with a barely perceptible motion of his head, he indicated that Sean should continue to the scene.

Sean put his hand briefly on Cassady's shoulder, to both comfort his deputy and bolster his fortitude as he moved forward.

A young New York State Trooper whom Sean had worked with before spotted the sheriff and walked up to him.

"Evening, Sheriff," the trooper greeted.

"Evening, Tom," Sean responded.

"I understand that you and Jacob Ernst were best friends."

"Yes," Sean said, and the older man did not miss the past tense in the trooper's statement.

Were best friends . . .

"It's not good, Sean," the young trooper said, maintaining his professional demeanor. "Jacob has been murdered, and from the looks of it, it was an execution. Whoever did this was lying in wait, and he knew Jacob would be here or possibly even followed him. We're still gathering evidence, but there are no witnesses that we know of just yet. The two teenagers who found him were coming back from the movies. They're in shock right now—it wouldn't do much good for you to talk to them till later."

Sean nodded and thanked the officer. He steeled his emotions as he moved past the ring of medical staff, who remained at a distance as crime scene investigators searched for any evidence that they could find. He knew the protocol—to stand back at this point and let the investigators collect the evidence—but for all his consummate professionalism, Sean stepped over the hastily placed yellow crime scene tape.

All eyes followed the tall, uniformed man moving closer to examine the body splayed out pitifully in the dirt, and no one moved to stop him. Painted Post was a small town, and everyone knew the lifelong friendship between the sheriff and the victim.

For a moment, Sean stepped out of his body and let his professional mind take over as he took in the grizzly scene.

The old, green canvas coat Jacob had worn for many years was stained and still wet with blood. Jacob had been shot five times—once in each shoulder, once in each knee, and the final shot perfectly aimed at the old coon hunter's heart.

The shots were precise, professional, and meant to cause an excruciating death.

Sean knew the young trooper had correctly assessed what had happened here this night—this had been an execution—and a particularly vengeful one at that.

A crime scene investigator whom Sean had never seen before passed the yellow tapeline to join the sheriff. The young man knelt near Jacob's cold body and shook his head. "Those holes," he noted, correctly assuming Sean was listening, "were made by a high-caliber gun. I'm guessing a .45 at this point." The investigator began shaking his head. "This is unbelievable."

"What's wrong?" Sean asked.

The investigator looked at the sheriff, his face highlighted by the pulsing flash of the many lights that surrounded them, and it was evident the man was in complete amazement.

"Look at the trail," the younger man continued, directing Sean's attention. "The blood from where the first shot occurred is at least fifteen feet from where the victim finally fell. The entrance wounds are all from the front. This man had moved *toward* his attacker as each bullet hit! That simply cannot be! How could anyone have withstood that kind of punishment?" Again, the man's voice drifted into silence.

"You didn't know Jacob Ernst, son," Sean said as he heard his voice crack slightly.

The investigator then stood and walked away into the night.

"You tough, old bastard," Sean whispered as he stared harder at the unmoving form that had been his best friend.

Another detail emerged—one that drove rage within Sean. The assailant had slit Jacob's throat. While there was some blood around the cut's edges, the sheriff's seasoned eyes told him that the cut had been made after Jacob's heart had stopped beating.

This last wound had been inflicted purely out of spite.

Sean looked up and noticed for the first time two other bodies lying prone. There beneath the outstretched limbs of the oak that covered parts of Ryland Creek, also facing the likely direction of the attacker, were Jacob's two coonhounds.

Sean spied one final detail—a ringed tail was partially showing from the back of the hunting coat, indicating that Jacob had been coming out of the woods after a successful night's hunt. That meant that the murderer had likely been lying in wait, had studied his prey, and knew exactly what to expect.

The young state trooper's initial assessment had been correct—Jacob Ernst's murder had been long in the planning.

Sean stood, saying a silent prayer over his friend's body. "I'll find the sonofabitch that did this to you, Jacob," he vowed.

The police and emergency professionals around the scene knew the sheriff to be an honorable man, who would never do them any harm. But an icy chill ran up their spines nonetheless upon hearing Sean's oath to his fallen friend.

Sean moved back toward his vehicle. Deputy Cassady, now more composed, tried to intercept him, seeking to comfort his boss. Sean's powerful arm swept Cassady out of his path with little effort.

Having worked with Sheriff Covington for many years, Cassady knew not to follow.

The sheriff moved to the back of his police vehicle and placed both hands on the trunk of the cruiser. Sean's head sunk to his chest, his brimmed hat falling to the ground as he closed his eyes.

And the toughest man in Steuben County wept.

Jacob's obituary in the local newspaper read that the longtime lover of the local forest, a kind and good man, who for decades had chased raccoon amongst these hills, had gone home to meet his Lord.

Father Simmons came out of retirement to say the funeral Mass. Stella Wharton and Miriam Helm, both dressed in black, openly sobbed, their tears running down their faces as they embraced each other.

J.P. Smith gave a rousing eulogy that did not leave a dry eye in the church.

"Perhaps a great man and friend to us all has died," J.P. intoned. "But another legend in our hometown has begun."

In touching display, Mead went up to the closed casket and placed Jacob's old, gray fedora on the polished oak wood. The mountain of a man then knelt down with both of his large hands gripping the sides of the casket, his huge body shaking as his tears stained the ground.

However, the eldest son of Jacob Ernst stood several feet back, silent, staring hard like he could see through the wooden coffin at his father's body. For many a year later, the town gossips would comment on the unnatural stoicism displayed that day by Nathan Ernst.

For on that day, Nathan slowly rolled a small, stained rock between his fingers and spoke to no one except a final thank you to Father Simmons.

They buried Jacob in the corner of the cemetery by the old maple, next to the graves of his father, mother, and his wife, Rose. On the tombstone, the simple epitaph read:

Here rests a true coon hunter
Lying next to whom he loved most
and died doing what he loved best.

———•◦•———

The local and statewide newspapers likewise reported the murder investigation of Jacob Ernst. The lack of clues and the frustration of the law enforcement personnel at making any progress to identify the killer drove a collective angst throughout the small, rural town.

Finally, after nearly six weeks, despite the strenuous objections of the local sheriff, state crime investigation officials declared the trail of the killer had gone cold, and the mystery of who had killed Jacob Ernst remained unsolved.

———•◦•———

Nearly two months after Jacob's funeral, Larry Allen waited nervously in the middle of the night on an abandoned, dirt road. The moon was bright tonight, and he could see clearly all about him in the ghostly light. His hand shook violently now, and while much of the loss of motor control was due to indulgence in the illegal drugs that he peddled, his whole body quaked even more so out of fear. For the man whom Larry was to meet tonight had a reputation for ruthlessness. These meetings with the top thug of his primary supplier were rare, but Larry knew never to disobey the order given by this man.

Larry's drug-addled brain thought this midnight rendezvous, far from prying eyes, seemed entirely appropriate, particularly for his illegitimate line of work. Larry stood outside the gates of the local hunting preserve as directed. There were not many visitors to the preserve at night as the paying "hunters" who participated in these "canned hunts" were not the kind of people who liked to venture into the woods at night.

And some of the "temporary residents" had just arrived. Just inside the 8-foot tall, wire entrance gate, but still locked in a smaller cage, was a Russian boar with four of her piglets. The sow's fearsome head and its razor-sharp tusks would someday grace the wall of some rich man who would tell stories of his bravery in killing the cornered beast.

"Been waiting long?" A voice came from behind Larry that nearly caused him to jump out of his skin.

Turning to see the enormous man, Larry was both relieved and simultaneously terrified.

"What is this place?" the man asked.

"It's a shooting preserve, man. Rich folks like to come here and shoot exotic animals. Where's your car, man?" Larry dared to ask.

"How apropos," the other said, and while his words sounded sinister to Larry, this man emanated evil, so nothing seemed necessarily out of place. "And I left my car back on the main road. We wouldn't want anyone to figure out that you and I are connected. Part of the profession—I'm sure you understand?"

"Yeah, man, no problem," Larry answered.

"Good. You're carrying a weapon," the man said.

The other's acute observation skills always amazed Larry. "Yeah, man, this is my baby," he said, referring to his nickel-plated .38 that he patted gently in its shoulder holster.

"Wonderful! It carries six shots, right?" the man asked.

"Yeah, and I shoot hollow points, too," Larry said, beaming with pride.

"Well, I have a job that we need you to do. And you'll need that," the man said as he pointed a gloved hand at Allen's revolver.

"Sure, man! Just tell me what you need, and I'll do it."

"First, I'd like to thank you for the information on Jacob Ernst. He was right where you told me he would be," the other said, relishing some memory.

While Larry might not have had much currency of any form in his morality vault, he was not stupid. When the local newspapers reported the news of Jacob's death, Larry had not missed the fact that Jacob's demise was very near the location that he had provided this man.

"And of course, you told no one about our little conversation, correct?"

"You know me!" Larry sounded offended. "I know what happens when someone talks out of turn!"

"And you've been following Nathan Ernst as I asked you to do?"

"Yeah! He takes his dog for a walk along Ryland Creek Road all the time. It varies when he goes, except for Saturdays—he always walks to the bridge on Ryland Creek around noon on Saturdays."

"I know that bridge," the man said with a smug grin. "Every Saturday at noon, you say?"

"Like clockwork, man!" Larry reaffirmed.

"And you're certain he did not see you following him?"

"Oh no, sir! I'm good at sneaking through the woods."

"Very, very good," the man said with an approving smile. The hitman did not doubt the veracity of Larry's claim, as he highly suspected that Allen was exceptionally devious—a common trait amongst their kind.

"Now, this job I need you to do. Are you any good with that piece?" He motioned to Larry's handgun and continued, "Can you hit what you aim at?"

"I'm a great shot!" Larry said, ever more confident.

"Let's put your assertion to the test, shall we?" the man said, but his eloquent words were again overshadowed by the vile acts that Larry knew this man had ordered others to do or personally perpetrated.

"Those pigs," he said, pointing to the cage. "Why don't you practice on them? There's plenty of moonlight tonight, so I trust you can see to aim your weapon?" The man continued without waiting to hear Larry's response. "Do you have some bolt cutters in your car?"

"Yeah, man!" Larry was enthusiastic.

"Please use them to open the gate and then the cage," the other instructed.

"Sure man!" Larry was keen on the idea of showing off his marksmanship as well as participating in some criminal mischief. He immediately rushed to his car's trunk, opened it, and rushed to the gate, placing the long-handled cutting tool on the padlock. Larry looked back seeking permission.

The other understood the hesitation. "Please—continue," he said, raising his gloved hands, directing Larry to proceed.

Larry grinned wickedly, and with a bit of effort, he managed to cut through the old padlock. He opened the rusted metal gate, and they stepped into the game preserve.

"Here's the test, my friend," the man explained. "There are five pigs in that cage. How wonderful! You will cut the lock on the cage, open it, and then you are allowed five shots. When you are finished, I expect to see five dead pigs on the ground. Am I clear? Take five shots—and five shots *only*."

"I got it," Larry said, nodding.

"Begin," the man said with a gratuitous smile.

Larry went over to the cage and cut the lock. The adult and her piglets naturally huddled at the opposite end of the enclosure, unsure of what was transpiring. The young piglets squealed, and the sow grunted loudly. Larry reached inside his shirt and pulled out his handgun. Once steadied, Larry swung open the heavy cage door, which gave a loud creak.

The pigs could now see there was an opening from their confinement, but at first, the piglets remained huddled around the safety of their mother. It took about thirty seconds, but finally one of the piglets bolted for the open door. Larry fired quickly, his bullet found its mark, and the small pig fell motionless in the dirt.

"Well done! Well done!" the man applauded.

The next piglet was not far behind, but it barely got two feet past its dead sibling when Larry once again fired and dropped the animal dead.

This time, the man clapped deliberately but said nothing.

The adult female boar now lunged forward. Its primitive brain had managed to realize that the human was the enemy here, and when it came out of the cage, it quickly turned, not away, but instead ran straight at Larry.

Terrified by the onslaught, Larry fired not once, but twice. Both shots hit the boar in its head and dropped the massive pig in the dirt but three feet in front of him.

"Sorry man, but she charged me." Larry apologized, knowing that he had violated the rules of the contest.

"That is quite understandable," the other said, nodding. "Let's see if you make the most of your *last* shot."

Before Larry could turn his attention back to the cage, the next piglet had already cleared the pen, dashed for the forest edge outside the perimeter fence, and slipped off into the night.

"It seems that little piggy is running all the way home!" the man joked. His look suddenly turned stern, and he held up his index finger and said, "One pig left, one shot left."

Larry nodded that he understood, and the last piglet, now desperate and alone, jolted out of the cage, but once again, Larry's marksmanship proved up to his former boast, and the last piglet lie in the dust next to its mother and fated siblings.

"Excellent!" the man again praised Larry's skill.

"Yeah, man!" Larry said, looking at the carnage before him in the silvery light. "Nice shooting, huh?"

Before Larry could say another word, the large man had closed the distance between them, grabbed Larry's hand that still held the revolver, and used the web of his other hand to capture Larry's elbow joint. The man's powerful arms slowly but effortlessly moved the end of the gun to rest beneath Larry's chin. He could not drop the weapon since the man's vicelike grip held it in place.

"What are you doing, man?" Larry screamed between his clenched jaws. "I did what you asked!" He was begging now, and he knew, pleading for his life.

"Yes, you did precisely what I asked, and I thank you!" the man said with false gratitude.

"Why?" Larry screamed, knowing his life would be over in moments. He tried to hit the man with his other arm, but the assassin had skillfully stepped in so that his attempts to strike were ineffective.

"Well, you see, I don't like loose ends." With nothing further to say, the man forced Larry's finger down on the trigger to fire the last bullet through Larry's chin and into the brain. Blood splattered on his face, but accustomed to gore, the murderer merely let the body fall hard to the cold ground.

"As it turns out," the sinister man said, grinning at Larry's cooling corpse, "there are five dead pigs on the ground after all."

He stared at the motionless form, satisfied there was no need to position the body differently. Police investigators would believe that Larry's death had been nothing more than the suicide of a local figure known to be a petty drug dealer.

The man reached into his pocket and pulled out an expensive, white handkerchief to wipe the blood from his face. He had studied the terrain long before the encounter and felt sure the shots should have gone unheard. Still, the man was no fool, and he left the crime scene quickly.

When he made it to the end of the road, the man produced a penlight from his coat and signaled to his subordinate. Upon seeing the light, the henchman turned the ignition switch, and the vehicle's engine roared to life. The sedan pulled up quickly and stopped. The large man opened the door and entered. There was no need to direct his well-trained lackey on what to do next, and they sped away.

Ah, the man thought, just a few more lives to end before I can quit visiting this godforsaken town.

The final reckoning for the reproach could wait, though. For this man was good at what he did—superb in fact—and waiting for just the right moment was a skill that he had mastered a long time ago.

When the night had settled, and the other enemy had left, the one remaining piglet returned to the cage to find the cold bodies of its mother, siblings, and the dead human.

Its primitive brain could not comprehend what had happened this night, but it knew death, and felt something close to human rage. It seethed with its unique form of emotion, looking at the lifeless form of Larry Allen. It also instinctively sensed that it must leave now, for more of the enemy would arrive soon. With one last look at the lifeless bodies around it, the piglet escaped into the dark forest.

A few days later, the murderer calmly drank some coffee as he read the local Painted Post newspaper. Just as predicted, precisely according to his plan, the local police authorities had ruled Larry Allen's death as a suicide—the article concluding that it was a sad ending to a tragic life gone awry.

Perfect. The nefarious man grinned wickedly as his thoughts continued to play out.

Soon, he mused, this little drama ends.

Chapter 18

Retribution

Nathan walked out the front door with a leash in one hand. It was midday now, and the sun shone on a beautiful Saturday. All the hounds barked excitedly to see their master emerge from the house.

Nathan approached Seth's pen. The powerful, black hound roared in excitement as his master opened the pen door and snapped the leash on his collar.

"C'mon boy, let's go for a walk," he said, with just a hint of happiness. Truth be told, little brought Nathan Ernst much pleasure anymore.

Since Jacob's murder, Nathan had again retreated from the world of men although he made an effort a couple of times each week to see his brother. Mead and Sarah were newlyweds, and Sarah was pregnant with their first child. He would occasionally drive into Painted Post for supplies, but a cursory conversation with any well-wisher revealed a profound underpinning of sadness in the young man.

Whatever promise Nathan once had of being something in this life had died twice on a solitary, rural bridge.

The familiar walk's destination with Seth was the very bridge where Sharon and Jacob had met their fates. The routine had become an unsaid promise made to their memories. Nathan went there to listen to the creek's water rush below the small bridge. Even during inclement weather, he would still make the journey with Seth. The tough coonhound was not bothered by any weather, the unbreakable bond between man and dog supplanting any thoughts of physical discomfort.

Today would be no different—a quiet walk with only a few words of encouragement to Seth.

Nathan and Seth made their way along the country road. They followed Ryland Creek's curvy trek to the small bridge nearly a mile away. Now and again, Seth would catch some critter's scent and bound to the end of the leash. His strong arms would gently pull the dog back with a reassuring tone, promising that there would be a time for chasing wild game later.

Nathan still hunted ringtails with Seth. Continuing to roam these hills is what Jacob would have wanted, he reasoned.

In about twenty minutes, they reached the bridge. Nathan unsnapped Seth from his leash. The loyal hound knew to stay nearby and allow his master to stare into the cold water that flowed below the bridge. The canine could not comprehend the reason for his master's long silences, but Seth did understand that his role—wait and allow the man time to heal. When the time came, Nathan would hook up his leash and begin their journey home.

Nathan reached into his shirt pocket and pulled out the small, oddly stained stone. He rolled it between his fingers as he had a thousand times before—many occasions in this very spot. Looking down at the rock for a long period and facing the creek, Nathan cocked his arm to throw it. He held his arm in place for less than a minute, but then let his hand fall to his side, still maintaining his grip on the keepsake.

"Not yet," came the oft-made promise, barely above a whisper, while Nathan looked up at the bright sky. "Not just yet," he repeated and put the stone back into his pants' front pocket.

Nathan heard the sound of an engine and watched as a shiny black town car drove slowly toward him. That was unusual, he thought, to see such a luxurious vehicle on this backcountry road at any time of day.

It was even more surprising when the car came to a stop and parked on the far side of the bridge. The door opened, Nathan noting how much quieter it was than his old truck doors, and a man in a black suit, perfectly cropped beard, and dark sunglasses emerged. The man was huge as he stood to his full height and must have weighed well over three hundred pounds.

Seth instinctively growled.

"Easy boy," Nathan said, looking down at the hound and back at the man walking onto the bridge. "Lost mister?"

"Oh no." The big man smirked removing his sunglasses. "I've come here to find you, Nathan Ernst. Tsk, tsk! You really shouldn't be so predictable," the man said, scolding as if speaking to a child.

"How'd you know where to find me?"

"Oh, your old friend Larry Allen told me how you and your family like this road so much. It was only a matter of time before I found you here alone."

"Larry committed suicide a few weeks ago," Nathan thought to inform the man.

"Oh," the man said, leaning over slightly, sharing a secret, "it was no suicide." He then added in a matter-of-fact tone, "I killed him."

Nathan absorbed the news silently as the man slowly peeled off his coat, revealing a shoulder-holstered pistol.

"My name is . . .," the man began.

"Carlos," Nathan said, completing the other's introduction.

"Yes! My name is Carlos. I am flattered that you remember! Oh, this?" Carlos said, following the other man's eyes to the weapon strapped to his side. The menacing man pulled the chrome-plated pistol out of its holster and pointed it casually in Nathan's direction. "I won't need this," Carlos said smugly. He bent slowly at his knees, the killer never taking his eyes off Nathan, and placed the handgun on the ground.

Then Carlos pulled out a large, shiny knife expertly concealed in a small sheath at his waist. Carlos pointed the disclosed six-inch blade at Nathan in a similar manner as he had the pistol but just shook his head slowly.

"And no, I won't need this either," Carlos said with an air of regret, and with the same exaggerated motion, he gently set the blade beside the pistol—his "tools of the trade."

"But I should add—cutting implements are useful!" Carlos rose to show off his massive stature. "Why, you can use them to cut a brake line just ever so slightly. Now, you don't want to make the cut too deep."

Carlos motioned with one hand in the air, grabbing an imaginary strand in front of him. "If you cut it too deeply, the fluid will run out immediately, and the driver will sense a problem with her brakes far too soon.

"But if you cut it just right," Carlos now moved his hands in a sawing motion, "she won't realize that she does not have brakes until it's too late."

The thug paused to let his words sink in. While he did not see the other's spirit collapse as hoped, Carlos knew that Nathan had correctly understood what the hitman had perpetrated in cutting Sharon's brake lines.

The day that Nathan had lost his soulmate.

Part of Carlos was happy that his intended victim did not fall to the ground, an utterly defeated man. He wanted to physically break this country hick outright, knowing that an enraged opponent often made mistakes in a fight.

However, the sadistic part of Carlos was not overly satisfied with Nathan's continued silence. No matter, the assassin silently reasoned, he would have to get his final satisfaction by beating the life out of the man.

"You're just like your old man." Carlos continued his taunt. "He went down hard. I have never witnessed a man take five shots like that before." The predator saw in Nathan's eyes that the younger man made the mental connections and believed the murderer's every word.

Seth instinctively growled, but Nathan motioned with his hand, and the dog obediently stopped.

"Your dog will die just like your old man's mutts," Carlos said, staring in mimicked sadness at the hound and then slowly turning to face Nathan again. "Once I'm through with you, of course." Carlos's tone sounded of pure malice.

"Just like that cute little thing that bussed tables at the bar. She was your bride-to-be? Bet she was good in bed, too, eh?"

The big man remained disappointed at first as his prey stood, unmoving. But Carlos's profession demanded the ability to foresee an opponent's next move, and the hitman caught something in Nathan's expression.

"Oh my—she was a virgin! Tsk, tsk—what a shame! If I had known that, I would have done the honors just to let her know what a real man was like."

Finally! The sadist was satisfied for he could now see Nathan's eyes, suddenly burning with anger—undeniable hatred where there had been nothing previously.

Perfect, the antagonist thought. Now his prey would make missteps and be an easy target.

"Now, I saw you that day in the bar," Carlos continued while unbuttoning his white dress shirt's cuffs and rolling up the sleeves. "You never threw a punch the whole time—not like your brother and your old man. You only grabbed, pushed and pulled. I'm betting you can't throw a punch like that oaf of a brother. Mead, I believe is his name?

"Nor do I suspect that you can hit like that old, now dead, father of yours," Carlos said, spitting on the ground, remembering the thorough beating that he had taken at Jacob's hands.

"I had hoped that you and your brother were going to be hunting that night when I killed your father. I could have just been done with this messy business. But no!" Carlos said sarcastically. "You had to stay home that night and force me to wait in this pissant town to finish the job. For inconveniencing me so, you will have to pay for that.

"You do understand? I could not let your father's insult stand. It's not good for our reputation. People begin to lose respect, begin to no longer fear you if you do not always show them there is a reason for their fear. Killing Jacob Ernst was a necessity, I admit, but a duty I also enjoyed immensely.

"And now," Carlos said, spreading his arms wide and looking around at the quiet forested place, "you, too, are going to die in the same place as your father and the bride that you *almost* married. Kind of poetic in a way, don't you think?"

Nathan moved now, shoving his hand into one pants pocket, and removed something. He hesitated, glancing down at the object, but then suddenly threw it hard.

The small, round stone came so close to Carlos's left ear that the hitman felt the air move as it passed by. "Hah!" Carlos laughed derisively for what seemed to be a buffoonish attempt to assault the assassin. "You missed!"

Very clearly, as the stone landed in the creek water behind Carlos, a loud sound broke the forest's air.

Kerplunk!

"Not exactly," Nathan responded evenly, with no hint of fear.

Now a chill ran up Carlos's spine. The thug could sense in his opponent's tone the determination that seemed to run in the Ernst family. Carlos surged forward and unleashed a powerful right cross, punching Nathan solidly with all his might.

Nathan's head jerked, and he fell to one knee, looking at the ground from the considerably forceful blow, making no attempt to counterattack.

"I suspect that hurt some?" Carlos asked vindictively.

"What know you of pain?" came the words as Nathan knelt, but the voice that spoke was distinctly feminine.

The big man's eyes went wide with amazement. Although Carlos should not have recognized the voice, he somehow knew that it was Sharon Helm speaking.

Seth growled deeply and instinctively took a step forward.

"I've got this, Seth." Nathan looked at his loyal hound and waved for the dog to stay put.

"Oh, by the way," Carlos began, trying to regain his composure as Nathan stood again and looked at the murderer defiantly. "Did I mention that once I am through with you, I'm going to kill your brother Mead? I won't bother to fight him hand-to-hand, though," Carlos said, motioning with his head back to the weapons. "I'll just put a bullet hole in his skull.

"Of course, there is that young wife of his to take care of, too. Can't leave any witnesses, you understand." Carlos grinned maliciously as Nathan's lip curled ever so slightly. He hoped that he'd hit another mark in his opponent's psyche, which would make the pain that much more intense.

Carlos lurched forward, landing another devastating blow to his opponent's head. Again, Nathan fell to one knee, looking at the ground.

"You're going to die alone, my friend," Carlos assured, looking down at Nathan.

"He is not alone!" The voice, unmistakably that of Jacob Ernst, rang aloud once more in the land the old coon hunter had known so well. "And this forest stands against you!"

Carlos went pale as his blood turned to ice.

What was happening?

Nathan looked up, rising again to his feet with his eyes on Carlos. If there was any hint that the henchman's punches had damaged his enemy, it was not apparent.

Let it go! Nathan heard Sharon's voice in his head. He glanced down to his hand, watched his fingers curl into a tight fist, and then looked back at Carlos.

"And now my friend, this little soiree ends," the outsider said, shaken and unable to disguise the loss of his former bluster.

"You talk too much." Nathan seethed. "And you're not my friend," added the man from Painted Post, his voice his own once more, sounding like someone reading an epitaph.

Carlos threw his massive, clenched hand streaming toward Nathan's throat with what he was sure would be the final crippling strike.

Amazingly, the smaller man's left hand snapped forward, catching Carlos's fist, stopping it in midair as if the wicked man had hit a wall!

Carlos's mind screamed. *Again? Impossible!*

The hitman remembered that day in the bar, how Jacob had perpetrated the same unbelievable stunt, and Carlos felt cold fear permeate as he gazed into the unfettered eyes of Nathan Ernst.

With his right hand, Nathan struck the giant with such power! Carlos had *never* been hit that hard in his life—not even Jacob Ernst's punch had been that forceful. With that single punch, the big man's knees nearly buckled.

Nathan punched *through*—his long-held rage suddenly released like the waters of a massive dam.

"My father said that I had the hardest punch of anyone he ever knew." Nathan remained unbearably polite.

Nathan resumed his assault, landing blow after blow as Carlos staggered backward, unable to stop the coon hunter's fury. Each punch Nathan threw seemed miraculously harder than the last.

With each retreating step, the large man moved toward the bridge's edge. With one especially well-aimed punch, Carlos's face became covered with blood.

As the large man's consciousness began to fade under the vicious barrage, Carlos suddenly felt a strong arm grab his shirt, now stained with his blood, which kept him upright.

"Stay away from my family!" Nathan landed a final blow, which sent the man flying backways to land on the bridge's surface, with Carlos hitting his head hard on the bridge's metal guide rail.

The coon hunter stared down at the defeated hunter of men. "If I ever see you in Painted Post again, I'll finish this," Nathan growled ominously.

"Seth!" he called to his hound to leave this place. "Let's go." Nathan turned back to look at Carlos upon hearing a noisy motion as the bloodied man tried to get up. However, Carlos now held his pistol as he finally managed to stand upright on wobbly legs.

"You stupid country hick!" Carlos squeezed the words through his bloody teeth. "You just don't get it, do you? You're going to die today, one way, or the other." He aimed his weapon, though dizzy as he tried to see through the blurred vision of the one eye that had not already swollen shut.

A loud, long, vicious howl erupted from the forest. The eerie, booming sound seemed to come from everywhere, and nowhere, all at once. Nathan and Seth stood transfixed, but without fear, by the resonating sound that they had never heard before in the forests of Painted Post—their home.

"What was that?" Carlos could not hide the terror in his voice as he looked about the woods for the source of the terrifying sound to emerge.

Nathan looked squarely at the evil man who had despoiled the pristine forests of Ryland Creek. "I believe that would be Samuel—Sam for short," he said cryptically, yet somehow knowing that his assertion was correct.

Carlos was an excellent marksman, but in his battered condition and further shaken by the ghostly sound, his aim was off ever so slightly as he squeezed the trigger. The round missed Nathan's heart and instead struck deep into his shoulder.

While his body jerked under the impact of the bullet, Nathan regained his stance and stared back at the murderer.

There it is again, Carlos thought, seeing the son standing defiantly, just as Jacob Ernst had that night not so long ago. No matter, Carlos reasoned, trying to stem the rising panic in his chest. The assassin readjusted his aim, confident now that he would finish this country bumpkin.

Seth then roared, and with his incredible speed, charged Carlos.

Startled by the sound, the big man turned to face the rushing dog, pointed his gun, and fired repeatedly. The bullets, three in all, sprang up spurts of dust just behind the fast-moving canine.

Seth launched his considerable weight through the air, hitting the big man squarely in the chest. The bridge's guide rail caught the back of the man's legs just behind the knees, and both hound and villain began to fall over the bridge's edge to the sharp rocks below.

Two strong arms reached out to encircle the hound and pulled Seth back to safety as the gangster plunged over the side of the rail, shrieking and grasping for something to hold.

Moments later, the screaming stopped as Carlos impacted hard on the rocks below, instantly severing his spinal column.

The creek's shallow but cold water flowed about the paralyzed man as he saw Nathan holding Seth in his arms nearly fifteen feet above within the safety of the bridge rail.

Carlos listened to the last words that he would ever hear in this world as Nathan looked down at him in pity, and the blackness of death encircled the dying man.

"You gotta lead 'em," was all Nathan Ernst said.

Nathan was still staring down at Carlos's motionless body when he heard the sound of another vehicle approaching. He turned slowly, his wounded shoulder hampering his movement, and gently put Seth back on solid ground.

This time, the vehicle that approached was familiar—that of the local sheriff's patrol car.

Sheriff Sean Covington stepped out of his police cruiser with his tall form moving toward Nathan with purpose. Nodding his head as he looked at the black town car, it was clear that Sean was not surprised at what he was finding. However, what caused the graying law enforcement officer to show a paternal concern was the sight of Nathan's bleeding shoulder wound.

As Sean neared, Nathan motioned for him to look over the guide rail at the lifeless form of Carlos in the water below.

"He—" Nathan began.

"Fell," Sean quickly interrupted. "Yes, he fell plumb over the railing." Sean continued, "Damned guide rails can be dangerous when city folk, especially thugs from Chicago tend to show up."

Sean's insight into Carlos's identity confused Nathan.

"He drove his town car through Painted Post this morning," Sean explained. "I ran the plate numbers. It would seem that Carlos Leonard Renthro has something of a sordid criminal history. He was implicated in numerous crimes—murder, extortion, rape—but always seemed to beat the rap in Chicago." Sean paused and then added, "Other than visiting a local waterhole, I guess he never spent much time here."

"Carlos spent more time here than we knew." Nathan's words came out labored due to the pain from the gunshot wound. "He cut Sharon's brake lines and killed Larry Allen. He also said that he shot Pa five times and killed his hounds."

Sean's eyes narrowed at this news. "Those were details of Jacob's death that we intentionally never released to the public—neither the number of shots nor the killing of the hounds. This Carlos was the one then. . . ." His voice drifted off, a chapter closing in his life, and he leaned over the rail one last time to look at Carlos's corpse. "Yes, sir, Renthro accidentally fell over the damned rails." He continued to tap the rails with both hands. He then added venomously, "That piece of filth didn't fall fast enough or hard enough as far as I'm concerned."

Nathan grimaced, feeling the pain in his shoulder.

"You best get that taken care of," Sean advised.

Nathan nodded in silence and motioned for Seth to follow. The black hound fell beside his master as they began the long walk home.

"I probably wouldn't be here if Seth hadn't intervened," Nathan said, stopping to look back at Sean once more.

"He's truly an exceptional hound," Sean confirmed, looking at Seth with an approving smile.

The next day, Sheriff Sean Covington, the toughest man in Steuben County, announced his retirement from the police force.

The spirit of Carlos Leonard Renthro rose from his dead body. He could see Nathan putting the hound on the ground as he spoke with the uniformed lawman. The former hitman even saw the police officer look over the rail at his body, evidently satisfied that Carlos was dead.

Carlos's spirit screamed at a world now deaf to his voice. For all of Carlos's perfect scheming, for all the dastardly deeds committed without remorse, he had made one final, egregious and eternal mistake.

For Carlos had been a bad man—a very bad man.

And he had died in the forests of Painted Post.

Suddenly, an incredibly powerful force snatched Carlos. As he turned, his ghostly eyes beheld what he somehow knew to be the spirit of an ancient Native American. The chief's aura glowed bright white, emanating with power, and he held a tomahawk of fire.

Had Sheriff Covington or Nathan not been lost in conversation, they would have seen Carlos's body thrashing in that cold creek. Likely, they both would have deduced the convulsions were only the final death throes of a man who had met his deserved fate.

They would have been wrong about that.

Carlos tried to break the other spirit's grip, but he could not wrest himself free. The spirit took him through the air to a copse of large, mangled trees. Carlos realized that he could look inside these trees and see tortured souls. There were other evil men, just like him, trapped in the Black Oaks of Ryland Creek.

The chief pressed Carlos's spirit against one particularly gnarled tree, and slowly Carlos became absorbed into the tree itself. As he searched for help, the former hitman saw two other ghostly figures watching the ordeal silently. The chief stopped pushing Carlos, hesitating as he turned to the other ethereal beings, seeking final approval.

Carlos recognized them and screamed curses.

They did not look at him but rather stared directly at the chief. The taller of the two spirits then looked to the ground and nodded reluctantly with a grim resolution. The smaller figure turned away from the scene, knowing too well what was about to happen. With that final consent, the chief's spirit pushed Carlos's nefarious soul deep into the black oak.

Carlos's essence filled into the twisted limbs of the tree. His consumption was pure torture. He felt every insect boring into the wood like a thousand needles were sticking him. When the wind blew through Ryland Creek, and those tree limbs moved even more, Carlos's spirit cried out in sheer agony alongside the other evil people who had unwittingly died in this place.

To most in the world of the living, that agonized sound was only the creaking of the Black Oaks of Ryland Creek, benignly groaning under the weight of the wind.

Others who knew of the legends believed otherwise.

It was Painted Post, after all.

Chapter 19

Going Home

1993

N athan stepped out of his pickup truck in the middle of the forest and onto the soft snow that glistened in the moonlight. He reached into his vehicle, pulled out his .22 rifle, and threaded the weapon's sling with his right arm to have the gun rest naturally across the middle of his back. His face tightened for a moment as he felt a dull pain in his shoulder caused by the gunshot wound that he had received nearly nine years before.

Nathan's white hair hung loosely down to his shoulders. Although aged nearly thirty years, he looked much older.

He smiled, remembering the conversation with his brother only an hour before as Nathan had headed out to hunt this night.

"Be sure to be over in the morning. The kids want to see Uncle Nathan and hear about the coon hunt," Mead had said.

Nathan, the childless bachelor, had promised that he would join them, and he very much enjoyed telling stories to Mead's progeny, "little" Sharon and John.

"Oh, can I go with you, Uncle Nathan! Please, please, please!" Little Sharon had implored, tugging on her uncle's hunting coat.

Nathan looked down at his nine-year-old niece, barefoot in her pajamas, getting ready for bed. "I'll take you next time, honey," he said, bending over to kiss her light-blonde hair. He quickly added, "I promise."

It was fitting, Nathan thought, that someone should have the name "Sharon Ernst," and Mead and Sarah had made it so out of respect for love once lost.

"What about me?" John screamed happily, running around the corner, also dressed for bed, and vying for his Uncle Nathan's attention.

"Yes, you, too," Nathan said, grinning as he looked at Mead. "Now off to bed with you, before your mother gives me the what for!"

Both children laughed as they ran to their beds, thinking of the future when they would be able to hunt raccoon alongside their Uncle Nathan.

"Where are you going hunting tonight?" Mead asked when his children were out of sight.

"Ryland Creek," Nathan replied.

"Which hounds are you taking tonight?"

"Buck and Tye," Nathan said.

"They're good-looking hounds," Mead affirmed having seen the hounds on many visits to the Ernst farm.

As the brothers stood in the doorway, Mead grabbed Nathan's arm as his older brother turned to head to his truck and the waiting hounds.

"Nathan—the moon," Mead said, motioning to the familiar silver plate that stood over the darkening forests. "Remember what the legends say about the full moon and Ryland Creek."

"Pa knew," Nathan said enigmatically.

"Pa knew what?" Mead asked, not comprehending his brother's gist.

"Pa knew he was going to die that night. He wouldn't let me and Seth go coon hunting with him." Nathan stopped short of mentioning the specter he'd witnessed the night Jacob died, those many years before.

"Nathan," Mead spoke slowly and deliberately. "A long time ago, you told me that Ma's death wasn't my doing. Now I'll say the same to you. Pa was murdered that night. It wasn't your fault that you couldn't be there. The odds are that you would have been killed that night, too. There's no reason to feel guilty. You always take too much on your shoulders."

"Perhaps," Nathan said as he looked up at the large moon. After a short pause, he added, "Are you ever going to chase ringtails again, little brother?" He chided his brother, reminding Mead that he had not once stepped back into the woods to chase raccoon since Jacob's death.

"Someday, Nate," Mead said with no small measure of guilt in his voice. "Working and helping Sarah with these young'uns takes a lot of my time. But someday soon I'll join you again."

Nathan nodded, accepting his brother's promise.

"Are you going to have a family of your own, someday?" Mead asked ever so bluntly.

"My hounds are my family now," Nathan responded with a smile. While he had asked the question sincerely, Mead showed no surprise at Nathan's response.

The brothers then took one long look at each other as Nathan resumed his walk toward his truck. The coonhounds, sensing their master's proximity, barked excitedly within their coops.

As Nathan climbed into his truck and started the engine, Mead waved with a reminder.

"Don't forget! Sarah will have blueberry pancakes ready for you in the morning!" Mead shouted.

Nathan gave Mead one last look inside the truck's dimly lit cab and rendered a polite salute, acknowledging Mead's invitation. Nathan shifted his vehicle into drive and headed down the road.

Beneath that same full moon on the ever-dusty Ryland Creek Road, Nathan parked his truck. He stepped out and retrieved his walking stick from the truck's bed. The staff was over five feet long and slender but made of sturdy oak. The coon hunter needed the staff now since he was not as steady as he had once been running these hills in his youth.

It was the way of things, he knew.

Nathan reached for the latch and engaged it to drop the tailgate. Buck and Tye sprung from their adjacent coops as Nathan released the door catches, and the hounds raced down the trail into the forest. Both dogs had been on this hunt many times before and knew where to find a raccoon.

Nathan grasped his walking stick and trod along the path with his headlight following the hounds' tracks in the snow. He finally came to the spot where they had departed the trail and gone into the woods.

234

He walked another hundred yards and smiled when Tye, and seconds later, Buck, opened with their loud trail barks. They had found their prey and were in full pursuit.

Nathan closed his eyes, listening to the hounds bawling, and imagining his niece Sharon's bright eyes as she sat on his lap when he would retell this story to her tomorrow. She always wanted to know all the details of each foray into the forest; she was indeed an Ernst!

As the hounds continued to trail, Nathan looked down at the snow, finding a pair of huge tracks. These imprints were shaped similarly to a deer, but this woodsman knew immediately that this spoor was not that of any whitetail buck. These tracks were that of a pig—a large one, by the looks of it. He recalled the story of a wild pig getting loose from a game farm nearly thirty miles away. Further, this purported refugee was a dangerous Russian boar and to be avoided at all costs.

Nathan shook off a nagging fear. The boar would likely run in the opposite direction as soon as it heard the hounds, he reasoned. Still, the hairs rose on the back of his neck, and his senses heightened.

———— • ————

The boar heard them, and the rage that came so naturally, became unleashed. The hounds were easy to locate as their trail barks filled the night air. While it had been in this part of the forest for only a few weeks, the hog already had full knowledge of the lay of the land.

In its primitive mind, the pig knew that the Enemy would not be far behind the hounds. With its sheer power now, it feared nothing in these woods. There was nothing that it could not rend with its tusks. Tonight, it would meet the Enemy and let the man know that this forest belonged to it.

The hog moved its massive five-hundred-pound bulk effortlessly through the soft snow, which masked the sound of its approach. Although old now, having lived considerably longer than others of its kind, it showed no infirmities of age.

This night, there would be a final reckoning.

———— • ————

The chase continued as Nathan coursed the hounds and tried to keep up. The steep terrain and his age were not helping, he knew, but he walked on without complaint.

Pa never approved of carping, Nathan scolded himself.

The thought of his father caused his throat to tighten for a moment, and his gait slowed. The coon hunter shook his head to clear his mind.

Tye sounded a long locate howl. Buck, not to be outdone, immediately let out his treed barks, confirming the location of the raccoon.

"Well done, boys," he said aloud.

Nathan estimated that his dogs were only two hundred yards away. He would be there shortly.

The hounds were no longer moving and solely focused on their raccoon prey; just as it now sought them.

The boar tested the air with its long snout—its olfactory senses were even keener than that of the black and tan coonhounds. There was a slight breeze, and it quickly found the smell of the dogs.

There was something else in the wind! It could sense the Enemy, and it immediately determined the man's pending approach via the telling scent trail in the air.

It moved silently toward the hounds—toward conflict—to their shared destiny.

Whoa!

Nathan was thankful for his walking stick, as he had almost lost his balance while fording a small, iced-over creek as he headed to the hounds. He was still a little over one hundred yards away from them and berated himself for his slow going. The coon hunter knew better than to move too quickly through the woods, though—a lesson learned long ago.

"That coon isn't goin' anywhere, son."

Nathan stopped, startled as he heard his father's voice. He paused but then shook his head, thinking that he must be imagining things.

Nathan began moving through the forest again and passed through a copse of maples whose colorful fall leaves were now long gone. The lack of a leafy canopy allowed the moon to illuminate the white snow in the pristine forest. He turned off his headlight since the soft lunar glow was more than enough to see.

"Stop and see the wonder that is all around you. Feel the magic that is this place!"

Sharon's voice, his long-lost Sharon, rang so loudly in his ears that Nathan stopped again and glanced to his left from where he had imagined the sound emanated. There in the moonlight, the mist rose to form the shape of a young woman.

"Sharon?" Nathan heard himself say her name, as if listening to another speak. He ran toward the spirit, absently dropping his walking stick.

"All things return upon themselves, my beloved Nathan," the misty figure said.

Nathan heard the prophetic words and watched as the form gently dissipated but a few feet away from where he stopped. Just before the vision completely vanished, he was able to make out a ghostly, delicate hand reaching, beckoning him to follow. He felt no fear. Instead, an inexplicable calm entered him—a solace that he'd not known in many, many years. He gasped suddenly, not out of any sense of foreboding, but because he'd been holding his breath.

The hounds' loud barking broke him out of his reverie. Nathan walked back, stooped to pick up his walking stick, and reoriented himself to the hounds' barking.

Perhaps this would be the night, then. Nathan could not foretell what lie in front of him. What he did know was that he stood in the woods of Ryland Creek, in the land of the Painted Post, and anything could happen.

No matter, Nathan thought, God hates a coward.

And a smile slowly crossed the last coon hunter's face.

The boar's stealth had been perfect. The hounds had not picked up its scent as it had been careful to maintain its downwind trek toward them. Although its eyes were not as sharp as a canine, visual acuity was unnecessary now for it knew the precise location of the hounds.

Further, the canines remained focused, treeing beneath an ancient oak, adding to the chance of a complete surprise attack. It was an appropriate place as many things begin and end beneath oak trees on Ryland Creek.

By the scent now thick in the air, the monstrous hog judged that the Enemy had neared—just beyond the creek's bank. It would be only moments before the man arrived.

Its instinct took over, and it charged the hounds.

It would kill them instantly.

Then there would be just it and the Enemy.

Nathan came to another creek whose water's action through the centuries had washed out its banks, making it difficult to negotiate. He was now within fifty yards of his treeing hounds and clawed his way to the top of the steep bank.

His smile of relief at overcoming this last hurdle changed as his headlight caught the Russian boar's charge impact against Buck at the base of the tree. Nathan instantly reasoned that this was the creature whose tracks he had crossed earlier.

Similarly, he innately knew that this scene was all wrong. His dogs had been treeing a raccoon—not baying the boar.

That meant the boar had hunted his hounds.

And then Nathan knew that this animal was unlike anything he had ever come across in the woods of Ryland Creek.

It was after his hounds with the intent to kill.

And that Nathan Ernst would not allow.

The boar's charge and sheer power lifted Buck into the air. It was only a miracle of its poor eyesight and a slight misjudgment of the angle of its attack that allowed Buck to land on his feet shaken but unharmed. As the boar tried to reorient itself, Tye, now acutely aware of the danger, attacked the hog's flanks, causing it to turn from Buck.

The boar tried to maneuver, but now its bulk caused a disadvantage.

It had lost the element of surprise, and the pair of hounds worked in unison.

Buck used the large oak to his advantage, hiding his approach from the boar, and the large hound attacked the hog's exposed side.

The dance of death continued as the hounds and pig turned in ever-tightening circles in the snow. The canines knew instinctively to stay away from the pig's sharp tusks.

As the fight continued, the boar's frustration grew steadily. It was not supposed to be this way, and its ear-piercing squeal sounded far more a cry of rage than fear.

Realizing it could not match the hounds' agility, the boar instinctively backed itself against the tree to protect its flank. This tactic mitigated some of the canines' quicker speed. Now the coonhounds stood, facing it head on.

A light like the sun shone in the boar's eyes, confusing it momentarily. It then heard two loud sounds and felt a sharp pain in its sides. Then it remembered! For it had experienced those sounds when it had been a piglet, albeit more deafening, the day its mother and siblings had died. The day it had come to hate the Enemy.

The bullets hit the intended target, even drew blood, but its tough hide thwarted any mortal wound. Nathan had brought the gun to bear when the boar and dogs had briefly separated, allowing a clear shot.

The last coon hunter knew that he was terribly under matched against this brute. Unloading every round of his weapon into that boar's sides still would not be enough to kill it immediately, if at all.

But he was a coon hunter, accomplished at taking aim at small targets at night, and he leveled the semiautomatic rifle again.

The third bullet entered the boar's left eye. It threw up its massive head and roared in protest at the pain. The angle was off slightly, and while blinded in that eye, the bullet merely lodged in the boar's eye socket and had not found its mark into its brain.

Pure instinct drove it now, and the boar charged the closest hound. Tye had not been ready for the sudden burst of speed, and the boar struck its prey. It lifted the hound into the air, its tusk cutting deeply into the hound's front shoulder. Luck was on the dog's side as the blow was not mortal, but the wound was debilitating and stole the hound's agility.

There was blood in the snow now. The hound that the Russian boar had successfully wounded was back on its feet, but it sensed the dog was badly hurt, and that its target could no longer successfully evade another onslaught. The boar tensed for another charge—one more drive that would surely end the canine's life.

Again came the light with its sharp noises and stinging pain! Another well-aimed round found the boar's other eye, rendering the beast totally blind. With one final, loud crack, the next bullet found its way into the pig's brain. The boar felt the mortality of that last shot, intuiting it would not survive to feel the warmth of another morning sun.

The piercing sounds and subsequent stinging had stopped, and the boar knew not if the white light still shone on it. But that did not matter now—determined that it would not be the only thing to die this night. Even though bereft of sight, it still knew the wounded hound's whereabouts.

Nathan pulled the trigger again to hear the dreaded sound of the firing pin. His rifle was out of ammunition, and there was no time to reload. While the man knew his last few shots had been accurate, and the hog was moving blind and sluggishly, it continued toward the wounded Tye. Further, rather than run to safety, the brave coonhound refused to back down.

The boar was now but a few feet from the black and tan hound. One more lunge, one last raking of its sharp tusks to rip open the rib cage, and the dog would be finished.

Then the massive creature heard a solid "thud" in the snow. Something stood between the boar and its intended purpose. It sensed the Enemy directly in front of it! Roiling with revenge, the hog felt a renewed energy even in these final moments.

"You will not harm him!" Nathan shouted with a rage rivaling the boar's hatred. Over his head, he raised the .22 and brought it down with a vicious swing. Repeatedly, he struck the slowly moving, wounded tusker. Backing away inches as the pig still crawled forward, Nathan screamed with each downward thrust of the rifle's butt.

Suddenly the boar mustered another burst of strength, and with one swing of its massive head, tore the gun from Nathan's grip. The rifle cartwheeled into the darkness. The beast then turned its powerful neck again, lifting Nathan's body effortlessly, launching the man through the air.

Nathan struck one of the oaks, and the impact drove the air from his lungs. Luck still favored the man and his hounds, though. Nathan felt his heavy canvas coat, shredded by the boar as if lightweight cotton. Miraculously, the boar's tusks had not touched his skin.

The coon hunter quickly spotted his light, knocked off his head by the impact, which remained on. He reached for it, and his other hand hit something familiar—his oak walking stick! Nathan donned his helmet, grasped the stick, and charged back into the fray.

A searing pain registered in what was left of the pig's senses as Buck came from behind and clamped down on the boar's groin. It squealed as the able hound's strong jaws held and caused a drag toward Tye, its intended goal. Instead of attempting to shake Buck loose, the pig channeled its pain to give it more incentive to move forward toward the wounded, but ever-defiant, Tye.

The hog screamed as it sensed the Enemy was again in the fight and protecting the wounded hound.

With all the strength he could muster, Nathan brought the walking-stick-now-club down hard on the beast. Inexorably, the boar crept forward toward the man and hound. Repeatedly, he clubbed at the pig's head. His muscles begged for relief, but his iron will drove him on. His headlight fell off; its luminescence whisked away. But it did not matter, as the boar and man were so close to each other now.

Tye let out a roar. The hound moved around Nathan to latch onto the pig's ear and pull down to expose its throat. Buck maintained his grip to staunch the pig's forward momentum. Nathan's concentration was complete—nothing else existed except for the boar, his hounds, and the oak club.

The last coon hunter and his dogs fought as a team.

Desperately, the hog tried the same tactic of swinging its head, hoping to cut the Enemy. While it failed to score a direct hit, the strong oak walking stick snapped in half, with the lower half, akin to the rifle earlier, flying into the darkness.

But Nathan was ready this time.

The coon hunter maintained his grip on the upper half of the walking stick, which now ended in a sharp shard. With the rage that came so naturally, Nathan yelled, spun the stick around in a fluid motion, and brought the club-now-spear down with all his remaining strength. The sharpened staff penetrated the hog's tough hide, with the momentum driving the wood entirely through its body and skewering the animal against the earth.

Finally, the battle leaving Nathan at the limits of complete exhaustion, the boar slumped into the snow with one last, convulsive exhalation of air from its lungs, blood erupting from its snout, and then it breathed no more.

Nathan gasped heavily as he collapsed onto the massive, unmoving head. Tye released his grip on the hog's ear and moved slowly around cautiously, sniffing the dead animal. Buck, amazingly unscathed through the entire ordeal, released his hold on the brutish pig and came forward. For a moment, the trio sat unmoving there in the dark with the moonlight poking through leafless branches, and then both Tye and Buck started to lick Nathan's face as the hunter began to laugh. Nathan stood up and turned around to pick up his headlight with its light still glowing in the snow.

"Yes! We did it, boys!" he shouted to his hounds in a victorious cheer. "Little Sharon and John are going to love this story," Nathan confided in his hounds.

He imagined young John listening with mouth agape to "Uncle Nate" telling the story of the hounds and hog. Nathan could see Little Sharon's eyes sparkling as she listened intently to the forest saga—just as another Sharon had once a long time ago.

But somewhere, the last spark in the boar's soul reignited! The creature suddenly came alive and slashed its massive head upward into the Enemy. Its tusks easily penetrated Nathan's blue jeans, completely severing the femoral artery in his right leg.

Nathan's body arced as he screamed at the searing pain and reflexively grasped his wound.

The boar slumped to the ground with both hounds roaring, their powerful jaws biting into the hog's exposed throat. But the dogs' assault was pointless now, for the boar willingly released its spirit, and its bulk settled into the cold snow for the last time—its long-awaited vengeance, complete.

Nathan could feel the severe wound to his leg—his hand awash in blood that freely flowed. In his soul, the last coon hunter knew the injury was mortal, and he would not make it out of the woods to his truck in time for help. The peace that Nathan had felt amongst the maples but a few minutes before now returned. The rapid loss of blood quickly began to steal his consciousness away.

Convinced the hog was indeed dead, both hounds turned to Nathan. Like the man, they knew the boar's final blow had been fatal for their master. They whimpered softly as his breathing began to labor.

"My boys," Nathan said, patting each hound's head. Panic set in as he worried about his dogs' fate—and not his own.

"Don't worry about the hounds, son. They'll be all right," the familiar voice returned.

As the moonlight filtered through the tree branches, a tall man's figure formed in the mist.

"Pa?" Nathan said in a dream state, standing between the two worlds.

Both Tye and Buck looked directly at the ghostly form of Jacob Ernst and wagged their tails.

"Yeah." Nathan could see the shimmering image of his father Jacob smiling and turning to the hounds. *"They can see and hear me. They could all along."*

"It's time for you to come home, my baby boy." Another figure, this of a smaller but familiar, pretty woman, appeared next to Jacob—a vision that he inherently knew.

"Ma? Ma!" Nathan shouted, gasping as he tasted blood.

"The wait is over, Nathan. You have suffered your loneliness long enough," Rose Ernst's spirit spoke softly.

A third voice, one that had never left his heart or dreams, now filled Nathan's ears.

"There is so much that I want to show you. From this time forward, we shall make new memories without the need of stones."

Smiling as she always had, another ephemeral spirit emerged from slightly behind the figures of Jacob and Rose. Sharon's gossamer shape moved closer to Nathan, knelt beside him, and leaned over to kiss him. Nathan could feel something akin to a warm breeze cross his lips.

Then the ghost of an exceptional hound, the color of midnight, walked over to Nathan, staring at both Buck and Tye, who could clearly see the shining aura, and then the spectral hound turned his loving gaze back to his master.

"Seth!" Nathan said as tears streamed down his face.

Both corporal hounds caught the scent and sound of movement at the base of the oak. The raccoon that they had treed came down, beholding the scene. It was a simple creature, and while it had watched the battle between man, dog, and boar from its lofty oak perch, the raccoon did not comprehend what had happened then, nor what it was witnessing now.

Buck took several steps toward the raccoon, and without malice, just nodded his head. The ringtail, looking back one final time, turned and scampered away into the night.

The last coon hunter watched the scene between the raccoon and the hounds with a sense of closure as his vision faded. He smiled at the thought of the coon's escape and another chase.

But in those waning moments, Nathan knew his nights of running these rugged hills had ended. His body slowly eased into the snow as he breathed his last, his eyes still open as the ghostly figures by his side disappeared into the forest's mist.

Nathan Ernst had died that night fighting.

He had died while chasing ringtails with his hounds in the forests of Painted Post.

He had died while defending his family beneath the behemoth oaks of Ryland Creek.

And you can't ask for much more than that.

———— •◦• ————

A deep sense of foreboding washed over Mead as he parked his truck.

The big man put on his gray fedora and stepped out of his vehicle to examine the familiar, old pickup just in front of him. The tailgate was down, and the windows iced over by the frigid air—both signs telling Mead that Nathan's truck had not been started in many hours.

"Where's Uncle Nathan?" Little Sharon asked.

"Yeah, Pa, where is Uncle Nate?" John demanded more than asked.

"I'm not sure," Mead spoke plainly, managing to hide the concern in his voice despite the growing dread.

Mead stepped out of the vehicle, but as he neared his brother's truck, his heart froze, but not due to the wintry cold.

Deep in the forest, two hounds' voices pierced the frigid air in a long, mournful bawl. Mead had experienced that haunting call before—they were singing a last open.

Mead slowly turned to his children, who had also heard the hounds' call, and while they did not discern its meaning, the concern on their father's face soon reflected on their own.

"What's the matter, Pa?" Little Sharon asked, her small voice trembling slightly. "Where's Uncle Nathan?" she asked again, knowing from the change in Mead's countenance that her father somehow knew something that he had not known just moments before.

"Sharon," Mead said, but his look seemed distant, "take your brother and stay in the truck. I will be back soon with your Uncle Nathan." While the words should have been comforting, the intuitive girl held her worried look.

Mead started his truck's engine to keep his children warm inside the cab and again instructed them to stay put. He easily found his brother's tracks in the snow and set off at a quick pace. As he followed the trail, he saw where Nathan had knelt to examine a set of unusual tracks. Like his brother, Mead immediately discerned that the spoor belonged to that of a wild pig.

As Mead rounded a bend in the trail, he saw Buck and Tye, their heads hung low, slowly walking toward him with their tails wagging in recognition. With dread, the man also noted the large gash and matted blood on Tye's shoulder—a wound that he had never seen on any coonhound.

"What's the matter, boys?" Mead asked as he patted Buck's massive head. "Where's Nathan?"

In perfect communion with his request, the hounds turned and began down the path. Buck and Tye then stopped together and looked behind to ensure that Mead walked behind them.

"Take me to him." His words choked in his throat, somehow knowing what he would find there in the forest of Ryland Creek.

Mead followed the hounds' lead, which retraced Nathan's path in the snow. The big man moved quickly through the woods that he'd known as a boy. When he finally arrived beneath the oak, he read the snow's story, the final chapter in his brother's life.

Nathan's body lie but a few feet in front of the enormous boar. Both lifeless forms had large ovals of red crimson snow around them, and where their blood had met and overlapped, the redness was brightest, still somehow wet and not yet frozen.

Tye went over and draped his body across his fallen master's chest. The hound barely lifted his head to watch as Buck and Mead approached. Tye let out a low growl, warning Mead to stay away.

"It's okay, boy," Mead said with his voice breaking while trying to reassure the loyal hound that he meant no harm. "It's time to take him home." After a few moments, Tye reluctantly moved, allowing Mead to come nearer.

Mead stared at Nathan's motionless figure. His brother's eyes were open and frosted with a white glaze. Nathan's cold stare looked up into the oaks with a serene smile—a peaceful look on his brother's face that Mead had not seen in a very long time.

A sudden breeze from the otherwise placid morning knocked his hat from his head onto the ground. As Mead knelt to pick up the hat, he laughed and sobbed.

The big man slapped his hat back on his head and looked into the blue morning sky as the sun rose above the eastern ridge. Standing to his considerable height, his eyes welling with tears, Mead managed to smile, and began nodding his head slowly.

The hounds moved closer but stared beyond the big man with their tails wagging. Following the dogs' stare, the man could not perceive anything out of the ordinary in the forest of Ryland Creek that so demanded the hounds' attention.

But Mead believed in his heart that they could see something far beyond his human senses.

Mead then knew.

Yes, he understood.

"I reckon he's already home," Mead confided softly in the two hounds.

Epilogue

After Nathan's death, Mead moved his growing family into the Ernst family homestead and took care of the coonhounds as he had as a boy. More times than he would like to admit, the large man found himself staring at the small graveyard beside the barn that was full of small mounds and crosses.

There were the names that he quickly remembered.

Duke. Cilla. Storm. Luke.

Damned Mule.

All the crosses were wood, except for one large, cement monument that displayed one name in boldly carved letters: "Seth."

However, there was one faded, ancient, wooden cross that Mead held dearest, written in the penmanship of a child that read: "Moses."

Mead closed his eyes and heard the hunts from the past rush upon him. He heard his father telling him to keep up, and Nathan's voice explaining that a decaying branch in the middle of an old swamp was in fact not a skeletal hand.

And Mead could hear the hounds singing.

Yes! He could hear the hounds.

Mead opened his eyes to resurvey the quiet cemetery.

Sarah now carried their third child, but her gumption, even during this first trimester of life, drove her to make the old farm a home once again. She insisted that they would name their third child, if a son, Jacob. If the child were another girl, then she would be named Rose.

Mead whole-heartedly agreed.

The leaves were changing color now as fall came, and young John and Little Sharon begged their father to take them coon hunting "like

Grandpa and Uncle Nate once did." A quick look at Sarah told Mead that he should honor the request, as they knew coon hunting was in their children's blood.

Mead loaded Buck and Tye into the truck with his two young children riding in the front seat and talking excitedly about the upcoming hunt. Mead pulled off the road at a familiar spot. When he let the hounds go, he noticed that they did not go immediately into the woods.

That's strange, he thought, but then Mead realized that this was the first time that these hounds had returned to Ryland Creek since Nathan's death.

With a glance at their new master for reassurance, the hounds quickly began running side by side down the trail.

"Tye!" Little Sharon, now preferring to be called by her nickname "Lill," shouted to the departing dog.

Upon hearing his name, the coonhound stopped as Buck continued into the night. The older hound then ran back to stand in front of the young girl.

Sharon knelt down and felt the healed scar across Tye's shoulder. Then she took the big hound's head in her small hands and gently kissed the dog on top of his head.

"Go get a coon, boy," she said softly.

Tye quickly turned to catch his hunting mate but then stopped once more to look back at Little Sharon. "Hurrumph!" the hound barked, and with a shake of his head, continued down the trail, disappearing into the night.

Mead smiled while watching the exchange.

As they waited for the hounds to open, Mead began telling his children of the legends of his youth—stories of old wells, swamp ghouls, and friendly spirits in the moonlight. His children listened intently in the dark with mouths agape.

Then Tye's barrel voice filled the night air. Soon Buck opened, and Mead explained to Little Sharon and John how the dogs were now tracking the raccoon.

With an air of mystery, Mead told his children that the dogs were headed toward the Black Oaks of Ryland Creek. Both children held their breath—terrified and excited—as he shared the tale of an ancient Native American chief's triumph, and the subsequent entrapment of evil souls.

"Pa, when I grow up, I'm going to hunt raccoon just like Grandpa Ernst and Uncle Nathan," John declared.

Mead's light played upon John's smiling face. The father knew that it was more than just the white light from the headlamp that caused his son's face to beam brightly.

"Me too!" Little Sharon shouted. Like her mother, she was not one to be one-upped.

"But Pa! Didn't Grandpa Ernst and Uncle Nathan die when they were coon hunting?" John's former enthusiasm waned as his question seemed suspended in the air.

Mead paused but acknowledged, "Yes they did, son."

"Well, maybe coon hunting isn't good for our family, Pa," John suggested.

The mountain of a man knelt on one knee beside John. "Coon hunting is about living, son," Mead explained. "Being out here with your hounds—in these forests—that's what it means to be truly alive."

In the moon's silvery light, the children understood their father's simple lesson.

Little Sharon suddenly noted the rhythmic changeup in Tye's voice as the hound sang in the dark. "What's Tye doing now, Pa?"

The giant smiled, proud that his daughter had correctly identified the difference in the hound's barking cadence.

And knowing that all things returned upon themselves, Mead explained with a single word.

"Treed."

About the Author

The author with Seth

Joseph Gary Crance was born in Upstate New York near his hometown of Painted Post. He spent hundreds of nights with his father and their dogs, chasing raccoon through the hills of this scenic land. After a career in the U.S. Air Force, he returned to Painted Post with his family, back to the woodland hollows of his youth. Mr. Crance is a member of the New York Outdoor Writers Association.

An Exceptional Hound

Book II of the Ryland Creek Saga

Twelve-year-old Jason Canton longs to become a coon hunter when a chance meeting in the woods with Nathan Ernst and his legendary coonhound, Seth, sets the youngster on a path to learn the lessons about the forests and life.

But something powerful and malicious has entered the forests of their Upstate New York hometown of Painted Post—something not entirely of this world.

It will test the skills and stamina of the Ernst family with Jason and his friends to confront this deadly marauder.

It will rely upon the strength of the bonds between hunters and their dogs.

It will require an exceptional hound.

The Legends of Ryland Creek
Book III of the Ryland Creek Saga

Young Sharon "Lill" Ernst finds solace in the woodlands of her rural hometown of Painted Post. With her family, Lill has grown up following their coonhounds in the nighttime forests.

Andrew Renthro, orphan but heir apparent to a vast empire of drug dealers, has been ordered to prove his worthiness. Andrew leaves his native Chicago—a teen who eagerly seeks revenge for a father he never knew—and his success means destroying the unsuspecting Ernst family.

But the forests of Painted Post don't belong solely to the realm of man. Stories of guiding spirits, ghostly hounds, and hideous beasts abound in this mystical place of wooded hollows, streams, and pathways.

For many trails converge and diverge in the oak-strewn hills of Painted Post.

Some paths lead to redemption . . . while others may end in certain doom.

But all have the potential to become legend.

The Master of Hounds

Book IV of the Ryland Creek Series
Coming Summer 2020

College student Jacob "Matthew" Ernst has a unique ability to see through the eyes of his hounds. For now, he needs a break from his studies. It's summer in Upstate New York, and Matthew has planned a long hike amongst the beautiful hills of his hometown of Painted Post. With his faithful young coonhound, Monk, he is looking forward to a long, uncomplicated time in the woods.

Logan Willoughby wants to belong, but she's fallen in with the wrong crowd—a motorcycle gang with a long list of criminal exploits. However, the price of admission may be a price too steep for her to pay.

A chance meeting puts Logan and Matthew on a collision course. Each will learn the wisdom that only the forests of Ryland Creek can impart.

But Logan knows too much. She's become an end that can ill afford to remain loose, and the gang will do whatever is necessary to protect their own interests.

The only thing that stands between her and the gangsters is The Master of Hounds.